AF117810

ALICE K. ARENZ

The Case of the Bouncing Grandma

Book 1 of the Bouncing Grandma Mysteries

By

Alice K. (A. K.) Arenz

Copyright © 2015 by Alice K. Arenz

Forget Me Not Romances, a division of Winged Publications

Previously published by Sheaf House

All rights reserved as permitted under the U.S. Copyright Act of 1976. No part of the publication may be reproduced, distributed or transmitted in any form or by any means, or stored in a database or retrieval system, without prior permission of the publisher.

This book is a work of fiction. Names, characters, places, and incidents are the product of the author's imagination and are used fictitiously. Any resemblance to actual events, locales, or persons, living or dead, is coincidental, except for the instances where they were used in conjunction with a business on purpose.

All rights reserved.
ISBN: 979-8-8691-3932-0

!

Chapter 1

Confined to a wheelchair and bored out of my mind, I found watching the neighbors move in at the end of our cul-de-sac more entertaining than anything on TV. But the storm front that settled over us early this morning managed to take away even this questionable diversion.

Other than the mysterious man with a limp hanging around the moving van in the middle of a downpour early on, things were pretty dull.

Once it stopped raining, I expected the action to pick up, but it didn't. Even the people who flocked to dead end streets for the sheer joy of driving around the circle at the top stayed away. Several hours had passed since I witnessed any real activity, and what I did observe seemed, well, a little odd.

The realtor, Elsie Wilkes, came by while it was still sprinkling. She removed the For Sale sign from the yard, walked around the van a couple times, and ended up on the curb closest to my side of the street. After staring at the house she'd recently sold, she darted to her car and shoved the sign into the trunk, her head bobbing in every direction. Peculiar behavior for anyone else, but when it came to Elsie, peculiar was the norm.

Rex Stout's visit was stranger. After parking his old white Caddy in front of my place, he walked all the way around the cul-de-sac, returned to his car, then pulled it into the driveway near the unattended van. He got out of the car, stood for awhile in front of the house that once belonged to him, turned, then disappeared up the ramp and into the truck. Since then, I'd neither seen nor heard anything or anyone.

The breeze coming through the open window was fresh and clean, adding to my desire to be out of this chair and working in the yard. I hated being so sedentary. The inactivity made me feel useless. Worse, it made me feel old—and that was something I refused to be for a very long time.

With one hand still on the curtain, I turned and gazed out across the living room. There was bound to be something I could do that would make me feel useful—and keep me from this less than admirable form of diversion.

Interference from both the wheelchair and curtains stalled my attempt to move away from the window. As I struggled to untangle myself, the sound of a woman's shriek had me back at my post in a flash.

Two burly men stood on the ramp leading down from the massive moving van. Between them lay several large carpets piled haphazardly atop one another. The upper one was partially unrolled revealing a rich forest green pattern. I could barely see the woman beyond the giant spirea bush that edged our properties, but her voice was crystal clear. And she wasn't happy.

"Do you have any idea what you've done?" She screamed. "You dropped that even after I told you to be especially careful with the rugs. Can't you follow the simplest instructions?"

The man in the rear said something, his deep, gruff tone the only thing to carry on the breeze. His arms waved in what I perceived as a threatening manner until the other man silenced him with a look thrown over his shoulder.

When the woman disappeared, the men bent down, picked up the partially unrolled carpet, and hefted it onto their shoulders. As the man in the rear stepped over the carpets remaining on the ramp, his boot caught on the corner of one near the top. He shook himself free, then continued on his way.

A pale object protruding from the end of the rolled carpet captured my attention.

"That's a foot." I whispered.

I pulled back from the window, closed my eyes, took a deep breath, then looked again. Sure enough, a foot dangled out the back of the rug.

"Andi!"

My daughter magically appeared in the doorway, hands on her hips, a frown on her pretty face. "Who was it always said we were supposed to mind our own business?" Moving past me to the window, she sighed as she shoved the wheelchair away from my post.

"Andi, you need to take a look out there. At the carpets."

"Mama, I know you're bored, but really, spying on the new neighbors?" She fussed with the curtain, straightening it out before turning back to me.

I found the role reversal more than a little amusing, though a bit irritating under the circumstances. I needed to get a better look at that carpet.

"I wasn't spying," I insisted, struggling to maneuver closer to the window. "I was just—looking. Besides, honey, you really need to take a peek out there right now."

"You've been watching those people for the last three days, and while it may be fascinating, it's not very polite." The stern look gave way to one of curiosity. "I'll bet they have
some incredible things."

Wasn't that what I was trying to tell her? "Nothing as incredible as what I just saw. Please, Andi, just one look and tell me what you see."

Frowning, she lifted the panel she'd just smoothed into place.
"Well?"

"Well, there's a bunch of rolled carpets sitting on the ramp."

"That's all you see? Nothing sticking out the end of one of them?" Had my desire for excitement caused me to hallucinate?

"See for yourself."

She helped me back to the window and raised the curtain for me to peer out. Just as she'd said, there were several nicely rolled carpets—no foot. *Take a deep breath, Glory. Look again.*

No foot.

"Are you okay, Mama?"

I nodded. No way would I tell her what I thought I'd seen. I'd never live it down. Instead, I tried to downplay my interest in the newcomers.

"There's been quite a racket with doors slamming, people yelling. You know that's not normal for our neighborhood."

Having lived at the end of this small cul-de-sac for the last twenty years, I pretty much knew what to expect from the surrounding area. Even with the change of family dynamics—kids growing up, death and divorce—and homes bought and sold, there had never been this kind of activity.

Of course, I never thought I'd see a body part wrapped in a rug before either.

"They *do* have a lot of stuff, don't they? A lot of people too. Though I suppose most of them are the movers."

I thought about reminding her of the mind-your-own-business rule but didn't think it was appropriate at the moment.

"Maybe an extended family. Like that old movie *Yours, Mine & Ours*," I mused. "They don't make them like that anymore. Lucille Ball, Henry Fonda..."

"Sure they do, Mama. They're remaking all the old movies, modernizing them."

"Ruining them," I muttered.

"Anyone here?" My sister's voice rang out from the kitchen, followed by the clomp of running feet.

"Walk!" Andi called as my seven-year-old grandson appeared in the doorway.

"Gramma!" Seth grinned up at his mother, then proceeded to me at a far more sedate pace.

I opened my arms and hugged him to me. He was warm and smelled of fresh air and little boy... a heavenly aroma if ever there was one.

"How was the last day of school?" I asked, determined to put what I thought I'd seen out of my mind, chalking it up to my general state of boredom.

"Bor-ring! Don't know why we had to go anyway. It rained, and we didn't get to go outside or nuthin'!"

"Never have liked the last day of school," sighed my sister Jane, who had also been Seth's first-grade teacher. "Too much to do and not enough time to do it."

" 'N you made me stay till you got it done," Seth pouted.

"And it didn't hurt you one bit." Andi pulled Seth's Chiefs cap from his head, smoothed his fair hair, and relieved him of his backpack. "So, did you pass?"

"Ah, Mommy, 'course I did. I know the teacher!" Seth threw a grin toward his great-aunt and giggled. "Gramma, how's your leg? Is it gettin' all healed up?"

I glanced to where the said appendage sat propped on the special ledge of the wheelchair and tried to ignore the intense itching that seemed to begin every time I even thought about it.

THE CASE OF THE BOUNCING GRANDMA

"It's getting better and better every day," I assured him.

Though I doubted my own statement, I was determined to maintain a positive attitude.

"Good, then we'll be able—"

"I don't think Gramma's going to be able to do much of anything for a while, kiddo, so don't be making any plans."

"We'll be back to our adventures in no time—"

"Mother!" Andi's brows drew together in a warning glance.

"Adventures? Is that what you call skateboarding down Walnut Avenue?" Jane didn't bother with a warning; she gave me both barrels. "You're not a kid, Glory Harper. You should have known better."

"Gramma was awesome."

"If they had fixed the street rather than putting that steel cover over the hole—"

"And without a helmet or pads." Jane continued.

"—I would have been fine. The wheels just couldn't jump the lip of the cover—"

"And body armor," Jane persisted. "By fifty you should wear body armor if you're going to attempt something so foolish."

"—and then the Pearson boy pulled out of his driveway like he was going to a fire, so I tried to swerve."

"You're nearly fifty-two and should have more sense—"

"Aunt Jane."

"Fifty-two years *young*, Jane. Young. Besides, it's not my sense that's lacking."

"What would you call it then? Of all the fool—"

"You should try it sometime—"

"Mama! Okay, enough."

Andi put out her arms and made the "safe" sign—like this was a baseball game and she was the umpire. It was clear from her expression that she believed we should end this conversation. I had to withhold a laugh as I looked from my sister to my daughter. Their frustration was due to my repeated efforts to remain a fun grandmother, which had caused me a few minor injuries in the past. The adventure in skateboarding six weeks ago was by far the worst.

I still believed they were in collusion with my doctor to put me into this wheelchair. There was no way I could have damaged my leg as badly as they'd said. I mean, I had been able to get up and walk over to the sidewalk before collapsing.

Jane plopped down in a nearby chair and pushed her bangs off her forehead. At fifty-five, she still had her figure and could easily pass for her mid-forties. Her shoulder length dark hair had only a sprinkling of grey, and it wasn't because she colored it—she never had.

In contrast, my blonde hair only remained that way because of the abundance of grey that refused to accept every color my beautician had thrown at it—and boy had we tried to cover it! With my color-resistant hair, a few additional pounds, and the lines I'd developed during Ike's battle with cancer, I guessed I looked about ten years older than my sister. That didn't sit well with the youth and stamina I still professed to have.

"What?" Jane asked.

"Huh?"

"You were staring."

"Was I? Must be the pain meds." I winked at Seth, who started giggling again. "You guys staying for dinner?"

Andi shook her head, her own shiny blonde curls dancing across her shoulders. "Jared's calling tonight. He wasn't sure when, so we'll be missing Bible study." She stretched her arms high above her head then lowered them around Seth. "How about it, kiddo. Should we skedaddle home so we can wait for daddy's call?"

Jared was about to be deployed to the Middle East. When his National Guard Unit was first called up, we prayed he'd get to stay home, maybe go with a group down to the hurricane-ravaged South.

Jared, always one to look on the positive side, figured he could make more of a difference in the Middle East, where many of his fellow soldiers were at the end of their tours and ready for a well-earned reunion with their families stateside. He wasn't thrilled about leaving Andi and Seth but knew they were safe in God's hands—if not her mother's.

"Wish he didn't have to go." Seth sauntered over to me and knelt before the wheelchair, his small hands testing the plaster covering my leg.

"That goes double for me, kiddo," Andi said with a catch in

her throat. "But we're going to pray for Daddy, all his buddies, and everyone else over there. Right?"

Seth laid his head against my leg and sighed. Meeting my eyes, he whispered, "I just don't want him to go home to Jesus like Pa-Pa did."

Andi grimaced, watching my face and waiting for a reaction.

In the three years since Ike lost his battle to lung cancer, we'd all tried to fill the gap left in Seth's life. In the process, we became closer to one another, which aided in our own healing.

Sure, it also made me a little more daring, a little more active—or, perhaps that was proactive. I knew the special relationship Seth had enjoyed with his grandfather those first four years of his life could never be replaced. Not even by what he affectionately called his "Bouncing Gramma."

After Andi and Seth left for home, Jane seemed to reawaken and stirred from her chair.

"I thought I'd fry a little chicken in some olive oil and toss it onto a nice salad. How does that sound to you?"

"You're terrific, you know that?" I grinned. "Not only have you willingly moved in to help me, you cook like an angel!"

She batted the back of the chair. "If you don't stop being so nice to me, I'll stay forever."

"Do you hear me complaining?"

Jane's laughter echoed through the hallway as she made her way to the kitchen.

Actually, I'd asked her to come live with me about three months after Ike died. She'd sold her house in Kansas City and moved to Tarryton to be closer to "the rest of the family."

With our parents out touring the country, the only ones left around our hometown were Andi's little family and me, so it hadn't taken a lot to figure out what she was doing.

Her own husband had died from a heart attack the year before, and although Jane always gave the impression of being a regular Rock of Gibraltar, she was really a pussycat. Still, by the time she'd been here six months, we knew that as much as we loved one another, we couldn't live together. She got a little house a few blocks away, snagged a job teaching first grade at the elementary school, and we became best friends.

A gentle breeze blew the curtain into my face, and as I

struggled to disentangle myself, I heard the same female voice from the house across the way.

The woman was no longer in sight by the time I resumed my position, sans the pesky curtain, but a few words drifted in to me: *careful, valuable, irreplaceable.*

A quick glance acknowledged the same men had returned for another carpet. They lifted it up from the ramp and onto their shoulders without incident, but when they reached the sidewalk, the man in the rear appeared to have a problem. They stopped for a moment to give him time to shift his hold, then continued on their way.

My mouth dropped open, and this time when I attempted to move closer to the window, I did so easily.

As the men and their burden disappeared from sight, I saw the confirmation—there really was a foot hanging out the back of that rug.

Chapter 2

It took a moment for my brain to wrap around what I'd just witnessed. I reviewed the last few minutes, running the scene through my mind, searching for alternative interpretations. It didn't play out any differently. I had no doubt it had been a human foot.

"Jane! Jane, grab the phone!"

Once again I found myself fighting the curtain. It stuck to my face then to the wheels of the chair. I heard Jane running down the hallway toward me, calling my name in panic.

"Glory, what is it? What happened? Are you hurt?" Her worried face peered into mine as her hands searched my body for injury. "Is it your leg? Your heart? Oh, Glory, not your heart?"

Don, Jane's husband, had been fine one moment and dead the next. A massive heart attack felled the giant of a man who had never been sick a day in his life. Now, as I tried to reassure my sister that I was fine, I realized how much she feared something like that happening again.

"I'm fine. It's not me." I told her again and again. "I just need the phone to call 911."

With a look of panic on her face, Jane darted across the room and grabbed the phone. Without bringing the handset to me, she dialed.

"What's our emergency?" She asked, her hands shaking as the tinny voice on the other end asked for information.

I held out my hand, but Jane didn't move toward me.

"There's been a murder." I couldn't believe how calm my voice sounded. Neither could I believe the blank look my sister gave me. "Jane, they're waiting," I urged.

"Uh, could you hold on just a sec?" Jane put a hand over the receiver and gave me one of those stern expressions I was certain she used on wayward first graders. "There's been a murder?" She spoke slowly with a great deal of deliberation.

"It seems obvious. I don't think anyone alive would allow themselves to be rolled into a carpet." I continued holding out my hand, waiting for her to give me the phone.

Jane raised her hand from the receiver and wagged her index finger at me. "What are you saying?"

I struggled with the wheelchair until I was finally close enough to grab the handset from my sister. "Sorry to have kept you waiting."

While the operator sputtered, obviously wondering what was going on, I rushed into an explanation of what I'd witnessed. As she questioned me, I remained calm, gave her my address—though I was certain she already knew it the moment she answered our call—and was assured someone would be there shortly. I hung up and handed the cordless handset back to my sister, who stared at me as if she were measuring me for a straitjacket.

"You saw a body?" Jane felt behind her until she connected with the arm of a chair. Sinking onto it, she crushed the phone to her chest as she continued to stare at me.

"A foot," I corrected her.

"A foot."

"Um." I wondered if there was something I should do for Jane. The shock was overwhelming her. At least, I assumed it was. It's how I'd felt when I spotted the foot.

"What about the moving men?"

"What about them?"

"They didn't see the foot?"

"Not that I could tell. I think they were concentrating on the rug. After they'd gotten yelled at for dropping—"

"Glory, do you have any idea what you're saying?"

I nodded as I took in her disbelief. "I wouldn't have called 911 if I didn't."

"Glory—"

I heard a car pull up in the driveway. The slam of doors that echoed through the open window caught my attention.

Had they sent more than one car?

"Hold that thought," I told her, knowing she'd need to answer the door in a moment.

THE CASE OF THE BOUNCING GRANDMA

When the bell rang, Jane rose from the chair, set the phone back into its base, and walked to the door as though in a trance. Her pale face flushed as she showed two police officers—instead of the one I expected—into the living room. Whether it was the extra officer or just the unusual circumstances, Jane looked like she could pass out any second.

"Gloria Harper?"

"Glory," Jane and I corrected simultaneously.

Both young men seemed vaguely familiar, but that wasn't unusual. Tarryton isn't very big, and if I hadn't seen them in their official capacity, it was likely I'd seen them shopping or even at church.

"I'm Officer Bradley, and this is Officer Roberts," the older of the men spoke up, his delivery reminiscent of Jack Webb's from the old *Dragnet* TV show. I wouldn't have been a bit surprised to hear him say, "Just the facts ma'am" in that perfect monotone.

"Dispatch said you saw a murder."

"That's not quite right, Officer." I smiled up at him but was met with stony silence. "I reported a murder, yes, but I didn't see it happen."

Officer Bradley turned to Jane, who shook her head.

"Sorry, gentlemen, this is her story."

She circled around the two men, watching them as they studied me. I could see the gears turning in my sister's brain and knew I'd get no help from that quarter.

"Did someone tell you about this murder, is that it?"

"Not at all. It's all very simple, really." I spread my hands out on my lap, flexing fingers that had suddenly begun to tingle.

"I heard some noise from next door, so I peeked out the window. The moving men had dropped what looked like an expensive Oriental rug, and one of the owners had yelled. Shrieked, really."

"And that's when it happened, ma'am?"

"Did you see the weapon? Would you recognize the perpetrator?"

"No, and no, and um, no. I mean, it was later."

"Later?" I think Roberts asked that. They looked so much alike, both in uniform, both of them standing with their hands on their fully loaded belts, their buckles, buttons, and shoes shining.

"Right. When they came back to get another carpet, the woman must have followed them. I couldn't hear everything she said, of course, but I did hear enough to tell you she was

insisting they handle the remaining rugs with care. She said they were irreplaceable."

"And one of the guys did something to her—"

"No, she left. Most likely returned to the house."

"Mrs. Harper, I hate to rush you, but every second counts in a murder investigation."

"Yes, yes, of course. I am sorry." I took a deep breath then spit it out. "The second carpet had a body in it."

"Did they drop that rug too? Is that when you saw the body?" They were getting excited now. One of them even reached for the communication device near his shoulder.

"I didn't actually see a body. I saw a foot."

The hand came back to the belt as the face tightened. "A foot."

I nodded. "The man in the rear readjusted his hold on the rug. As he hoisted it back up, the foot sort of dangled out."

"Dangled?"

"That's right." I saw Jane roll her eyes just before she sank onto the sofa.

"But you didn't see a body? Didn't see a body being wrapped up in the rug?"

"No. Just the foot."

The officers exchanged a glance, then one of them—Roberts, I think—gave me the once-over.

"You're Glory Harper."

"That's right." Hadn't we already established this?

"The Glory Harper who released a skateboard on Walnut about six, seven weeks ago, which resulted in a three-car pileup at the intersection of Walnut and Barry?"

"That's her," Jane volunteered a little too eagerly.

"The same Mrs. Harper whose grandson called 911 a few weeks earlier in need of assistance to extricate his grandmother from the springs of a trampoline?"

"They've nailed you."

Throwing my sister a scathing glance, I said, "I slipped when I was trying to get off the thing and somehow got wedged in. Seth

THE CASE OF THE BOUNCING GRANDMA

was only trying to help."

"Mrs. Harper—" this time I was sure it was Bradley giving me the evil eye—"you said they were taking this rug with the dangling foot *inside* the house."

"I assume that's where they were taking it."

"Ma'am, does that make any sense to you?"

"No, but I don't think like a murderer."

"Of course you don't. But don't you see, it doesn't make sense for them to be carrying a dead body *into* the house. They'd want to get rid of it, not keep it."

What he said made perfect sense, but I knew what I'd seen. "True, but they're moving. They couldn't very well have left it wherever they came from. Even I know that would have been stupid."

I think the doorbell saved me from further humiliation. As Jane got up to answer the door, the officers conferred with one another. When she showed another man into the living room, both officers gravitated to him.

Jane rolled her eyes as she passed me and mumbled, "You hit the jackpot this time, little sister."

Answering her would have meant taking my attention from the more interesting spectacle before me. Though I couldn't hear what was being said, watching the three men interact was fascinating.

After some whispering, with frequent glances directed at me, the officers showed themselves out. The new guy gazed from me to Jane then back again. Twice I thought he was about to say something, but both times he appeared to change his mind. While he was mulling over what he was there to discuss, I deduced from his lack of uniform that he must be a detective.

"I'm Detective Rick Spencer."

Aha! I was right.

The detective held his hand out to Jane, who seemed to develop a sudden shyness. She took his hand, dropping it almost immediately as if it were too hot to touch. When he turned his baby blues on me, I felt my stomach sink to my feet—or at least to the one not enclosed in an embarrassing cast.

"And you are Gloria Harper."

He extended his hand to me, and for a moment, I forgot what I was supposed to do with it. His dark blue eyes peered out of a ruggedly handsome face that reminded me of a younger Harrison Ford. He even had a build like Ford's when he played Indiana Jones.

"Glory," I corrected him when my tongue reduced to normal size. I shook his hand, finding his grip strong and capable.

"Glory, not Gloria?"

"When our mother was in labor with her, the only thing she could say was 'Glory, glory, glory!' "

I stared at Jane, mortified. I needn't have worried; the detective's eyes were shining, and a smile creased his face.

"Interesting story," he said taking a seat in a nearby chair. "I'd like to hear more of it someday. Right now, we need to get back to this body you've seen."

"Foot." Jane again, sticking her foot in where it didn't belong.

"Right. Did you see it too, Miss—"

"Calvin. Jane Calvin. And no, I didn't. I was in the kitchen getting dinner together. Which reminds me..."

Jane smiled her apologies and hurried from the room. I hadn't smelled anything burning, so maybe dinner would be saved after all.

"So you saw a foot poking out of the end of a rolled-up rug."

"That's right. Twice. The first time was when one of the men tripped over the rug as they were carrying another one. I asked Andi to take a peek, but the carpet had been rolled back up by the time I convinced her to look out the window."

"Andi?"

"My daughter," I told him, trying not to lose my momentum. "Anyway, it was when they returned for the second carpet that I was sure. I mean, the foot just popped out when the mover shifted his hold."

"And he didn't appear to notice it?"

"Not that I could tell. But you know, his back was to me."

"All right. Was this the foot of a male or a female?"

"Female, I think. I'm sorry, I just can't say for sure."

"Don't worry, you're doing great. Now, did it have on a shoe, a sock?"

"Neither. It was nude," I answered.

"Odd."

"Um." I was getting a bad feeling from Blue Eyes. Though he was asking all the right questions, I got the impression he wasn't taking me any more seriously than the other two had done. "You think it's possible they are in this as well? Maybe one of the moving men put the body in there." I shook my head. "No. That scenario doesn't work. The one about the movers."

"No," Blue Eyes said solemnly.

"But you *will* check into it, won't you? I know how it must sound, moving a body into a house rather than out of it, my only having seen a foot, and all that. Still, you have to admit it has to be a dead body rolled up in that carpet. I can't imagine the person was alive, unless they were drugged. Then you could be looking at a kidnapping and not a murder."

Why had I just kept talking? And why, for heaven's sake, had I begun to babble? It couldn't be those incredible blue eyes that studied me so closely. It's true I've always liked Harrison Ford, but this wasn't him, and I was a married...

Not married. A widow.

"I sent the officers over to take a look around, see if they can talk to the new owners. Beyond that, there's not much we can do. We'll find out who the people are, run a little background check, but..."

"Not enough evidence to get a search warrant."

"Exactly. And there could be a logical explanation."

There could be, but I was certain my interpretation was the correct one.

"You've got a bit of a *Rear Window* thing going on."

"Excuse me?"

Blue Eyes pointed to my leg propped up on the wheelchair extension. "You know, Jimmy Stewart, Grace Kelly, *Rear Window*. Hitchcock."

"Oh, yeah." I tried to see the humor in his remark, but all I could think about was how Stewart's character kept insisting there had been a murder, and no one believed him.

Until it was almost too late.

18

ALICE K. ARENZ

Chapter 3

Detective Rick Spencer, who I appropriately dubbed Blue Eyes—no offense to Sinatra, but he couldn't have held a candle to this guy—had an incredible smile. It was a bit lop-sided, and the laugh lines around his mouth deepened as his entire face lit up, causing his eyes to crinkle ever so slightly at the corners. I had no idea why I noticed these things. Maybe it was the shock of what I'd seen, or maybe it was his weird resemblance to Harrison Ford.

I couldn't remember the last time I'd taken such an inventory of someone of the opposite sex. I mean, I'd had the man of my dreams for twenty-five wonderful years. Ike had been everything a girl could want. We had been soul mates, friends, and lovers. He was God's perfect gift to me, and I hoped he'd felt the same.

"Mrs. Harper?"

Pulled from my reverie in the nick of time, I smiled over at the detective. "I'm sorry, did you say something?"

"I asked if you knew anything about your new neighbors."

I shook my head, hoping it would help reactivate my brain and erase the brooding I'd been about to start.

"No. We were surprised Rex Stout decided to sell the place after his family owned it for so long." I didn't mention what I knew of his mother's will or my curiosity regarding Rex's sudden ability to break it and sell the property. Still...

"I don't know if you're familiar with this subdivision, but it was originally part of a large estate."

Blue Eyes nodded. "I know Stout. He was my insurance agent before he decided to—"

A knock on the door interrupted our conversation. He was kind enough to get up to answer it. I wondered what was going on and wished my leg would hurry up and heal; I hated sitting around like a bump on a log.

The low murmur of voices just inside the front door was accompanied by the sounds coming from the kitchen. Jane was humming, not slamming pots and pans—a sign the chicken hadn't burned.

Detective Spencer returned to the living room by himself. He stood with his feet spread about shoulder width, his hands folded in front of him.

"That was Officer Bradley." He punctuated this statement with a hint of a smile. "The doors were open next door, and he got a chance to peek inside before someone came to talk with him."

"And?" I prompted.

"There were a couple mannequins in the foyer."

"Mannequins?"

"Yes. It appears one of your neighbors is a seamstress."

"A seamstress?" Dear Lord, tell me I don't sound like a parrot.

"Right. It was confirmed when Bradley commented on the mannequins. Other than being a bit rattled from their move, your neighbor was very cooperative." He spread his hands and smiled. "Anyway, it appears what you saw was one of those mannequins. Does that make you feel better?"

"Yes. I mean, no. I mean—" If I shook my head one more time my brain might explode. "I know what I saw."

"You know what you *think* you saw. And hey, I'm sure it was alarming to see the foot sticking out the end of the carpet. But it wasn't real. Just a hunk of plaster."

I started to open my mouth to protest but figured it wouldn't do me any good. Besides, if I alienated the detective I might never see him again.

Now, where had that come from?

"At any rate," Spencer was saying, "it looks like they wrapped the mannequin in a carpet to keep it from getting broken."

"Is that what they told the officers?"

"Not exactly." Blue Eyes cleared his throat. "In case you were right, and it *had* been a human foot you'd seen, we didn't want to spook them."

"I see." I said, though I didn't see at all. True, we wouldn't want to play our hand to let them know we were on to them, but...

THE CASE OF THE BOUNCING GRANDMA

"So the officers didn't tell them what I saw?"

He nodded. "They mentioned a disturbance in the neighborhood that warranted their going door to door."

"Did they?"

"Excuse me?"

"Did they go door to door? I mean, you sent two cars that pulled into my driveway, and the officers came into my house first. Did they go across the street to the Devlins' to add credence to the statement, or did they just leave after reporting to you?"

He seemed taken aback by the question, then his eyes did that crinkling thing at the corners again, which almost led me astray. Almost.

When he didn't answer, I continued my own line of questioning.

"If your officers didn't go over to the Devlins', or even farther down the street, then these people will know the call originated from here. If they used the mannequins as some sort of tactic to throw you off track, my sister and I could now be in danger." Watching *Law And Order* three times a week hadn't been for nothing!

"I don't believe you have anything to worry about, Mrs. Harper."

"Glory," I said, aware he still hadn't answered my question. "So?"

"So if you have any more questions or problems, feel free to give me a call." He handed me a business card that included his extension.

Until today, I hadn't even known that Tarryton had a detective unit or that the police department was big enough to have multiple extensions.

"Detective Spencer?" I halted his advance toward the front door. He turned back around, giving me a full measure of those incredible eyes. "What happens if I'm right?"

"Then sooner or later it'll come out, and we'll take it from there."

"In the meantime?"

"Try to relax," he said. "And stay away from skateboards."

Chapter 4

Jane entered the room, wiping her hands on a dish towel. She scanned the area, then turned to me. "He's gone?"

I nodded, still burning over his closing remark and the knowledge he'd known who I was all along—at least my, er, reputation. Even if the comment had been said in jest, it still stung. Especially after Blue Eyes and I seemed to get along so well.

"If you don't pull in your tongue, I'll have to tell your doctor."

He was my doctor, really, but ever since my visit to the emergency room for this leg, Jane and Dr. Steven Acklin had been ogling one another. Not that it was unusual; the esteemed orthopedist and Jane had been sweethearts in high school eons ago.

When Don came into the picture during college, Steven, away at medical school, lost out on the prize. It was obvious to anyone who saw Acklin and Jane together now that he'd never gotten over her. Maybe that's why he'd never married.

"Earth to Glory." The "prize" now had a frown on her face and her hands on her hips. "So, what did they say?"

"Our neighbor's a seamstress."

Jane, used to my minimalist way of expressing myself, didn't mimic me as I had the detective. She simply nodded in a manner that said she understood everything left unsaid. Maybe it came from working with children, the uncanny way she had of deducing things. Though if truth be told, I'd known plenty of six and seven-year-olds who could spin a tale without ever getting to the point.

It was a trait that frequently carried into adulthood and could be a source of frustration and confusion. At least to someone with my limited attention span...

"Well," Jane said, wiping her hands on the towel again. "Dinner's on the table and we need to get to it. You ready for tonight?"

Was I ready for tonight? What a question. Was I ever ready for those occasions when I was forced before the spotlight to speak?

"As I'll ever be."

Jane's eloquent answer was a grunt.

"Do you need more time to prepare?" She took hold of the wheelchair and pushed me toward the kitchen.

Now it was my turn to grunt. "It wouldn't help." I shook my head. "You and Andi got me into this—"

"For your own good."

"Why is it every time a person is forced to do something outside their ordinary boundaries someone tells them it's for their own good?"

"You don't like the Bible study class?"

"That's not what I said."

"Stretching beyond your comfort zone may be—"

"Uncomfortable?"

"Exactly what you need," she retorted.

Jane positioned the chair at an angle so I would have access to the table and the beautifully arranged chicken salad.

Nestled in a bed of romaine and iceberg lettuce, the lightly fried chicken bits were accompanied by fine slices of carrots, celery, radishes, and cucumber. Alongside my plate were a small dish of broccoli and a bottle of my favorite dressing.

"It's a work of art," I told my sister as she sat opposite me. "I don't know how you make everything look so—"

"Artistic?" Jane finished for me. She said the blessing then picked up her fork. "You didn't answer my question, you know."

A mouthful of salad gave me a moment's reprieve. It wouldn't make much difference though. We'd been over this ground many times before.

"I like the study group just fine," I answered in between bites.

"But?"

Ever since the medical community began suggesting shyness wasn't necessarily a normal human attribute, people were no longer allowed to state they were shy and introverted. Now you had some kind of disorder or something that could be whisked away by a wonder drug. Or so they would like you to believe. They might be right in some instances, sure. But it didn't apply to

THE CASE OF THE BOUNCING GRANDMA

people like me.

No, I didn't like the spotlight—though it had been on me plenty in the last couple of years. I avoided public speaking, didn't do well at parties or among large groups of people, and I generally took a long time to warm up to new people. It wasn't that I was unfriendly; I was just shy. Ike used to say I was socially retarded, that Jane had gotten all of the outgoing, extrovert genes. It hadn't been a slam either. He'd understood me better than anyone ever had and rarely pushed me beyond my comfort zone. Jane and Andi weren't so accommodating.

I placed my fork next to the plate, and after taking a swig of water, chose my words with the utmost care. "I enjoy the fellowship, the concentration on Bible passages. I even enjoy the others' take on the verses."

"But you don't think it's necessary for you to take your turn at leading the group."

Bingo! Throughout our growing up, whenever I was at a loss for words—okay, not at a loss, more at an impasse for expressing myself with tact and aplomb—Jane stepped right in and completed the thought with a minimum of effort. Our mom used to shake her head and frown at us.

Janie, if you don't allow Glory to finish her sentences she'll never learn to express herself properly.

Mom's sweet voice sounded in my ears. She may have felt that way most of the time, but I'll bet she wished for a return to the days when Jane spoke for me whenever I became obsessed with an idea or situation and spouted opinions from my soapbox. My mother determined I had a bad case of opinion-itis. And to date, there didn't seem to be a cure-all for that.

"Are you still mooning over that detective?" The smirk on Jane's face seemed to hold more behind it than the words implied.

Why did I get the feeling she knew something I didn't?

"Did he look familiar to you—and not just Harrison Ford-*Indiana Jones and the Last Crusade* familiar?"

Jane shook her head as a look I couldn't decipher flitted across her face. "No, but I'm not as acquainted with Tarryton's finest as you are."

"As I recall," I said evenly, "you were also taken by the gentleman. I was beginning to wonder if your hasty retreat into the

kitchen was a sign Dr. Acklin wasn't the be-all and
end-all in your romance department."

"Glory Harper!"

It surprised me she didn't include my middle name in that exclamation. If she'd really been upset with me, she'd have used our maiden name as well. Talk about a mouthful.

"Just do me a favor." I winked. "Don't break the poor man's heart before he gets me out of this cast."

Jane's blush spoke volumes, and I wondered if things between her and Dr. Dreamboat were progressing faster than I'd imagined.

"You're spacing again."

"Oh, uh, sorry. Maybe it's all the activity lately."

My sarcasm was met with a roll of her eyes.

"I suppose spying on your new neighbors *is* tiring."

"Okay, so it's not among the top ten approved forms of entertainment. And before you say anything, I'll admit I should be ashamed of myself, and would be, if I wasn't certain there's something strange going on."

Jane pushed back from the table. "You're not going to start with that foot again!"

"Actually, it starts with Rex selling the house in the first place. You know as well as I do, his mother blocked that in her will."

"Rumor."

"Fact. *She* told me it was to preserve the Stout inheritance."

"Not our business." Jane picked up our plates and carried them to the sink. "Henrietta was a dear, sweet woman who didn't deserve a son like Rex."

She'd get no argument from me about that. But discussing Rex Stout and all his foibles wasn't on my agenda.

"There was a mysterious character over there this morning."

"Oh? And what constitutes *mysterious* to you?"

I refused to allow her facetious tone to get to me. "What would you call someone who hangs around a moving van in the pouring rain?"

Jane turned back to me, narrowing her eyes. "And you can't think of a single reason for the guy to be there?"

I hated when she forced logic into the mix.

"Maybe," I conceded. "But you didn't see the strange way

Elsie acted when she came by for the sign."

"Elsie. Strange. Think about it."

"O-kay." I sighed. "But Rex—"

"Glory, are you listening to yourself? You sound like one of those old busybodies we used to make fun of as kids."

This none-too-pleasant picture hit me between the eyes, and my mouth slammed shut.

Once Jane secured all the dirty dishes into the dishwasher, she wheeled me toward the bedrooms. On the way through the living room, she flipped on the TV and turned up the volume.

". . . Though Parker's lawyers deny any wrongdoing in the Lantana Development acquisitions, the case..."

"That man can't seem to stay out of the news," Jane said as she deposited me inside my room. She set the walker in front of me, shaking her head over whatever news story the snippet came from. "You want to try getting up on your own?"

That was the understatement of the year. Being mobile again—on my own power—and not forced to rely on this blasted wheelchair was one hurdle I was ready to sail over. The problem is my balance. The cast is so heavy that every time I attempted to stand with crutches or use the walker, I tipped over.

Ever patient, my sister helped me up and assisted me into the bathroom. Once she was sure I wasn't going to fall and become a beached whale, she went off to do her own freshening up.

Later, in the car, Jane gently pointed out the buttons I had mismatched. While I fixed them and tried not to be embarrassed, she hummed a tune I didn't recognize. My mind being what it is, I knew I had to do something quick or I'd latch onto the tune and replay it over and over again while I tossed and turned that night.

"Detective Spencer said Rex Stout had been his insurance agent before everything blew up." Out of all the things I could have chosen for conversation, where had that come from?

"Doesn't surprise me. Rex had business from people in all walks of life. That was the one good thing to come out of your skateboarding fiasco."

Two of the three cars involved in trying to avoid the runaway skateboard had been insured through Stout. I imagine it was a shock to discover the premiums they'd given their agent never made it to the insurance company. Always resourceful, Rex managed to do some sleight of hand and got his clients covered. Still, the incident had been enough to make insurance investigators nervous. The next thing we knew, Rex was in a lot of trouble.

"I'll bet Henrietta was rolling in her grave," Jane said. "All that pampering and money and look how Rex abused it. Broke and in trouble within two years of her death!"

"First, you can't tell me he wasn't dipping into the family cache long before his mom died. And second, Henrietta has likely pestered God Himself for her own lightning bolt to shock some sense into her son."

"Or fire and brimstone." Jane laughed.

We stopped in front of the Hobbses' residence, not surprised to see half a dozen cars already there. Marla Hobbs loved entertaining and was constantly hosting church functions. Even when confined to a wheelchair after a hip replacement a year ago, she'd been the number one hostess in the community. For our purposes, it was a good thing her husband Gordon never got around to removing the ramp to their front door.

Meeting and greeting, smiles and laughter, little cakes that looked as if they'd been taken directly from the pages of a Betty Crocker cookbook, punch in delicate glass cups, and Marla flitting around like a nervous honey bee—it was enough to make my stomach churn. I smiled the smile, laughed the laugh but couldn't face the food.

If I could have fled, I'd have been out the door in a flash. Instead, with Jane looking down on me like she would one of her wayward first graders, I clutched my Bible until my knuckles turned as white as I figured my face already was.

I'd avoided this moment for more than two years. Whenever my turn came to lead, laryngitis, strep throat, or the flu struck me down with perfect timing. All through the New Testament and partway through the Old, I managed to be an onlooker, a backseat non-participant, taking in what was said and storing it up to use when I reread the chapters
in the privacy of my home.

There were some great thinkers in this little group, or so they believed, and discussion ran the gamut from one end of the doctrinal spectrum to the other. While I thought many of these ladies just liked to hear themselves talk, I knew the majority were

THE CASE OF THE BOUNCING GRANDMA

serious about studying the intricacies of the Bible and their faith. I wanted to learn all I could from them; that didn't mean I wanted first-hand participation.

Marla was clapping her hands together to get everyone's attention when I spotted Elsie Wilkes on the other side of the enormous living room. Elsie isn't just a realtor. She's also the only person in Tarryton who knows more about its citizens than they know themselves. A born gossip, Elsie is always happy to share any and all information for a price—you just have to be patient and willing to sit long enough for her to weave her tales in her own inimitable way.

"Ladies, ladies." Marla bestowed her welcoming smile on the masses—or at least on the twenty of us who were there. She patted her perfectly coifed hair as she awaited the requested silence. "Before we begin, let us bow our heads for a moment of prayer. Elsie?"

A moment? Elsie? Lord have mercy. Literally.

In her defense, it was a nice prayer, relatively simple for Elsie Wilkes, with no overt messages of gloom and doom and "what's this world coming to?" That was good, in and of itself. She even added a reminder to God to watch over Jared and his unit as they joined our other forces in the Middle East. I liked that. A lot.

When the prayer ended and the activity in the room shifted to the many chairs placed around the edges, Jane leaned down and whispered in my ear.

"You're on, kiddo."

Marla's introduction was a bit more elaborate, giving a history of where we were in our studies and where we were going.

"As you all know, Isaiah was the son of Amoz." Marla's voice was clear, precise, and, as always, authoritative. "But what you may not be aware of is that he was martyred by being sawed in half."

In the stunned silence that followed this revelation, she turned to me.

"Glory."

All eyes were glued to me in anticipation. I cleared my throat, swallowed audibly, and opened my Bible.

The words spoken by Isaiah, as dictated by God, poured forth, gaining strength the further I got into the chapter. The abject

sadness and loss God felt for His people, their betrayal,
    and all the chances He had given them always made me want to cry. Tonight was no different.

"Your New Moons and your appointed feasts My soul hates; They are a trouble to Me. I am weary of bearing them."

My voice no longer shook, and I was there with Isaiah urging Israel to penitence, to bow before God in righteousness and faith and not out of some perverted habit. When the chapter ended, I was spent. My heart and soul ached for God and for the people who had failed him. Kind of like me. There had been a gulf between God and me since Ike's death, something I had been unable to bridge. Why had God taken Ike? Was there some fault in me, in the way I lived?

As usual, I pushed these thoughts aside, refusing to give them any credence. Ike's death had shaken my faith but not my beliefs.

I knew God was still there. I just wasn't sure how closely He was listening.

For a while, discussion on the chapter was organized, and people waited their turn to voice their opinions and to share insights. Then someone had to ask how Marla learned the information regarding Isaiah's martyrdom. Soon, all semblance of chapter discussion was banished and the larger group broke into smaller ones.

Some of the ladies gravitated back toward the refreshment table that contained those too-perfect cakes; others carried on conversations from where they were sitting. I did my best to ditch my sister and headed for Elsie Wilkes.

While I was homing in on her, Elsie was coming straight toward me. We met somewhere in the middle.

"I understand there was some activity around your place this afternoon." Elsie smiled one of her I've-got-you-now-sucker smiles and offered me one of the two cups of punch in her hands.

Not wanting to offend her, I took the proffered drink.

"Um" was all I answered, knowing this would entice her to say more. I took a swallow of the punch and found it not as sweet as I expected.

"I didn't catch the numbers," Elsie was saying. "A customer came in right at the moment the scanner came on."

She knew the call numbers, what they stood for? *Thank you,*

THE CASE OF THE BOUNCING GRANDMA

Lord, for distracting her. While she expected news, a kind of give-and-take sort of thing, I wasn't about to tell her what I'd seen—she'd broadcast it all over the county before I even made it home tonight.

"They said something about looking for more witnesses to the accident a few weeks back." There, that sounded logical.

"Accident?" Elsie frowned. "Ah... your accident." She nodded, the frown still creasing her face.

When she began looking around at the crowd, I knew I had to capture her interest before she walked away. "Did you have any trouble with the sale of the Stout property?"

Obvious there, Glory, I thought. Too obvious.

Elsie eyed me for a millisecond before she pulled my chair over to a nearby loveseat. Sitting on the edge of a cushion, she leaned toward me, her eyes bright and conspiratorial.

"Isn't that something how things happen, Rex pocketing money that isn't his, gambling and running wild?" She shook her head. "It's a crying shame Henrietta's wishes for the property couldn't be carried out, but what was the judge to do?"

Okay, I'm following this. Sort of.

"Then it was a good thing the house sold." I offered.

Elsie nodded and took a delicate drink of her punch.

"Good? More like remarkable, considering the will stipulated the estate was to remain in Stout hands. You know how much Henrietta wanted grandchildren to carry on the Stout legacy."

I nearly choked on that—knowing what a philanderer Rex was, it was hard to believe there weren't some unclaimed Stout children running around somewhere. Elsie's wistful expression stopped me just in time.

"I don't know how they managed to get around it," she continued. "But it's likely what kept Rex out of jail. Well, that and the love and respect people had for Henrietta."

That same kind of sad, pensive look flitted across her face as she sighed. But her mercurial personality banished it in the blink of an eye. Had I not been paying attention, I never would have seen the slip in Elsie's demeanor.

"Though it's a shame about Rex's inheritance, the history of the people who bought the place is truly exciting. Have you met them yet?"

I shook my head, still playing catch-up on the conversation.

"They started moving in a few days ago."

"Wonderful. I really did like the girls, you know. Twins."

"Excuse me?"

"The twins were the ones I dealt with most of the time, the ones who *actually* have all the money. I didn't care as much for the father or the brother, and I only saw the mother at closing. Still, it's obvious they're wonderful people."

"Elsie, you lost me."

I didn't bother to tell her I'd been lost since the beginning of our conversation; I was too afraid she'd start all over again. And was it me, or did she seem particularly fond of the word *wonderful*? Did so many *wonderfuls* really mean the opposite?

"The family, silly. Their name is Midas, and it certainly suits them to a T. They're the folks who won the big lottery a couple months ago. Though the girls bought the tickets, they're sharing the winnings with the whole family. Isn't that nice? Such a Christian thing to do." She leaned forward, her voice lowering. "This is all in confidence, Glory, very hush-hush, you understand. They don't want just anyone knowing who they are."

"Aw, there you are." Jane swooped down on me like she hadn't seen me in days instead of just a few minutes.

"Elsie was just telling me a little about our new neighbors." *And I still have a lot of questions I'm sure she can answer.* Like why people with so much money would use a move-it-yourself moving van...

"Lovely girls," Elsie offered with a smile. "Not as educated and refined as you, Jane. Perhaps you could give them a few pointers."

To the unknowing listener this would be a compliment. To anyone who knew the history between Steven Acklin, my sister, and Elsie, this was a perfect time to duck... or at least beat a hasty retreat. Jane chose the latter.

"She's never forgiven you for coming back to town," I told my sister as she wheeled me down the ramp and over to our car.

"As if she ever had a chance with Steven! Besides, she's had thirty years to try to get his attention."

"She was too busy going after Rex Stout to notice the good doctor."

THE CASE OF THE BOUNCING GRANDMA

Jane practically shoved me into the car, then stood on the sidewalk huffing and puffing as she worked on collapsing the wheelchair. Few things in life got under my sister's skin; rarely did they manifest in fits of anger. But give her a face-to-face with Elsie Wilkes, and Jane would turn several shades of red until you thought steam might come out of her ears. I didn't know the details of what was between them and wasn't sure I wanted to know.

By the time we got back to my house, Jane and I were carrying on a normal conversation. She didn't ask about the information Elsie shared regarding our new neighbors, nor did I offer to tell her. I thought that was best for now.

Jane helped with the nightly ritual of duct taping a lawn-and-leaf bag over my cast so I could get a bath. Once I was out of the tub and tucked into bed, she said goodnight and went to her room down the hall.

I switched on the TV and found a *M*A*S*H* episode I hadn't already seen a dozen times. I didn't see it this time either. All I could think about was the foot I'd seen hanging out of the rug that afternoon.

No matter how many good-looking police detectives told me it was a plaster imitation of the real thing, I wouldn't believe it. I knew what I'd seen, and it wasn't part of a mannequin.

Outside, a loud thump from the direction of the old Stout place startled me. Sitting at attention, I hit the mute button on the remote and waited. Even after several minutes, there was nothing but the chirp of crickets outside my bedroom window.

I eyed the walker at the side of the bed, there for emergency trips to the bathroom. I thanked God there had never been any emergencies—my less-than-adept usage of the thing would have left me in a puddle long before I hit the linoleum. Still, it was there, and the wheelchair was just a little way across the room.

I shut off the TV and lay there barely breathing. I wondered if Jane was asleep. With the door closed, it was impossible to tell if she was watching TV in her room, reading, working, or whatever...

Okay, this was silly. If I wanted to get up and go to the den, I could do that. I was a grown-up and didn't need to ask for permission.

While I might not need permission, I wasn't altogether certain I could do this alone. After six weeks, I'd become so dependent on

33

other people to get around, to do even the simplest things, that I was almost afraid of trying anything on my own. And that had to stop.

Now.

With far less grace than I would have liked, I swung myself to the edge of the bed and grabbed the walker.

Chapter 5

I was definitely out of shape—or maybe that's more out of shape than I had been before my close encounter with the concrete on Walnut Avenue. The exercises designed to keep the upper body in tip-top condition during my sort of confinement might have worked better if I'd taken them a bit more seriously.

Still, after a lot of gasping and panting, and more sweat than I would ever admit to being capable of producing, I not only managed to get from bed to walker to wheelchair, I also maneuvered myself down the hallway and into the den without knocking too much paint off the walls. Jane would be proud of me—after she finished bawling me out for doing it in the first place.

I didn't bother turning on a lamp, just rolled up before my desk and switched on the computer. As it hummed to life, I pulled out a notepad and loaded the printer with paper. Once I found the information I was looking for, I wanted to make sure I didn't lose it. Printing was for everything I could get to cooperate, notes for the rest.

It's a marvelous tool, the computer, with the ability to tap into news and information from all over the world. Marvelous as long as no one tapped into mine. Jared and Andi made certain I was equipped with programs to capture and delete spyware, eliminate viruses and worms before they could do any damage, limit the amount of spam, protect me from phishing, and control cookies.

It sounded very technical and reminded me of the professors I worked with at the local college. They talked that way too. For my part, I figured as long as the machine did the things I asked of it, without giving me messages like "fatal error" and "irretrievable data," then we could be friends. I had a marked aversion to comments of "user error" and was doing my best to eliminate that phrase from my vocabulary.

I logged onto the Internet, adjusted myself in the wheelchair with the keyboard balanced on my knees, and settled in for a night of Googling. That's when my conscience assaulted me with Jane's voice calling me a busybody. I paused with my fingers hovering over the keys, deciding a reevaluation of my motives might be a good thing before pushing onward. After all, Jane wasn't the first to accuse me of the unsavory activity of spying. And to be perfectly honest, that *is* what I'd been doing. Still...

All the strange goings-on day *and* night—doors banging, loud voices, and everything else—it couldn't help but draw attention. And with me stuck in this blasted chair, I was helpless,

pulled in like a moth to a flame. Not the best analogy perhaps, but basically accurate.

Then, of course, there was the moving van parked on the street almost like it was on display. I mean, if those people really wanted privacy, they could have pulled the truck into the driveway where the enormous privet hedges on either side of the property lived up to their name to keep things hidden.

Except for that small area near the front. And my giant spirea bush blocked most of that anyway.

I pulled my hands back from the keyboard and tucked them beneath me. I couldn't believe I was sitting here arguing with myself! For goodness' sake, it wasn't a matter of national security, just curiosity.

Well, that, and the need to figure out who that foot might belong to.

Okay... it wasn't spying, it wasn't just being a busybody. This could be a case of life or death. I might be the only thing standing between someone's chance for survival...

Breathe. Get a grip, Glory. Remember what Jane said about logical explanations.

The Stouts', no, the Midases' driveway was really too narrow to accommodate a truck that size. Rex had discovered this several weeks earlier when he cleared out the house. At least the new people hadn't made Rex's mistake of backing across the lawn to the front door. The new grass put in after that fiasco was finally taking off.

See, logical.

Except for that foot.

Taking a deep breath, I flexed my fingers and went to work.

Using what I'd learned from my esteemed colleagues in the computer science department, and from my seven-year-old grandson, I put quotes around the Midas name, hit enter, and waited to see the search results. The sheer number of hits had my head spinning.

Okay... let's try Midas and lottery. Jackpot!

Again, there were a lot of hits. Scanning headers and blurbs, I attempted to find some sort of timeline for the media frenzy surrounding the Midases' lottery win. I finally gave up, and clicking the first entry, found myself staring into the beautiful faces of Chandra and Chelsea Midas, the twins dubbed "The girls with the Midas touch." It was a little cheesy, but you could tell from the smiles on their faces they didn't mind a bit.

Tall, willowy brunettes who looked more like models than most models did, Chelsea and Chandra quickly became media darlings, and not only in their home state of South Carolina. There were articles from newspapers across the country. One story suggested they were being considered for starring roles in an upcoming Spielberg film, another that they had been signed to write a book on their life and how they came to buy the ticket that made them multimillionaires.

The girls themselves appeared very humble. Though they ate up the attention and mugged for the cameras, they were consistent in declaring the winnings would be split between

their parents, their brother, and themselves. The family elected annual payouts rather than one lump sum, and even splitting it between the five of them over the next twenty-nine years, each share was more money than most people would see in a lifetime.

Everything I read about the twenty-year-old Midas twins made me like them. Despite their sudden wealth and popularity, they appeared to retain an innocence and naïveté that was touching. Their first expenditures included a sizable donation to the church they attended the last ten years, as well as improvements to homeless shelters across South Carolina. When asked about these donations, they smiled and blushed, stating they just wanted others to share in their good fortune.

And what did they want for themselves? Their answer was simple and straightforward: They wanted to get the college education they had put off all this time.

After the initial excitement, the desire to get out of the media whirlwind had the girls refusing interviews and striving to stay away from prying eyes. I understood their reasoning. I mean, winning the lottery had to be both a blessing and a nightmare. The sudden abundance replaced an existence of scrimping and saving, but it also brought a constant flow of people with their hands out.

Learning to cope with the media on top of the constant demands for attention and donations had to be overwhelming. Then there was the responsibility and management of their winnings, making sure taxes were paid, investments were researched...

The more I thought about it, the more it resembled the nightmare side of things. I empathized with their need to relocate. What I didn't understand was why they came here, a thousand miles from where they'd lived, to a place most people never heard of. Tarryton's biggest claim to fame was a small college that didn't even have a decent football team. The lack

of excitement may suit the parents, but I would think the girls might prefer the bright lights of a big city. I didn't get it.

As I peered closely at the faces on my monitor, looking from their glossy hair into the deep brown of their wide eyes, I got a strange sense of *déjà vu*, which was totally ridiculous. Hundreds of kids pass through my office at the college every year, but these young women had never been to college, never been to Missouri. So where was this feeling coming from?

The little cafe curtains on the window danced in the cool breeze. The fresh night air, filled with the heady scent of roses, vibrated with the song of crickets. Somewhere, a dull thud and an odd clang echoed through the darkness—probably someone working late in their garage. At night, even a slight noise was magnified here in the cul-de-sac, the reverberation building intensity as it might in a canyon. Just the kind of thing that could make one curious.

The sound of souped-up motors caught my attention. I didn't have to go to the window to know one of them would be Nick Pearson's hot red Mustang convertible. You could almost set your clock by Nick and his pals. Since he'd gotten his license earlier this year, he made it a habit to speed up the cul-de-sac around midnight, spin around the circle, and then peal out with a squeal of tires back down the hill.

I knew his parents tried to curtail his nocturnal activities, keep him at home and away from the kids he'd been hanging with, but it didn't appear to be working. It was a shame, too; he used to be such a nice boy.

There it was, the squeal of tires and gunning of a motor. I hoped the kids didn't plow into the moving van and hurt themselves.

I raised my wrist and turned it so I could see my watch in the light coming from the monitor; Nick was right on time. As the sound dissipated, I added a prayer that he'd get home safe and sound.

While the printer played catch-up on the pages I'd asked it to print, I continued to search the faces of my new neighbors. The brother, Frank Midas, didn't look like the kind of person you'd want to meet on a street in broad daylight, let alone in a dark alley. His hooded eyes seemed shifty to me, and the consistent smirk he had for the cameras gave me the creeps.

I estimated his age in the mid to late thirties, and from the poses he struck to the way he played with the small spot of whiskers beneath his lower lip—a so-called soul patch—I figured he believed himself a ladies' man. The way he handled questions from the media proved he thought pretty highly of himself. His lack of education hadn't held him back—at least, in his own mind.

There was speculation about Frank, about his status as the twins' half brother, and about his cocky attitude. One reporter broached the subject of his incarceration on an assault charge and was quickly hushed by the beautiful sisters.

Ah, a suspect. It wasn't just his previous jail time. I suddenly realized Frank Midas was the "moving man" who'd tripped over the rug then later lost his hold on the carpet with the foot dangling out the back.

Okay. Let's do this scientifically—or at least in a similar fashion to what I'd seen on *Without A Trace*. I pulled a piece of paper from the ream and wrote "Foot in a rug" at the top of the page. From there, I drew a diagonal line and wrote "Frank Midas."

That would do for now.

I found little on the mother and father. Every photo I came across showed Helen and Darrell Midas always on the periphery. Of course, the main attraction was the twins, but that hadn't kept Frank away from the cameras. When the girls were presented their check, he was standing between them, an arm around each of his sisters. Sure, the parents were there, but not up front—they'd stood behind their children where you could barely see them.

While it seemed a little odd to me, I understood how all the attention could make a person uncomfortable. I would be. Still, it was disappointing not to find a clear photo of either parent.

The more I read and studied the pictures, the more uncomfortable I felt. It wasn't just Frank Midas's surly expression, the elusive parents, or the fact they ended up in the house next door—which was still hard to believe. Some things just didn't add up—like why they moved themselves when they had all that money at their disposal. Perhaps it was a privacy issue, a way to keep their new location out of the public eye. After all the publicity, that would make sense.

Right?

And if the one "moving man" was Frank Midas, was the other his father or another family member? Did it really matter?

It might, if it came to keeping a confidence of the deadliest kind.

Though nothing I read or saw in this research gave me the slightest hint into the mystery of the dangling foot, as I gathered the pages from the printer, I couldn't help but wonder which of these people might be capable of murder.

Chapter 6

"Glory Adele Montgomery Harper!"

Okay, there it was, the dreaded moniker that told me I was in big trouble. Raising my head from the desk, I swiped at a piece of paper that stuck to my cheek. As I gazed up at my sister, the expression on her face softened a little, but only for a moment.

"How can you expect to get better if you stay up all night?" Jane removed a pen from behind my ear and shook her head.

"I wasn't up. I was sleeping. Or was until you hollered at me." I would have moved away from the desk but didn't want to risk running over Jane's feet.

Jane strode behind the wheelchair and angled us toward the door. "I need to get to work. We have some in-service meetings this morning. I'll be back to pick you up for your doctor's appointment at one. Is Andi bringing Seth over?"

"She didn't say anything. I assumed she didn't have to be at the meetings."

Andi's part-time status as a kindergarten teacher didn't require her to be at some staff meetings. This time, however, I figured it had more to do with Jared's deployment than anything else.

Jane deposited me at the kitchen table and set a plate of toast in front of me. I wouldn't fight her over my dislike of breakfast this morning; I didn't feel like being clobbered—

verbally or otherwise.

"I brought in last night's paper." She put it down next to me, so I was able to read the headline: "Tarryton New Home of Super Lottery Celebrities."

"There goes the neighborhood." I smirked, gazing up at my sister.

"Those poor people should have been warned about Elsie

Wilkes. Oh yes, I heard her telling you they wanted to keep a low profile."

"Hush-hush was how she put it." I shook my head. "This was the kind of thing they were trying to escape."

"Well, the cat's out of the bag now." Jane stared down at me. "I'll put another lawn-and-leaf bag in your bedroom along with the duct tape. You have ink all over the side of your face, and I don't even want to know what's stuck in your hair."

She sighed and crossed her arms over her tiny midriff.

"On second thought, I'll put the things in Andi's old bedroom so you can use the shower stall. Now I know you can manipulate that walker—"

"Jane." She hates being stopped in mid-sentence, but I thought I'd risk it anyway. "Thank you."

"What?"

"For all your help."

"Um." She uncrossed her arms and stared at me a moment longer before she left the kitchen.

She returned a couple minutes later, her book bag slung over her shoulder, her keys in hand. "See if you can stay out of trouble between now and noon. And be careful getting in and out of the shower."

"I've got your number on speed dial."

My attempt at humor failed to draw a grin. Maybe she'd slept funny.

"You'll be in a better mood once we see Dr. Steven," I told her as she grabbed for the door leading into the garage.

Not even that elicited a smile. She left without so much as an acknowledgement.

I wondered what might be bothering Jane. Her irritation at finding me asleep in the den was out of proportion to her normal congenial personality. While it was true she didn't always approve of my behavior, she never voiced it in a mean-spirited way. Though I was sure she wanted to at times.

Eyeing the toast, I grabbed the jar of grape jelly Jane had left on the table for me, and slathered enough on the bread to feed a very small third world country. It still didn't look appetizing.

So if it wasn't something I'd done that was eating at my sister, what could it be? I knew it couldn't be work related, which left...

Dr. Dreamboat!

I tossed the now soggy toast back onto the plate and clapped my hands. *This* was getting interesting.

The rest of the morning passed smoothly; even using the shower stall and dressing wasn't as difficult as I anticipated. I did worry about not hearing from Andi and wondered what

was going on. I didn't want to call her regular phone in case Jared was trying to get in touch with her, and I couldn't find her cell number—I couldn't remember what I'd done with my cell phone at all. Using my landline to call my cell flitted briefly across my brain, but the idea just seemed too silly.

Despite the incredible amount of pull the window exerted, I exercised my rather anemic willpower and avoided it for most of the morning. Yet from where I sat across the living room, I could see the moving van was still parked in front of the old Stout—Midas—place. It looked different from yesterday, but that was probably just because the sheer curtains gave it a kind of wavy outline.

Try as I might to keep my mind off the Midas family, my thoughts kept returning to them and the foot I'd spotted. No matter how many times I tried to convince myself the cops were right, that it was just part of a mannequin, my head insisted they were wrong.

I picked up the James Patterson suspense I was nearly finished reading and tried to concentrate.

Were the Midases finished unloading their belongings? Had they found the body in the rug?

That was a silly thought. Someone in the household had to know the body was there and must have a plan to deal with it.

Unless, by some remote chance, someone outside the family had taken advantage of the van sitting around the last several days and dumped the body. The thought brought a shiver of apprehension along with a vision of the man with a limp lurking by the van in the pouring rain.

But if that had been the case, that the crime had been committed by a third party, the police would have been notified by now. Right?

I gazed back down at the book, once again trying to concentrate on the words in front of me.

Could it be my fascination with mysteries, suspense, and crime dramas that led me to see something that just wasn't there? Had my boredom and overactive imagination been working overtime?

How long would it take for me to stop questioning my every thought, every mood? Had I always been like this?

Was there an echo in this room, or just in my head?

Setting the book on a nearby end table, I glared at the cast-encased leg propped on the wheelchair extension. If I didn't get out of this thing pretty soon, I would be nuttier than one of those stale fruitcakes passed around at Christmastime. It wasn't an appetizing thought.

Around eleven-thirty I heard the rumble of a bad muffler on the street in front of my house. I recognized the sound. It was the old Dodge pickup owned by the Midas family or someone helping with the move.

Going to the window, I watched the pickup back partway into the Midases' driveway, yet angled toward the moving van. A man rose from the bed of the truck. The driver came to his assistance, and they lifted a small chest freezer down to the ground.

"Looks like it came from a dump," I muttered, noticing how banged up the freezer appeared even from this distance.

I was about to lower the curtain when the driver, who'd just gone up the ramp and into the van, began to shout. He shoved a dolly down the ramp and over to where they'd set the freezer.

I couldn't hear what was being said, but it was obvious he was angry. While he strapped the freezer to the dolly, the other man went over to the truck and peered inside. This time I heard one of the words: *cops.*

Now I realized why the van looked different; the logo appeared to have been altered with some kind of paint.

Just as things were getting interesting, Jane's car pulled up the street and into the garage. I let the curtain drop back into place and moved away from the window. I wanted to share what I'd just seen but thought it might be better to test the water first.

Jane was in much better humor—probably the anticipation of seeing Steven Acklin. She was so full of news from the school that I hated to interrupt her. I just let her chat away while we ate a light lunch.

THE CASE OF THE BOUNCING GRANDMA

"Find anything interesting in your research?" Jane asked when we were on our way to her favorite doctor's office.

"I'm not sure." I told her, surprised she'd brought it up. "I can't figure out why anyone who just won over *fifty million dollars* would move here, but other than that..."

"You know they don't get all their winnings right away. They would be on some kind of payment schedule. Then, of course, the IRS has to have its percentage. I think I read somewhere that it could be thirty percent or more. That's a big chunk."

"But Tarryton? Why here?"

Jane shrugged. "It's a nice, quiet, out-of-the-way community where nothing much happens. Most of the time." She stopped at a red light, and I followed her gaze to my cast.

"Like I'm the only one who makes news around here. Have you forgotten Sticky Fingers Rex?"

"I don't have to live with him."

"Good thing too, or you and Dr. Dreamboat would be in real trouble."

The doctor's office wasn't busy when we got there, and we were hustled right in. The first thing on the agenda was an X-ray of the leg. Afterward, we were ushered into a consultation room to await Dr. Steven.

Jane fussed with her hair while peering into a stainless steel paper towel dispenser. I didn't attempt to assure her she looked terrific; she wouldn't have taken my word for it anyway.

I couldn't help but smile over my sister's infatuation for my doctor and loved being able to take some credit for getting them together. Sure, they saw one another at church, and Steven had called her a time or two over the last few years, but it wasn't until I broke my leg that the sparks began to fly. Then again, maybe the sparks had been waiting until Jane felt more able to handle them— and Don's death.

When Steven Acklin entered the room, his dark eyes instantly sought Jane. His smile was infectious even when it wasn't bestowed on you. I found myself smiling back, despite being ignored.

"Jane you look wonderful."

He brushed a hand through hair more gray than brown, then held that same hand out to my sister. She blushed, shook his hand, then sat in the open chair.

Up on the examination table, I cleared my throat and lifted my plaster-covered leg.

"Ah, Glory." He tore his eyes from Jane and gazed down at my leg. "The X-ray looks good. As long as you behave yourself, I think we can take the cast off next week."

Jane about choked on the words *behave yourself.* I was ready with a quick comeback, but one look at my sister told me I'd better hold it.

"And what would entail my behaving myself?"

I tried my best to give him a sweet and innocent smile. Not that he would have noticed; he was back to ogling Jane.

"Just continue to baby your leg. Don't try to be Superwoman and overdo," he answered without turning back to me. "I know you didn't get along with crutches, but you'll have to get used to them. And it would be a good idea to do that before we remove the cast."

He tore his eyes from my sister and met my gaze. "You need to remember that you won't be able to put any real weight on the leg for some time, which is where the crutches come into play. We'll get you into PT, and they'll help you work the muscles, give you strength training exercises, things like that."

"Ah, no trampolines?"

"Glory!" They were paying more attention to me than I'd thought.

"Joke, guys. Okay?"

"Are we still on for dinner Saturday?" Dr. Dreamboat asked my adoring sister. The way the two were eyeballing one another definitely gave me the crowd status, as in three's a crowd.

I tuned out the exchange, concentrating instead on the news that the cast would soon be history. And as much as I hated the admonishment, he was right about the need to get proficient in the use of crutches. Surely I'd get the hang of it once I was free from this hunk of plaster.

The way Dr. Steven presented the new set of crutches to my sister, you would have thought it was an engagement ring. While their starry-eyed glances were sweet, it was becoming a little old. Besides, I was anxious to get out of there so we could check on Andi and Seth.

"You two going steady yet?" I asked after the doctor left us

THE CASE OF THE BOUNCING GRANDMA

near the waiting room.

"Going steady?" Jane pushed the wheelchair access button to open the doors to the outside. "For someone so young, you certainly use old-fashioned terminology."

She was throwing my words back at me. Hey, I was up for the challenge.

"When's the dude going to lay some major bling on you so you can hook up on a permanent basis?"

We giggled all the way to the car.

Once ensconced in the front seat, I decided to dig through my fanny pack on the off chance my cell phone was actually where it was supposed to be. I lifted out my checkbook, wallet, a wad of tissues, and lo and behold, there was the phone!

"How the devil do you manage to get so much junk in that little thing?" Jane asked, sliding behind the steering wheel.

"Magic." I pressed the one-button-dial for Andi and listened to the phone on the other end ring until the answering machine picked up. "Sweetie, it's Mama. Jane and I are just leaving the doctor's office and thought we'd drop by. See you in a bit."

"She's probably out with Seth." Jane said, reaching over to pat my good leg. "You're worrying for nothing."

"I'm not worried. Not really. It's just..."

"I know, Glory. They'll be fine, you'll see. All of them."

Jane was my hero. Despite everything life had thrown at her, she remained strong and optimistic. She'd always wanted to be a mother, and her love of children led her to teaching. While she and Don prayed for a baby of their own, they taught Sunday school, took in foster children, and poured out their love on every child who crossed their path.

They doted on Andi, mourned when I couldn't have another baby, and were finally able to rejoice when their own was on the way. Years after they stopped "trying" for a baby, they suddenly found themselves preparing for twins. I stole another glance at my sister, took in the serenity on her lovely face, and said a little prayer for those tiny infants, lost at the end of her second trimester so many years ago.

Jane was not only the greatest sister anyone could ever want, she was also my best friend. We'd seen one another through good times and bad, and I'd watched as tragedy brought out a strength

47

she insisted belonged to God, not her. Her life was a true testament to her faith and God's grace.

"Why are you crying?" Jane asked as she pulled into Andi's driveway.

"I'm not," I sputtered. "The sun's in my eyes."

Andi answered the door, her eyes red and swollen. She swiped at the tears with the back of her hand and stood aside so we could enter the house.

"I just got your message. I was dropping Seth off at Mindy's so he and Nathan could play. They need the distraction as much as I do."

The heart-wrenching sigh that issued from my daughter had me wanting to take her into my arms to comfort her. But right now, I knew it was better to wait for her to come to me.

"Did you hear from Jared?" I asked.

Andi nodded. She led us into the living room and asked if we wanted anything to eat or drink—she got that trait from her aunt.

"He didn't call last night; I got an e-mail this morning. He said everything was on the QT, and it might be a while till I heard from him again." Her soft eyes filled with tears. "I was doing good, honest I was, then I thought about what Seth said yesterday. I'm just so scared, Mama."

Jane joined us, and we had a three-way hug, followed by a prayer asking God to place a circle of protection around Jared and his buddies. Afterward, Jane regaled Andi with the incident that led three policemen to my house the day before. It wasn't long until laughter replaced the tears.

"A foot? Ah, Mama, how on earth could you believe it was real?"

"I think she's out to prove us all wrong," Jane winked at my daughter, and they both giggled.

"Fine, laugh at my expense. I don't mind. I know what I saw. You would've seen it too, if you'd looked when I told you to."

"Right, a mannequin." Andi gave me a quick hug. "We're not laughing at you, honest we're not."

"Speak for yourself," Jane told her.

Now, what was I thinking earlier? That Jane was my hero? I'd forgotten to add that she was also my tormentor.

"But two police cars? Oh, Mama, what will the neighbors be

thinking?" Andi shook her head, causing her long blonde curls to dance across her shoulders.

"That's when Detective Spencer arrived," Jane was saying.

"Spencer? You mean—"

Jane shushed Andi with a cock of her head in my direction. What was that all about?

"Do you know him?"

Andi's eyes widened, and she stole a look at Jane before turning back to me. "All the officers are part of the fire department. You know that. Jared and I've met them at one time or another."

"You're trying to change the subject, Glory." Jane interjected. "It's time to fess up."

Refusing to remain the brunt of their discussion, I decided it was time to add my two cents. "Jane was so struck with the guy she couldn't even shake his hand. You never saw anyone exit a room so fast."

"I had chicken on the stove."

"A likely story."

Jane stuck her tongue out at me in a very unladylike and immature manner. I followed suit, thrilled to see I was rubbing off on her.

"As for the rest of it," I continued. "Whether you believe it or not, I did see a foot—and not that of a mannequin. And I'll bet the old chest freezer they got today is where they're going to put the body."

"Glory, tell me you didn't call the cops about your latest theory." Jane appeared horrified at the idea.

Just to turn the tables on her a little, and torment her, I waited a beat before answering. "No, I didn't call them. Yet."

The conversation went downhill from there. When Jane and Andi brought up the dinner date I'd missed because of the skateboarding accident, I knew it was time to go home.

How could they believe I'd deliberately broken my leg just to get out of their matchmaking attempt? Besides, if I'd been trying to weasel out of the blind date with their mystery man, I would have figured out a less painful way to do it.

As we were leaving, Andi's friend Mindy Allen arrived with Seth and Nathan in tow. One look at Mindy's face proved she wasn't doing any better with the news about their husbands than Andi was. After a quick hug and kiss for my grandson, Jane and I were heading home.

And I was trying to devise a plan to get into the Midas house.

Chapter 7

"Cookies? You want me to make cookies?" Jane flashed me one of those looks that made me feel like my hair was standing on end or my head wasn't screwed on right. I found myself smoothing my hair and testing the scrunchie that held my ponytail in place.

"It would be the neighborly thing to do," I told her, pointing toward the road to make sure her attention remained on her driving.

"Under ordinary circumstances, perhaps, but you've accused these people of murder."

"I did not." My protest was honest. After all, I hadn't accused anyone in particular of murder, just insisted a body was in one of their carpets. That didn't actually constitute an accusation. At least, not toward any one individual.

"You called the cops on them."

"They don't know that. As long as the officers did their job right, anyway."

"Glory, I don't think—"

"It's the right thing to do, Jane, to welcome them to the neighborhood. Especially after Elsie betrayed their trust and handed them to the press."

That was a sound approach. Would she buy it?

"I don't know," Jane hedged.

We turned off Barry Road and onto Walnut Avenue, past the scene of the accident

caused by the runaway skateboard. Just a few more blocks and we'd be home. I wanted her convinced by the time we pulled into the garage.

"You make the most marvelous cookies. And it's the perfect

treat after all the work they've had moving."

Jane loved to cook, and her baking was top-notch. She always volunteered to help with church suppers, took meals to the elderly, and contributed so much to every bake sale in town that between her and Marla Hobbs, no one else needed to do anything except show up to buy.

"Ah, come on, Glory. You're not fighting fair."

"They'll see you coming with a plate of cookies, and—"

"Wonder what this loser is after." Jane sighed. "Maybe if the story hadn't been in the paper—"

"And that's precisely why we *need* to do this!" The perfect opening. "Don't you see, they came here to escape the media frenzy, make a new start? Their realtor, the person they've confided in, has broken their confidence, and they have to be wondering if they've made a mistake coming to Tarryton after all."

I was on a roll now—and we were about to pull into the garage. "See there, the moving van's gone. They have even more ahead of them now. They'll be so busy—"

"A cake would really be better," Jane mused as the garage door closed.

"Your cakes are divine, Janie, but cookies are faster." I had her hooked now.

Once inside, she was off and running—mission accomplished.

Now I had a legitimate reason to get into the Midas house.

Wow, the Midas house. It was strange to think about that grand old place without the Stout name attached to it.

After the wear and tear of three generations, Henrietta had improved on the original and updated everything shortly before her death. Nothing was too good for future generations of her family. She just hadn't counted on her only son turning into a thief and a scoundrel.

The delicious aroma of freshly baked cookies filled my nostrils. I sniffed the air and detected the scent of oatmeal.

A healthy choice that could be made even better with a decadent helping of chocolate chips, or fun and chewy with gumdrops, like our mom used to make. This was definitely an excellent idea.

Twenty minutes later, I held a Styrofoam platter of cookies on my lap while Jane pushed my wheelchair across the street toward

THE CASE OF THE BOUNCING GRANDMA

the Midases' driveway.

"Give it up, Glory. You wanted cookies, you got cookies."

"But oatmeal with raisins? With *raisins*, Jane? Not everybody likes raisins."

I knew I didn't. All those dreams of delectable cookies with special treats hidden inside had been dashed. Raisins!

"They're a good, healthy treat. Now quit your bellyaching and show a little gratitude."

"I am grateful. Truly I am. Thank you for going the extra mile."

Why not something normal like chocolate chips? Why hadn't that little package of gumdrops on the counter spurred her imagination and reminded her of when we were kids?

"You don't sound grateful," Jane grumbled behind me as we made our way up the sidewalk that ran from the street where the van had been parked straight to the front door.

"And right now, you need to be *very grateful indeed*."

I'd forgotten about the three steps that led to the porch. There was no way Jane could get me up there short of dumping me out of the wheelchair, which she might be considering at the moment.

"Any brilliant ideas?" she asked, her voice leaning toward the snide.

I surveyed the area, then remembered there was a side door that opened right into a butler's pantry in the kitchen—no steps. I was about to suggest heading there when the front door opened.

"Well, I'll be!" One of the Midas twins stared down at us, a hand patting her chest. "Y'all startled me," she laughed. Her dark brown eyes crinkled at the corners but remained wary.

"We brought you some cookies." I held up the plate and smiled. "I'm Glory Harper, and this is my sister, Jane Calvin. My house is the one just to your—er, right."

"How thoughtful of you to think of us. I can smell the cookies from here. Oatmeal, aren't they?"

"With raisins," Jane added.

"My favorite!" The girl's eyes lit with glee. She left the doorway where she'd hovered and skipped down the stairs.

"I'd like to ask you in, but we've got a bit of a problem here." She regarded the wheelchair a moment, then turned back to the steps.

53

"We don't want to impose," Jane spoke up as I was about to offer the alternate route. "You were on your way out."

"Out?" The girl looked confused. "Oh, that. I was going to the mailbox. Right now, even junk mail is exciting." She giggled. "There's another door down here a bit, if you don't mind going through the kitchen."

As we followed her, the young woman bubbled over, obviously thrilled to have company.

"This house is so big it takes getting used to," she threw over her shoulder. "Every day I find more and more to love about it and that enormous backyard. Daddy and Frank are going to put in a fountain and—"

She turned to us, her cheeks blossoming in a full-blown blush. "I apologize for going on like that, but you're the first ones to come by. Well, that's not altogether true."

Jane poked me in the back and leaned down to speak in my ear. "Here it comes."

I knew she was referring to yesterday's visit from the police.

I held my breath, crossed my fingers, and prayed she was wrong.

The girl held the door open for us. "Our first day here, a kid with his face painted a deathly white came by asking for a job. I'd never seen so many piercings in someone's face before." She shivered. "Very weird."

"It was probably Nick Pearson from farther down the street. He takes getting used to."

Or not. I made a mental note to add Nick and his parents to my daily prayers. It wouldn't hurt to include the kids he hung with either.

"Well, Daddy wasn't as pleasant to him as he should have been, I'm afraid."

She led us into the long hallway that connected to the front of the house. As we neared the living room, I realized that a lot of the furniture was familiar—and not because I'd seen it unloaded from the van.

"These belonged to Henrietta."

"The former owner." She nodded. "Most of our stuff wasn't very nice—not nice enough for this place anyway. They had all these wonderful things in storage and asked if we'd be interested in any of it. To tell the truth, we bought most of the furniture and all the carpets. If we'd known in advance, they wouldn't have had to take everything out of here in the first place."

All that money and they bought the former owner's stuff? Did that make sense?

I twisted around in the wheelchair and flashed my sister a questioning glance. Jane shrugged, pointed to the girl, and mouthed, "Behave."

In their defense, the pieces they'd chosen were antiques in excellent condition, so maybe it wasn't as odd as I thought.

Still...

The living room contained most of the furniture I remembered from when Henrietta had been alive. The only thing missing appeared to be the large painting of her and Rex that once hung above the fireplace.

"You ladies just make yourselves at home." She held her hand out for the platter of cookies. "Where are my manners? I totally forgot to introduce myself. I'm Chandra, Chandra Midas."

The corner of her mouth twitched, and her blush deepened as she relieved me of the plate. "I'll make us some lemonade to go along with these cookies." She scooted out the door with a little wave.

Jane pushed me over to the sofa and then sank onto it. She looked hot and tired, which made me feel like a heel for giving her a hard time about the cookies.

"Sorry about the grousing," I told her. "Your instincts were right on target."

She could have said "I told you so," but didn't. She accepted her victory with grace—and a self-satisfied chuckle.

"We'll show that idiot a thing or two. Can you believe—"

The girl who entered the room stood stock-still, staring at Jane and me. Since her clothing was different, I figured this must be the other twin.

"Uh, um, excuse me," she sputtered. "I didn't know we had company." Her mouth tightened, and streaks of red ran from her neck into her cheeks. She didn't appear happy to see us.

"We're your neighbors," I told her, hoping to set her at ease.

"From the blue and white house." She nodded. "I've seen you folks out in your yard a few times." There was no smile or welcome in this girl's expression.

"There you are, Chelsea!"

Chandra entered the living room carrying a tray laden with a pitcher of lemonade and glasses. She'd taken the cookies off the Styrofoam platter and arranged them onto a china plate I recognized. Rex must have sold them his mother's china too.

Chelsea followed her sister but didn't take a seat. She hovered nearby, her eyes darting from us to the doorway. With everything they'd been through, I expected them to be guarded, even suspicious, but her attitude went beyond that. Was she the one with something to hide—like a body?

"This is Jane and..." Chandra frowned slightly. "...Glory. Right?"

"Very good. You got it right the first time. Everyone wants to call me Gloria."

I threw my sister a look I hoped would keep her from repeating the story of how I'd gotten my name. I still couldn't believe she'd told that detective yesterday.

"I like Glory much better." Chandra grinned. "Chels, look, they brought our favorite—oatmeal raisin."

As Chandra placed the tray on the coffee table, her sister eased closer to the rest of us. After inspecting the spread on the tray, she must have decided the cookies were worth putting up with a couple of strangers. She sat on the smaller sofa opposite us and helped Chandra serve the snack.

"They know that boy, the one with all the piercings."

Chandra handed me a napkin along with a couple of cookies.

"Do you think he's into vandalism?" The other girl's attitude hadn't softened just because we'd brought their favorite dessert. If anything, she seemed even more guarded.

"I hope not." I recalled the morning's incident, the angry men, and the logo of the truck looking as though it had been painted over. "Has something happened?" Okay, that wasn't as smooth as I'd have liked.

"Chels, this isn't the time—"

"The least they can do is give us his name so we can tell the cops to check into him."

"Nick Pearson," Jane offered with a tight smile of her own. "He's a little off the wall and hasn't been running with the best crowd. Still, I thought he had more sense than to do anything illegal."

"Well, someone has." Chelsea Midas's dark chocolate eyes were hard as she regarded Jane and me. "We've had nothing but trouble since we got here. As bad as it's been, last night was even worse. The lock on the van was busted and someone destroyed what was left inside."

She sat back against the sofa and took a bite of her cookie. "These are really good, by the way. Thanks for bringing them over."

She might like the cookies, but she didn't appear to like us—at all. My attention went to Chandra. Her lowered eyes and the renewed blush on her cheeks spoke volumes; her sister's behavior embarrassed her.

"The cookies *are* wonderful," Chandra said, finally raising her eyes to look at us. "I've never had better. You'll have to give me the recipe."

"I'd be happy to," Jane responded with a smile that I knew was intended to put both girls at ease. It might work on Chandra, but I was betting Chelsea was a harder sell.

"I'm sorry you've had problems," I said. "This really is a nice neighborhood, and Tarryton's never had much crime."

I fiddled with the cookies Chandra gave me. If I wasn't careful, I'd end up with a lapful of crumbs, which really wasn't such a bad thing. It would keep me from having to eat those dreaded raisins...

"You have no idea what it's like to open a dresser drawer and find a dead squirrel inside. What kind of person would put rotting carcasses in a moving van full of furniture? You can't imagine the stench—"

"Chels," Chandra pleaded.

Out of the corner of my eye, I saw Jane lower a cookie back onto the napkin in her lap as she covered her mouth.

This talk of death and decay wouldn't be sitting well with my sister's delicate stomach.

It wasn't doing mine much good either.

"We should have said something when the police were here yesterday, but we didn't want to cause any trouble."

Chelsea's voice remained cold, unrelenting. "With all the cops at your place, we thought there might've been a break-in there too."

Though I wanted to know more about the sabotage of their belongings, the subject matter wasn't good for getting to know one another. We needed to break the ice, get Chelsea to see us as friends, not the enemy.

I peered over at Jane and found she'd developed a fascination for her glass of lemonade. Since I was on my own, I might as well go for broke.

"Actually, they were checking into an accident that happened a few weeks back." I grimaced and patted my cast.

This was the most logical explanation I could come up with, short of telling them about the foot in the carpet. And if I couldn't laugh at myself...

"I, uh, lost a skateboard on the hill, and it ended up causing a three-car pileup."

"You were on a skateboard?"

Chelsea's amazement brought an ornery gleam to her dark eyes. My gambit may have worked; she already looked friendlier.

"She was," Jane joined in. "She was trying to show her grandson how easy it was. I think it lost something in translation."

"Guess you're no Tony Hawk, huh?" Chandra said with a giggle.

I looked at Jane to see if she knew who this Hawk guy was. She simply shrugged.

"Just for the record, who's that?" I hated showing my ignorance, but in this case there wasn't any choice.

"He's a professional skater—skateboarder—that Channy used to idolize," Chelsea answered, her eyes rolling at the blush forming on her sister's cheeks.

Though it meant more ribbing about my skateboarding incident, I was glad sharing it worked as I'd hoped. As both girls relaxed, we began the process of getting to know one another. They'd been through a lot since winning the lottery, and trusting strangers wasn't easy for either of them—especially Chelsea.

"We're trying to get things together so we can enroll at the college this fall," Chelsea told us with a sigh. "We were homeschooled, but we did take the SATs. That was a while ago, though."

"Then, of course, we're from out of state," Chandra said. "So we're not sure how that will be handled."

"I don't think you'll have any trouble getting into the school here. It's a small college, but we have a lot of great programs and instructors. I'm on leave right now, but I've worked there for several years, so if you have any questions or concerns, I can probably point you in the right direction."

This brought a genuine smile to Chelsea's face. It was like someone had turned on a light inside her.

"Are you an instructor there?"

The choking sound from Jane had all eyes trained on her. She mumbled, "Pardon me," then turned her gaze to me.

"I'm not a teacher, no, but I've worked as a secretary or admin in several departments over the years. The admissions office will help you figure things out."

"I've never met anyone who's been homeschooled through senior high. I admire you and your parents." Jane set her empty glass onto the serving tray. "That had to have been difficult."

"Not for Mama," Chandra chimed in. "She can do anything she sets her mind to."

"We moved around a lot in the early years, so having Mama as a teacher meant we never had to get used to a new school," Chelsea added. "Then, when we moved to Brees Run, we were out in the middle of nowhere, so it was the perfect solution. Mama says that once she got started on our lessons, it was so much fun, she didn't want to stop."

"I've been impressed with the quality of education and curriculum of most homeschool programs," Jane said. "But as a teacher, I'm concerned about the socialization issue. I know there are homeschool groups formed to give children almost as much interaction as they'd have at school, and they sound impressive. Still..." She crossed her legs, her expression thoughtful. "There's something to be said for formal education. But perhaps that's just my old-fashioned take on it."

Was this dangerous ground? Not wanting to risk our tenuous relationship, I searched for something to change the subject.

The mannequins.

"Which one of you is the seamstress?"

I didn't think the question was funny, but both girls started laughing.

"I'm sorry, Glory," Chandra said, coming up for air. "The one thing Mama hasn't been able to teach us is to be good at sewing. We're all thumbs when it comes to anything even remotely associated with it. Mama's the one with the talent."

"She made all our clothes for the longest time, even brought in extra money sewing for others."

Chandra nodded at her sister. "That's right. She wanted to be a designer, but it just wasn't in the cards. Maybe now we're grown and we've got the lottery money—"

A noise from the hallway had all of us turning toward the room's entrance. A slender woman stood just inside the living room, a frown creasing her brow. She had auburn hair lightly frosted with streaks of gray and icy blue eyes that reminded me of a cold winter's day. Though she wore jeans and a simple T-shirt, she exuded an air of sophistication and arrogance that seemed out of place—especially when compared with the twins.

"I didn't know we had company." If possible, her voice was more frigid than Chelsea's had been earlier. "Are we having some sort of party, girls?"

Once again, Chandra's face flushed, and she lowered her eyes. In contrast, Chelsea stared straight into the woman's eyes, stood, and walked toward her.

"Mama, I'd like you to meet our neighbors from the little blue and white ranch next door." Chelsea took hold of her mother's arm and drew her into the room. "Glory and Jane, this is our mother, Helen Midas."

Helen inclined her head in our direction. "Charmed, I'm sure." She didn't sound charmed. She sounded angry.

That voice! She was the woman I'd heard yelling at the moving men, who'd told them to be especially careful with the carpets.

"They brought us cookies as a housewarming gift," Chelsea continued. "Wasn't that nice?"

The older woman's expression softened slightly as she patted her daughter's hand. "That's lovely, dear. However, your father and brother will be back any moment and we don't want to be caught playing now, do we?"

THE CASE OF THE BOUNCING GRANDMA

Helen Midas gazed at the remnants of our snack with what I perceived as barely contained disgust. When her icy stare fell on Jane and me, her mouth tightened into a thin, harsh line.

Jane peeked at her watch, tapped the face, and stood.

"And we really must be going." She took my glass and the napkin filled with broken bits of cookies, and set them on the serving tray.

"It was nice to meet all of you," Jane said, grabbing hold of my wheelchair.

"It certainly was." I held my hand out to poor Chandra, who seemed mortified by what was going on.

What was going on anyway?

Chandra took my hand and gave it a gentle squeeze. "Don't forget to give me that recipe."

"I second that motion," Chelsea said with a grin that seemed to waver at the corners.

Helen Midas didn't utter another word as the girls led us out of the room and back down the hallway to the side entrance. The twins thanked us again for coming over, but their attitude had stiffened considerably since the arrival of their mother.

As Jane and I headed home, I couldn't help but wonder why Mrs. Midas had been so upset to find us with her daughters.

Of course, in my mind, it always came back to the foot—and to the dead body I was certain it was attached to.

Chapter 8

"That was fun." Jane's voice dripped with sarcasm.

"But interesting. Didn't you find it curious they have Henrietta's stuff? Right down to her china! Makes me wonder if Rex kept anything. I mean, even on his worst days, I always thought he loved and respected his mother."

"When it comes to Rex Stout, nothing surprises me."

Jane's droll comment was right on target. She would know too, having gone through school with him. Besides, if a man could steal from his insurance customers, what wouldn't he be capable of doing?

Jane collapsed on the sofa, closed her eyes, and stretched her arms above her head. "If I ever wonder what it's like to be skewered and roasted over a spit, remind me of Helen Midas's welcome. Talk about rude!"

"I don't think it was quite that nice."

An intense itch was tickling its way along the back of my leg in the cast. I tried to readjust my position in the hope it would help. It didn't.

"What's with all the wiggling?"

If I let on, she wouldn't take her eyes off me. "You have any idea how uncomfortable it is to sit in this thing all the time?"

Jane frowned at my comment and stood. "Every time I offer to help you to the sofa or into a chair, you remind me that you want to remain mobile. Well, sweetie," she said, patting my back, "you're as mobile as you're going to get without using the crutches. And if you want to sit someplace more comfortable, all you have to do is say so. I'm going to get the paper. I think I saw it on the porch when we were coming back from the Midases'."

Once Jane was out of sight, I scooted over to where she kept

63

her knitting. The set of long, plastic needles should do the trick. I weeded through the basket, bypassed the smaller metal needles, and grabbed up one of the plastic fourteen-inchers.

"Glory Harper, give me that!" Jane plucked the needle from my hand just as I was about to lower it beneath the cast. "See what I have to put up with?"

I looked up to find Detective Spencer next to my sister. The amused light in his eyes brought instant heat to my face—and it wasn't a hot flash either.

"That's a formidable weapon," the detective said with a smirk.

I did my best to appear unfazed by their comments.

"What brings you here, Detective?"

Blue Eyes was in uniform today, which I found a little odd since he'd worn a suit yesterday. Did he alternate between suits and uniforms according to whim, the day? Whatever the explanation, he certainly filled it out nicely.

"There was some trouble at your neighbor's last night." Detective Spencer accepted Jane's offer to sit and chose an overstuffed chair facing me. "We're checking to see if anyone saw or heard anything out of the ordinary."

"Not me," Jane told him. "I conked out around eleven-thirty and didn't stir till morning."

Both of them turned to me.

"I was up for some time," I admitted. "Can't say I heard anything unusual. The twins mentioned the van had been broken into."

There was the slightest rise in the detective's eyebrows.

"Ah, so you've met your neighbors."

"As a matter of fact, we just came back from a visit. They seem like nice girls."

I wasn't sure if Blue Eyes noticed it, but I did—that little hesitation before the word *nice*. That was Jane for you; always looking for the best in everyone. It was something I needed to work on.

"From the sound of it, this wasn't the first time they've had problems."

I tried to assess what the detective might be thinking but decided he was inscrutable. Of course, he would have learned that in the police academy.

"What makes you say that?"

I'd seen this before on *Law And Order*—let the person talk to find out what they know and maybe they'd incriminate themself. Since I didn't know anything, it wouldn't work on me.

"That's what they told us." I answered. "They've been having trouble since they began moving in and wished they'd taken the opportunity to mention it when the officers were there yesterday."

Detective Spencer nodded. "They mentioned a kid—"

"Nick Pearson," I volunteered.

"That's right. You know the boy?"

"Not so much anymore, but I had him in Bible school several years ago."

Again, the nod.

"Detective, I know you're trying to be discreet, but it would help to know what you're after."

I got a strange feeling his questions were more of a pretense, that he wasn't actually here in a professional capacity. It was the way he kept looking at me that made me wonder what was going on. Was it just my imagination?

And what happened to the temperature in here? I was roasting!

"Have you noticed the Pearson kid or anyone else hanging around the van?"

He didn't seem bothered by the heat in the least. He sat at attention in his long-sleeved shirt, no sign of perspiration in sight.

"Even though I've watched some of what's gone on next door, it doesn't mean I'm glued to the window all day and night."

Jane's harrumph did little to help my disclaimer.

"I didn't mean to imply—"

"Of course, you didn't, Detective Spencer." The glare my sister aimed my way had me reevaluating my statement—and my attitude.

"I'm sorry," I told him. "After yesterday, I guess I'm on the defensive."

He didn't appear to have been offended. As a matter of fact, he acted amused.

"Someone's been playing nasty tricks on your neighbors, and they were suspicious about the kid I mentioned." Despite his serious tone, his incredible eyes seemed to dance as he looked at me.

"Because they didn't hire him?" Jane asked.

"Midas and his son said the kid was angry, kicked the side of the van."

"I can see him doing that," I said, noticing for the first time the small amount of salting in the detective's dark hair. Perhaps he was older than I originally thought. "But, I think it's a stretch to believe Nick would break into the van and destroy their property."

In spite of the bad crowd Nick hung out with and the weird things he was into, I couldn't imagine him being guilty of what Chelsea had described.

"The family admits to being lax in securing the van every night—locking it. They felt the initial damage was more of a prank, a kind of payback."

"The girls said dead animals had been thrown into dressers and other things. That doesn't sound like a prank to me." If I mentioned the carpets and tried to tie all of this to the foot I'd seen yesterday, would he think I was crazy?

"Perhaps, but that's how they saw it. However, last night things escalated, which is why they called us."

"And the lock was broken this time?"

"Smashed up pretty bad."

"Not cut?" I could tell both of them wondered what I was getting at. "Don't you see? Sounds echo up here, especially at night. If someone smashed the lock while it was on the van, well, a noise like that would wake the soundest sleeper."

Blue Eyes had a sort of *ah-hah* expression on his face now. "And you didn't hear anything to equate with that?"

"Not really. Though there was something," I said, remembering what I'd assumed was someone working in a garage. "It was kind of, um, a thud followed by a dull clang."

"Any idea what time that would have been?"

"A little before midnight."

"You're sure?"

I nodded. "It was right before Nick Pearson did his nightly number."

"Excuse me?"

"He has this habit of speeding up the street, cutting kitties, and then speeding back down the hill. Every night around midnight,

THE CASE OF THE BOUNCING GRANDMA

like clockwork. I think it has to do with his curfew." I shrugged. "After he'd gone, I glanced at my watch."

"That's it?"

Had my forehead creased or something to give me away?

"I was trying to remember if I heard the second car follow Nick down the hill," I told him.

"Second car?" He leaned forward again, a thoughtful look on his handsome face.

Cut that out, Glory!

But no matter how many times I admonished myself, I just couldn't help it. He was definitely worth looking at.

"Glory? Are you going to answer the detective?" Jane's voice pulled me out of the fog.

"Sorry. Um." Okay where was I? "Yes, two. Like I said, you could set your watch by Nick and his friends. Two cars, both with souped-up motors and those boom-type mufflers—

though Nick's is by far the loudest. It's a little hard to miss them. Whether you're up or not."

"Now that you mention it, I did hear the cars. I was just dozing off and the sound startled me. And you're right." Jane nodded. "It was right at midnight."

"We've got the time established. Now what about that second car?" Spencer prompted.

"I'm not sure. I'm certain Nick's Mustang went back down the hill, but if they were in sync..."

"You do realize the outside of the van was vandalized as well. Spray painted."

Just as I'd suspected.

"Since I wasn't watching, I can't really help any more than this. Sorry."

The phone rang, and Jane excused herself to go into the kitchen to answer it. The moment she left, Detective Spencer's professional persona slipped away. He leaned forward and flashed me a smile that lit up the room.

"I'm guessing you know all about the Midases by this time." There was an odd gleam in his dark eyes that gave me the impression he admired me—though where the thought came from, I had no idea.

"Some," I admitted. "Enough to wonder why people who just

67

won so much money would move themselves rather than hire professionals, why they relocated over a thousand miles from where they used to live to a Podunk town no one's ever heard of, and why they refurnished their house with the previous owner's possessions." Was he still listening? I'd know in a moment. "Then, of course, you have the questions of who they killed, why, and where they're hiding the body."

"Ah, you still don't believe it was a mannequin."

"No, I don't. And after everything that's happened, these rotting carcasses and ruined carpets are just a little too convenient, if you ask me."

"I saw the animals, Glory. While I admit to being curious about the things you mentioned, the Midases' story checks out. Other than Frank spending time in jail for a bar fight,

the rest of the family's squeaky-clean. With all the media attention on them following the lottery win, if there was dirt to find, someone would have found it by now."

"Maybe."

I wasn't convinced even if he was. Too many things just didn't add up—or the way they added didn't fit together properly.

I knew I wasn't wrong about the foot.

Since he didn't seem inclined to leave and I wasn't prepared to present any evidence to support my claim—mostly because I didn't *have* any evidence—a change of subject seemed appropriate.

"I, uh, didn't recognize you yesterday. Have you been in Tarryton long?"

Blue Eyes raised his eyebrows in an almost comical expression.

"A while."

"Anything in particular bring you here—other than the job?"

He sat back in the chair, folding his arms across his chest.

"Are you trying to check out my job qualifications, Ms. Harper, or is this inquiry of a more personal nature?"

His rich blue eyes twinkled, his amused expression totally disarming. I think my mouth fell open then, despite considerable effort to hold it closed.

"Actually..." Blue Eyes grinned. "I used to visit the area when I was a kid. Always loved the place. So when the opportunity arose, I followed my heart."

"That's... nice."

And that was a brilliant attempt at stimulating conversation, Glory! My next amazing feat should be banging my head against the wall to shake some sense into my oxygen-starved brain.

What was that he was saying? What had I missed while my mind was wandering?

"Well?" He asked, his rich, dark eyes searching mine.

"I—I'm sorry?" I couldn't have heard that right.

"Would you have dinner with me?"

Yep, that's what I thought he'd said.

I gulped in so much air I got the hiccups.

"I—uh, I don't think it'd work for me right now," I stuttered, pointing to my plaster-covered leg sticking out in front of me. Once again, I had to concentrate to keep my mouth shut—my jaw seemed bent on flopping open.

"When do you get out of the cast?" The mischievous gleam in his eyes made it impossible to look away from him.

"Monday," Jane chimed in from the entrance to the room.

The glare I threw her wasn't at all nice.

"Then how about a week from Saturday," Blue Eyes persisted with a grin.

I could feel my sister's eyes boring into my back, and with the detective watching me out of that oh-so-handsome face, what else could I do?

"I'd love to." I hiccupped.

* * * * * *

"Thanks for your help," I told my sister in my best sarcastic tone. "Now I've a date that I really don't need. Or want."

"Poppycock!" Jane laughed as she plopped into the armchair the detective had vacated only moments before. "You're thunderstruck by that good-looking detective, and you know it. You're just afraid to admit it."

"Thunderstruck? I don't think so."

I could deny it, right? My prerogative, after all. Sure, I thought he was great to look at, but so were the twelve varieties of fudge in the candy store downtown. I wouldn't touch him any more than I'd risk putting my itching fingers and watering mouth around one of those decadent morsels. It was a strange correlation, a man and candy; both of them wonderful to look at, but getting too close to either of them could prove disastrous.

Besides, where did that put Ike? I wasn't ready to close the file on him. Yes, he was gone, but not forgotten. Never, ever forgotten.

"Glory?"

I stared up at my sister, working hard to keep my emotions in check.

"It will be good for you." She reached forward and patted my good knee. "It's normal to feel funny about dating another guy. You can't help thinking about Ike, that's normal too. But you know, kiddo, he wouldn't want you to be alone. He'd—"

"Yeah, I know." I choked back tears that threatened to fall. "We talked about it before—um, when he knew he didn't have much longer. It's just... I don't know. It's... I mean, I can tell you're happy going out with Steven, and I think that's terrific."

Jane patted my knee again. "You've got eleven days to get used to the idea. It's one dinner date, Glory. One. If you don't like it, you don't have to go out with him again. But..." She rose, came over to where I sat, and kissed me on the cheek. "If you *do* like it, you might just turn a new page in your life."

We decided on frozen dinners for supper. Though I would've been happy having mine nuked, Jane preferred the oven method. While we waited, I grabbed up the articles I'd printed off the night before.

Now that I'd met the twins, everything I read seemed to take on new meaning. The one thing that remained the same, however, was the sense of *déjà vu* I got whenever I came across a photo of Chelsea and Chandra Midas.

As I highlighted passages in the articles for further research, Jane pored over the evening's newspaper. After a few oohs and aahs and the snap of the paper being straightened, I looked to find my sister's brow furrowed, an anxious expression on her face.

"What's up?"

"Huh?" She continued to study the paper, fixated on whatever she was reading.

"Glory," she said after a few minutes. "Do you remember the story about the surrogate mother who ended up keeping her babies? It became quite a scandal, involved that hotshot real estate

THE CASE OF THE BOUNCING GRANDMA

developer in Kansas City, Adam Parker. He was in the news last night. Another of his shady deals, I'm sure."

I was lost. Had it been anyone but my sister, I'd figure I just hadn't paid close enough attention. But with Jane, this meant she was disturbed about something.

"I'm afraid it doesn't ring a bell," I told her.

Jane lowered the paper and gazed somewhere beyond my right shoulder. "It was back when I was pregnant, Glory. It was in all the papers, a horrible, convoluted mess." She shook her head, that faraway look still in her eyes. "By the time this young woman gave birth to twins, the Parkers were divorcing and didn't want the babies. Parker accused the girl of trying to scam him, humiliated her in the press, then proved his accusations to the court's satisfaction. In the end, the surrogate kept the babies."

"I'm sorry, I don't remember. It was a long time ago—"

"Nineteen years." One of Jane's hands went to her stomach.

I'd seen her do this any number of times since she'd lost her babies, mostly when she was distressed. This story must have gotten to her in a big way.

"So, why's it in the news now?"

"The girl—woman, Angelina Verona, is missing."

Though I didn't remember the story she'd related, there was something about the woman's name.

"Hey, were her children kidnapped or something?"

Jane nodded. "Right before their first birthday, eighteen years ago next month. And now, their mother is missing. Sad, huh? We should say a prayer for her."

Jane came over to me, and holding hands, we prayed for Angelina Verona's safe return. Jane included an addendum for the babies, lost so many years before. As she prayed, I wondered if it was the Verona children she prayed for or her own.

The rest of the evening was uneventful. We were both tired and ended up in bed early. I fell into a fitful sleep and awoke around three to voices off in the distance. I lay there, listening, and decided the sounds were coming over the hedge that separated my property from the Midases' backyard.

My imagination was off and running. What was going on? What could that thudding be? It wasn't metallic, it was more like...

Could it be? Was it possible?

71

I peered again at the clock, rose up on my elbow, and blocked out the normal night sounds. There wasn't anything else it could be, I concluded.

It was a shovel breaking through hard ground.

Chapter 9

In the morning, Jane wasn't interested in my latest theory regarding the disposal of the body. While she peeled potatoes and carrots to put into my large slow cooker, she pooh-poohed what I'd heard during the wee morning hours and chalked it up to my overactive imagination.

"Don't forget that Andi and Seth are coming over in a bit to take you to Kelly's."

"Oh?" Though I'd asked about going to the garden shop, so much had happened that it slipped my mind.

"I didn't tell you last night, did I?" Jane scooped up the beef she'd finished cutting into perfect cubes. She put them in the cooker and then poured a mixture of beef stock, bouillon, and water over all of it. "She called yesterday while Detective Spencer was here. I thought I told you."

Guess I wasn't the only one who was distracted.

Once Jane left for work, I showered and dressed in record speed. Maybe I really was on the mend. I was so encouraged by how well I did that I decided to try the new set of crutches. That didn't turn out as well as I'd have liked; I nearly tipped over and fell on the floor—a fate I was glad to avoid. Lying helpless as a beached whale wasn't on my list for amusement, though I did get a chuckle from recalling those old "Help, I've fallen" commercials.

While waiting for my daughter and grandson to arrive, I waded back through the Internet articles, hoping to find a clue to the mystery next door. Digging out my case diagram, I drew another line from the heading and wrote "Helen Midas" across it.

I was still struggling with where to place the twins and Nick Pearson in the schematic when Andi and Seth came bouncing in. Seth ran into my arms and hugged me tight.

"Ready to go flower shoppin', Gramma?"

"As long as we get our favorites," I said, returning the hug.

Every spring since he'd been able to walk, Seth helped me plant pansies around the trees in the backyard. Though we'd had to put it off longer this year than I liked, I decided my broken leg wasn't going to interfere with our tradition.

"You can't get down on your hands and knees, so how are we gonna do it?"

I rubbed his smooth little cheek and winked at him. "I can't, but you can." I pulled him close and whispered in his ear, "This way, you can get as dirty as you want, and no one can say a thing because you're working."

Seth giggled, then looked up at his mom. "Can I plant the pansies for Gramma, Mommy?"

"Not a problem, slugger." Andi leaned down and kissed my forehead. "What a terrific idea, Gramma," she said sotto voce. "However, before we leave, I need to check the Crock-Pot for Aunt Jane. We don't want anything to happen to the stew she's making for tonight's potluck."

"That's tonight?"

Another thing I'd completely forgotten. This was the week for our dinner at the church. Once a month we had a Potluck 'n Praise night. First you sampled delectable dishes from everyone in the congregation, then you sang your heart out to a combination of traditional and contemporary songs. Food for the heart, soul, and stomach.

Because of the wheelchair, we had to go out through the garage to get to Andi's car. The moment the garage door began to rise, I heard angry voices coming from the direction of the Midases'.

As we neared the car, I saw one of the twins in the street with Will Garrett, a reporter for the local newspaper. Actually, he was the only reporter the paper had. It didn't make him any less obnoxious.

"Could you please just go?" the girl pleaded, trying to move past him.

Andi closed the garage door and came to help me into the car. "I've never liked that man," she said, lowering the leg rest on the chair. "When we were in school, he was on the yearbook staff and

THE CASE OF THE BOUNCING GRANDMA

thought it entitled him to get in your face whenever he wanted."

"Doesn't look like things have changed." I could hear the frustration in the twin's voice and wondered why she didn't just push him out of her way instead of being so polite.

I had an idea. "Seth, run over and tell that girl we're ready to go."

"Huh?" both Andi and Seth responded.

"Tell her it's time for us to go to the garden shop, and I'm getting impatient waiting for her."

Like any little kid, Seth loved playing games. Thankfully, he knew me well enough to understand what I wanted. He tore off across the street before his mother had a chance to protest.

"Are you sure you know what you're doing?" My daughter regarded me, her eyes thoughtful. "I know you think you're helping, but—"

"We'll see what happens."

With her assistance, I slid onto the front seat. By the time Andi had folded the wheelchair and stowed it in the trunk, Seth had returned—holding the hand of the Midas twin.

"Bless your hearts for sending this gentleman over to save me!" The girl bestowed a smile on all of us. "I went out for a walk and that—that twerp was at the house when I got back. I tried to be nice, but he wouldn't let me alone."

I watched in the side mirror as Garrett remained where he was. But it wasn't long before he made his move.

"You might want to get into the car now," I said, as the reporter started across the street.

The girl ducked into the backseat, and while Andi made sure Seth was strapped in, I reopened my door and waited. Maybe I could convince him to respect her right to privacy.

What a dichotomy! I was about to lecture someone on respecting another's privacy when I'd been researching these people and trying to figure out which one of them was a murderer!

But what I was doing was different. Right?

"That's far enough, Will Garrett." Andi's stern voice got my attention.

"Come on, Andi, I'm just trying to get a story."

I closed my door enough so I could use the side mirror to watch what was happening. Andi met Garrett at the end of the driveway and now stood with her hands on her hips. I knew that stance; Garrett was in trouble. He just didn't know it yet.

"You're never *just* out to get a story. You're always angling for ways to get in someone's face to humiliate them."

"Now, Andi, you're just sore about the way I handled your mom's skateboarding fiasco."

There was something smarmy about that man. It made me want to wipe that insolent grin off his face. If I didn't have this cast...

"*You* handled?" Andi's laugh only made Garrett's smirk more impudent. "The problem with you, Will, is you never learned to distinguish between fact and fiction. It's a good thing your parents still have control of what actually gets into the paper. If they didn't, you'd have run it into the ground by now—or turned it into Tarryton's Fiction Tribune."

"What exactly are you implying?" He was in her face now, trying to use his substantial weight to intimidate her.

"Just stating fact," my daughter said, pulling herself up to her full 5'9", a good three inches taller than he was, and far more slender. It was unlikely he knew that Jared had taught her some tae kwon do, and if she wanted to, she *could* flatten him.

"You ever hear of the First Amendment? Freedom of the press ring a bell?" he persisted.

Andi had crossed her arms and was probably tapping her foot. Like Jane, she knew how to handle students who misbehaved—with a gentle yet firm manner. If my guess was correct, she was giving him one of those stern, uncompromising looks right now.

"I also have the right to get out of the driveway without being harassed. In fact, I happen to have Detective Rick Spencer right here on my speed dial. How would you like to deal with him?"

Oooh, she *was* good.

Wait a second. Why would she have Blue Eyes on speed dial? She hadn't mentioned knowing him, had she?

"Fine, you win. This time. Tell your friend that she and her family are news, and I intend to give the public what they want. I'll be back." Garrett turned and sauntered toward his car.

"I never meant for y'all to take the heat for me," the girl said from the backseat. "I feel so awful about it. I should go—"

"Stay put." Andi pulled her door shut and started the car. "He

THE CASE OF THE BOUNCING GRANDMA

hasn't left yet."

"I—I really appreciate this, but I should be fighting my own battles. Usually, I would. He just surprised me."

"Yeah, that's his style." Andi studied the rearview mirror.

"By the way, I'm Andi Wheeler, and the guy who saved you is my son, Seth."

"Sorry about not doing the introductions," I said, feeling a blush coming on. "I'm not sure who you are."

"Of course you're not," the girl giggled. "Chelsea Midas at your service." She held her hand out to Seth, and they shook. Seth gave her a sheepish grin.

"I think Garrett's going to sit there a while, so we might as well leave." Andi released the parking break and put the car in reverse.

"You think he'll follow us?" Chelsea asked.

"He might. But I wasn't joking about calling the cops. They aren't his biggest fans. They know what a pain he is. Just keep that threat in mind if he bothers you again."

The girl nodded, then eased back against the seat.

"You did a good job back there," I told my daughter. "I couldn't have handled it better."

I saw the gleam in her eyes and knew the compliment made her feel good. It was important for me to remember how capable she was—*and* that she was all grown up. That last bit is always the hardest.

"This is so cool." Chelsea's enthusiasm was in stark contrast to her attitude yesterday afternoon. "Going shopping like this is like we've been friends forever."

Andi's questioning glance increased my desire to uncover more about the Midas clan.

"We're glad you feel that way." I flashed the girl what I hoped was an encouraging grin. "Where's your sister today?"

Chelsea giggled again. "I'm sorry, it's not polite to laugh like that, but it *is* funny. We've been at the library, looking into colleges. I'm satisfied with staying here at Tarryton Valley, but Channy wanted the chance to see a couple others. Northwest and Missouri Western are both within a hundred miles, and their education programs have good reputations. I knew she wouldn't make arrangements to visit the campuses, so I made them for her.

Even got appointments on the same day." She chuckled. "Mama decided she'd better go along with her."

"I see." Though I didn't. There was a lot about this family I didn't understand. It went beyond the question of why the twins still lived with their parents. They both wanted to further their education, yet even with all the financial options available, it didn't appear either of them had attempted to get into college until now.

Then there was the strange behavior of their mother yesterday.

At least as far as Jane and I were concerned.

"Mama wasn't at all happy about it, but now we have the money for school, what can she say?"

By the time we got to Kelly's Garden and Landscaping, the girls were becoming friends, and Seth was in total awe of the slender brunette who kept giving him such handsome compliments. It wouldn't surprise me if he developed a crush on this older woman.

While Seth and I looked over the crop of pansies, Andi helped Chelsea set up an account so she could pick up some flowers as well. Soon we had a cart overflowing with our purchases, and Chelsea was making plans to attend our Potluck'n Praise dinner that evening.

"Mama and Channy won't be back till late, so this is terrific," Chelsea said, thanking us for the invitation.

She didn't mention anything about her father and brother, and I didn't ask. Despite my burning curiosity, this wasn't the time to press for information. It was obvious the kid needed to get out and among other people. The dinner would be the perfect outlet.

Before returning home, Andi stopped for gas. While she was filling the tank, Rex Stout pulled up next to her in a car I didn't recognize. As usual, the man's clothing reeked of money and success that everyone in town knew he didn't have. When Stout started talking to Andi, I wished I could hear what he was saying— especially when I saw she was biting her lower lip. It was a sure sign that whatever he'd said made her uncomfortable.

"I detest that man," Chelsea said.

I glanced back to find her almost huddled in the corner.

Was she trying to hide from him?

"Rex has his moments," I told her. "He can be the nicest guy you'll ever meet one moment and a snake in the grass the next."

"I've only seen the snake. I don't like to be nasty, but the house doesn't belong to him anymore, and he shouldn't be hanging around so much. I wish we'd never bought his mother's stuff either. Not that it isn't beautiful, it's just... He seems to think it makes him family or something."

Rex could charm the pants off a person if he set his mind to it. Just ask the people who'd bought insurance from him for years, never suspecting they were being swindled.

Then there were his three ex-wives and Elsie Wilkes...

But why was he coming around a house he'd been itching to get rid of from the moment his mother died?

"Maybe he's feeling sentimental," I said aloud.

"Maybe." Chelsea didn't sound convinced. "But I think it's got something to do with Mama."

I would have liked to pursue that statement, but Andi's return to the car interrupted the moment.

"Did you see what Stout's driving?" she asked, pulling out onto the street.

"It's a Lexus," Chelsea spoke up. "He came by last evening to show Mama. Though I don't know why he imagined she'd care."

I threw a look over my shoulder and found the girl still slumped in the corner and her expression far from the congenial one she'd had since we saved her from Garrett.

"Don't know why people insist on spending so much money on their vehicles," Chelsea mumbled. "I'm going to get something practical with good gas mileage. No reason to spend a fortune when you can get a perfectly decent car for half the price."

True, especially when you didn't have a fortune to rely on. It was kind of a surprise, though, coming from a girl who'd recently become a multimillionaire.

As for Rex, I'd like to know where he'd gotten the money for the Lexus. I'd heard he was still paying a hefty fine to the court. The house and furniture may have covered that, but I doubt it would have been enough to get the car as well.

"He's more like a weasel." The voice from the backseat was so soft, if we hadn't been stopped at a traffic light, I wouldn't have heard it at all.

I met Andi's eyes, her unspoken question matching my own.

What *was* going on with Rex Stout and the Midas family?

Chapter 10

Andi pulled into the Midases' driveway, and we all helped Chelsea unload her flowers from the trunk. With each flat we lifted out, she oohed and aahed in appreciation.

"Daddy and Frank have started landscaping out back. They were supposed to be picking up concrete and pavers today. It's a good thing Frank still has his old truck. I doubt he'd be happy hauling all that stuff in the one he's got his mind set on."

Could they have been up at three this morning to begin their landscape project? It didn't seem logical to me. Digging in your backyard in the wee morning hours suggested something far more nefarious. Disposing of a body seemed more likely.

While I still felt someone in the Midas clan was a murderer, I was positive neither of the twins was involved. This brought another thing into the equation I hadn't counted on—fear for the girls' safety.

The morning had been good for Chelsea. She had roses in her cheeks, and the friendliness of her voice was much more pleasant than the distrust and suspicion of yesterday. She'd become smitten with my grandson and fast friends with Andi. Getting her away from the reporter had been the best idea I'd had in a long time.

"If you want to go with Jane and me tonight, you can come over about four. Jane will want to get there early since she's helping set up."

"That's okay, Mama." Andi handed the last flat of Chelsea's flowers to Seth, who then carted them along the side of the house to a small patio area. "She's going with us."

Chelsea nodded. "I don't want to show up empty-handed, so Andi's taking me to the bakery. What did you call it?"

"Randi's Dandies," I told her. "Where just looking at their

displays can pack fifty pounds on each thigh without having to take a single bite."

The girl laughed so hard she had to hold her side. It was funny but not *that* funny. This kid had been under way too much pressure. The Potluck 'n Praise was exactly what she needed.

She offered to walk with me while Andi moved her car into my driveway. Seth stayed by my side, stealing sidelong glances at the new woman in his life. Once his mother had parked, he ran off.

"Come on, Bouncy, Bouncy!" he called over his shoulder.

"He's quite a character." Chelsea flashed me one of her broad smiles. "I think I'm in love. Seriously, though, why does he call you that? I heard him say it at the garden shop too. Well, something like that... um... more like 'my bouncing gramma,' I think."

I nodded. "That would be it."

Okay, how do I explain this to make it sound cute and not just weird?

"When he was little, and trying to figure out that two grandmother thing, Andi and Jared tried different ways to help him distinguish which of us they were talking about. Well, our names didn't work because Laurie and Glory sound too much alike. Seth finally made his own distinction. Since I was the gramma who jumped with him on the trampoline and played ball—"

"You became the bouncing gramma. Very cute. So what did he name his other gramma?"

I pictured Laurie Wheeler's face, which seemed to wear a perpetual frown. It had taken a very long time and a lot of work on everyone's part to convince Seth that Mad Gramma was not a good nickname. Though, to this day, Seth often referred to her with his own pet name.

"Nana." I told Chelsea. "She likes to be called Nana."

Chelsea stuck around to help us unload our flowers and carry them into the backyard. She was considering our offer of lunch but refused when she heard her brother's pickup pull into their driveway. After confirming the time to meet Andi later, she gave Seth a hug and ran home.

"Did that seem weird or is it just me?" Andi watched Chelsea until she was out of sight. "And what's with those comments about Rex Stout?"

THE CASE OF THE BOUNCING GRANDMA

"Her leaving like that was odd." I shrugged. "In character, though. When Jane and I were over there yesterday, we got along fine until Mrs. Midas showed up. Her cold shoulder routine was more like a blast of Arctic air. The twins were about as anxious to hustle us out of there as we were to leave. Makes me think the rest of the family would rather not have anything to do with outsiders." This was food for thought. "Anyway, as for Rex, he's always been strange."

We called to Seth and then headed indoors. When Seth went to the bathroom to wash for lunch, Andi continued the conversation.

"Rex was flirting with me," she said. "Back at the gas station." She shivered. "There's just something greasy about him, you know? I loved visiting Henrietta when I was a kid, was thrilled when she invited us over."

"You loved Henrietta as much as the chance to wander through that old house," I teased, hoping to get her mind off Rex and put her at ease.

"There was that." She grinned. "Still, I always hated when Rex was there."

"I know you did; that's why I'd ask if she expected him. He was her only child and she loved him, but Henrietta wasn't all that comfortable with him either."

Andi pulled out some bread, turkey, and other sandwich fixings. "I never liked the way he looked at you—or me. Gave me the creeps."

"Who gave you the creeps, Mommy?"

"That big spider you found out back." Andi poked Seth in the ribs and got him giggling.

Once lunch was over and we were sure Jane's stew was coming along fine, we went to work in the backyard.

Setting Seth loose with a trowel and a flat of pansies proved how closely he'd been watching me all these years. He positioned each plant around the base of the tree, stood back to size up the distance between them, then dug his hole and set in the plant. While he worked on the beds beneath the trees, Andi and I put petunias in the planters lining either side of the patio.

It was a warm day with a sky so blue you could get lost gazing into it. I closed my eyes and listened to my daughter's and grandson's laughter, to the spray of the garden hose, the birds twittering high above us... the crunch of a shovel slamming into hard ground, and the murmur of male voices filtering through the thick hedge separating the Midas property from mine.

Was I curious about what was happening next door? Sure. But right now, all I wanted, all I needed, was right here in my own backyard.

I opened my eyes in time to see Andi send a mist of water in Seth's direction. He let out a squeal, ran off, then ran back for more. This was definitely a touch of heaven.

"There you are."

I started at the voice, more because of whose it was than for any other reason. As I turned to face Elsie Wilkes, I brushed the dirt from my hands onto my jeans and saw the distaste Elsie had for the action. One thing could be said about our premier realtor— she was one well-put-together lady. Elsie always dressed to reflect her importance in the community, and today was no different.

"Elsie, what a surprise."

I indicated for her to have a seat on the only piece of outdoor furniture we currently had available—an old glider that had seen better days. I followed Elsie's gaze to the glider, noted her look of dismay as she smoothed the front of her navy linen skirt, and knew my pitiful welcome would be fodder for her gossip mongering.

"I—can't stay, Glory." Her grimace made it plain she would have liked to had I been more accommodating. She glanced beyond me to where Andi and Seth played in the water. "Are you folks going to the dinner this evening?"

"Wouldn't miss it."

Okay, Elsie Wilkes, Tarryton's information broker extraordinaire, would not come by simply to check if my family planned to attend the church dinner. Something was up. But I knew Elsie, and the one way to keep her from spilling her guts was getting ahead of her and attempting to force her to talk before she was ready. She was a master at manipulation.

At least, in her own mind.

"Gramma, look what Mommy did." Seth wasn't soaked, but he was pretty wet. His ear-to-ear grin told the true story; he was one happy little boy.

"Elsie." Andi plopped onto the glider. She lifted the tail of her

THE CASE OF THE BOUNCING GRANDMA

T-shirt and wiped some excess water off her face. "How's the real estate business?"

Andi was nowhere near as subtle as I was when it came to Elsie. She hasn't been particularly fond of her since Elsie told the entire congregation that Ike had died—a full month before he actually did.

"Booming. You know the development south of town? I've been asked to represent the builders." Elsie drew back her shoulders and puffed out her chest. Multi-ringed fingers went to her head in a futile gesture to fluff her stiff red-orange hair. "Once the models are ready, I'll be spending most of my time out there."

"Well, good for you." I flashed my daughter a warning. If there was something on the woman's mind, I wanted to know what it was. After all, someone as important as Elsie Wilkes wouldn't make a house call for no reason.

"Nice to see you, Elsie." Andi waved for Seth to join her. "We need to finish planting, slugger, so we can get home and clean up before church."

"But we gotta get Chelsea, remember?"

Elsie picked up on that. Her head snapped to attention as she stared down at my grandson.

"Chelsea Midas?"

Seth nodded, then ran back out into the yard. Andi and I exchanged a brief glance before she followed her son.

"She's coming to the dinner?" Elsie didn't appear happy about the news. What about all that talk of them being such "wonderful" people?

"That's right. Isn't that *wonderful?*"

If she noticed I used her favorite word, she didn't react to it. She had this odd look on her face, blanched and kind of green at the same time. It didn't do her complexion justice at all.

"Yes, yes, terrific."

It took her a moment to compose herself and slip back into the self-confident, self-important person she was. You had to admire her ability to switch back and forth like that so quickly.

"I take it you've become acquainted with your new neighbors then."

"We've talked."

"Mama, I'm sorry to interrupt, but I think this flat of

85

geraniums must be Chelsea's. Unless..."

The crimson blooms in my daughter's hands brought out the color in her sun-kissed face. I couldn't help but beam at her—and her timing.

"You're right, honey. She wanted those for the planter next to their side entrance. Just set them down for now."

I could be wrong, but I think Andi interrupted on purpose. Maybe she thought it would take the wind out of Elsie's sails.

I turned back to find my company had regained the color in her face. Plus some.

"I'm sorry, Elsie. You were saying?"

"It's..." She swallowed, pulled the shoulder strap of her purse against her neck, and stared me straight in the eye. "I've just discovered that the brother, Frank Midas, spent time in prison for assault with a deadly weapon. With you here alone, well, with Jane, I thought it imperative you were warned."

I didn't bother to let on that I already had this information. I didn't want to discourage her from telling me any other tidbits that might become available and help with solving my mystery.

"Thank you for thinking of us. I'll make sure we keep our doors locked and our eyes open."

Dear Lord, please tell me I wasn't too facetious.

"Good. Good. You do that. It just goes to prove that looks can be deceiving, if you get my drift."

I didn't, not really. I did get the feeling she was attempting to warn me to stay away from the family. Since I hadn't gotten a warm fuzzy from Mrs. Midas, I didn't foresee us becoming friendly. The twins were a different matter. I liked them and knew they were warming up to us.

Elsie scanned my backyard before returning her gaze to me. "I'd best be going now. I'm showing a property to Rex Stout in a bit, and I don't want to be late."

"Rex is thinking about buying another place?"

She nodded, resuming her air of superiority. "Well, he can't continue renting now, can he?"

I watched her leave, wondering about her comment.

Which led me back to the question of where Rex had gotten the money for his Lexus, and why he was bothering the Midas family. If I wasn't careful, I'd be competing with Elsie in the

THE CASE OF THE BOUNCING GRANDMA

information game.

"Mommy, Gramma, I'm caught!"

I followed Seth's voice to midway up the old oak tree that stood just this side of the privet hedge. He was barely visible from the patio, tucked among the oak's majestic branches. And while those branches were thick and strong, it wasn't much of a comfort when my grandson was stuck twenty feet up.

Don't panic, I told myself firmly as I struggled to wheel the chair out there.

Andi was already climbing the tree and talking to her son in a soothing voice. When I finally got a good look at Seth, I realized the soothing wasn't for him, but for his mother.

"Don't be scared, Mommy. I'm okay. I just need you to get my belt loop off the limb. It won't let me move." He gazed down at me and frowned. "I think it's the part you and Aunt Jane tried to trim, Gramma. It's growin' back and grabbed me."

"You just hold on, okay?" I could see what he was talking about now. Somehow, the small limb had managed to slip through his belt loop enough that no matter which way he turned, it kept him trapped. Seth was good at keeping his head; he never panicked.

As for Andi, she didn't care for heights, and climbing trees had never been her thing. Stepping from branch to branch, with her eyes on Seth, she would do just fine—as long as she didn't look down.

"Hey, Gramma, I can see Chelsea from here!" Seth waved his arm, then looked down at me. "Guess she can't see me, huh? Maybe if I yell—"

"Seth David Wheeler, you keep those hands on the branches and eyes there too!" Andi's voice was stern and reflected her fear.

"It's okay, Mommy. Honest." Seth did as he was told and fastened both hands on a sturdy branch above him.

"You all right, Andi?"

She'd pulled herself up to a thick bough, stopped, and leaned her head against the tree trunk. Even from where I sat far below, I could see her legs were trembling.

"I just need to rest a moment," Andi called out. "Don't move, Seth. Okay? I'll be there soon."

I checked my watch. It was nearly two-thirty, which meant

Jane would be home any time. If worse came to worst, she could climb up and bring them both down. The thought seemed to produce my sister from out of thin air. She joined me beneath the tree, holding her breath as Andi set to work on the branch holding my grandson hostage.

"Do you have a pocketknife?" Jane's voice was calm, but the hand that settled on my back revealed her concern.

"No. And this silly thing won't let go."

I could hear Andi's frustration building. We needed to get them down. *Now.*

"Andi, honey, can you help him get out of his shorts? Seth, try to back up just a bit—hang onto the branch above you. The big one."

Seth did what I suggested, and while he clung to the branch, Andi reached up and unzipped his shorts. It took a bit for him to shimmy out of them, but once he had, he pulled the pants off the limb and began talking his mother back down the tree.

Andi was still shaking when her feet touched the ground. "That's not an experience I want to repeat."

"But I love climbin' trees, Mommy. That's never happened before."

Jane put her arm around Andi's shoulders. "He's fine, you're fine. God had you both in the palm of His hand." She kissed Andi's cheek and rubbed Seth's close-cropped head. "I think you both need to get cleaned up for church. What do you think, slugger? Can you amuse yourself while your mom gets a hot bath?"

"I hate climbing trees. Always have, always will," Andi mumbled.

I held my arms out for my daughter, and she melted into me. She would be missing Jared right now. I hoped I could be a close second-best.

It didn't take long for her to recover, and I was proud that she didn't lecture Seth or tell him he was to quit one of his favorite pastimes.

"Did your mother share her news?" Jane's mischievous tone had Andi pulling back from the embrace before I was ready to let her go.

"What news?" Andi quickly rubbed a hand across her eyes,

THE CASE OF THE BOUNCING GRANDMA

most likely to remove all sign of tears.

The way they were both staring at me gave me the feeling of being under a microscope.

"I've got a date."

There, I'd said it. Not loud, but loud enough that it felt as if I'd dropped a bomb in the midst of us.

Andi's eyes danced as she gave me another hug. "And with whom is this date?"

"Detective Spencer," Jane answered. "At this rate we'd be here all day trying to pull the information out of her."

Both she and Andi laughed as a sudden rush of heat flooded through me. "Don't you have a stew to see to?"

Jane put a hand to her mouth and rushed into the house.

I picked up the flat of geraniums, set them on my lap, then followed Andi and Seth out to their car. I could still hear the murmur of voices in the Midases' backyard and decided to deliver the flowers to Chelsea. Besides, it would give me an opportunity to check out what was going on over there.

"Hey, Gramma," Seth said as he climbed into their car. "How come there are so many big holes in Chelsea's backyard?"

"Maybe they're for all the plants she bought today." Andi tested his seatbelt before shutting the door.

"Nah, they're way too big for that." He giggled. He shoved his hand through the open window and signed, "I love you."

"See ya later, Bouncy, Bouncy!"

I threw my grandson a kiss and returned the sign.

"I can give those to Chelsea when I pick her up." Andi indicated the flowers on my lap.

"That's okay. It's not a problem for me to run them over. I'll see you guys later."

There was a short incline to the end of the driveway and from there it was mostly flat. I was nearing the end of my confinement in this wheelchair and was finally getting the hang of going it alone. Of course, it seemed to work a lot better on concrete than it did on carpeting.

When I wheeled into the driveway next door, I just followed the sound of digging and voices. The gate between the house and garage was open, with the front half of a pickup sticking out. At first, I wasn't sure there was enough room for the wheelchair, but

89

the remaining space proved larger than I expected.

I thought I'd find Chelsea, her father, and brother hard at work on their landscaping project. In my wildest imagination, I never believed I'd see that beat-up old freezer sitting in among the pile of wood and pavers. Even stranger was the extension cord that ran from it into the garage. Was that a padlock on the freezer?

"What do you want?"

I tore my eyes from the freezer and met the surly expression on the man's face. The harshness of his voice fit the brawny muscles spilling out of his torn work shirt. Dirt and what might be cement covered his overalls. But what caught my attention were his massive hands.

"I'm Glory Harper from next door. These flowers are Chelsea's."

He didn't look down, didn't stray from my face. "I know who you are, lady. You're the looky-loo who can't stop gawking at us."

"Daddy!" Chelsea and her brother appeared from the other side of the house. She hurried past her father and over to me.

"I thought I picked those up at the store." She smiled as she took the flat from my lap. "Thank you so much for bringing them over."

Chelsea set the flowers on top of the freezer then turned to her father. "Daddy, this is the nice lady I told you about. Glory, I'd like you to meet my father, Darrell, and brother, Frank."

I tried to return her smile but was sure it fell a good bit short of its mark. It was hard to be pleasant when you had a couple of Neanderthals looking as though they'd like nothing better than to rip your head from your shoulders.

"Nice to meet you," I offered. I held out my hand but neither man responded.

Chelsea frowned at both of them.

"Wouldn't want to get you dirty." Frank had the same insolent grin I'd seen in the photos.

He was definitely the man who'd tripped over the carpet; I was sure of it now. He appeared to size me up and then dismiss me. His father, whom I'd now identified as the other "moving man," also refused to accept Chelsea's encouragement for civility.

"We've got a lot of work to do. Can't be stopping for company. Chelsea, go get that hose again. And make sure the

THE CASE OF THE BOUNCING GRANDMA

water's on this time."

Chelsea mouthed an "I'm sorry," then ran to do what her father asked. Once she was out of sight, both men turned their backs on me. It was rude but probably for the best. I didn't know how much longer I could have stood their hostile stares.

"All righty then. Have a good day, gentlemen."

It took a little doing, but I got the wheelchair turned around and was headed back through the gate when I heard the tinny notes of a cell phone ringing. I knew they had to hear it too, but no one moved to answer the phone.

Darrell Midas was suddenly next to me. "Just get on home, Miss Looky-Loo."

I glanced up at him and knew this wasn't a man to tangle with. He fisted his large hands and smacked one into the other as he glared at me.

"Do yourself a favor and don't come around no more. If'n my girls want to see you, they know where to find you."

That's neighborly—not. However, it might be safer in the long run.

I shouldn't do it, but...

I grinned up at the churlish oaf, and in the sweetest voice I could muster said, "Have a great day."

As I rolled out of the driveway, I couldn't help but add, "And by the way, your freezer's ringing."

91

Chapter 11

"Come on, Glory, we don't have time for this." Jane continued peeling carrots for the veggie tray without so much as a glance in my direction.

"I'm telling you a cell phone had to be inside that freezer."

"And you told him it was ringing?"

"Not exactly," I admitted. "I was almost to the end of the driveway, so I imagine he'd returned to the backyard."

"That's a relief. Look, you've made a breakthrough with Chelsea; she's coming to the church tonight. It's obvious those girls need our friendship. Do you want to put a rift between us because of this crazy notion of yours?"

"Of course not. And I resent that." I finished washing my hands and rolled to the counter where Jane was working.

"So?"

"So? So? Do you keep your cell phone in a freezer?"

She heaved a sigh and glanced at me. "Glory, you've got to stop this. It's not healthy."

"The body—"

My sister shook her head and began to calmly cut up a stalk of celery. I could see this was going nowhere fast. Until I was able to prove I was right about the body, she would remain unconvinced. Jane was a Missourian through and through; *Show Me* were her bywords.

I grabbed a jar of sweet midgets and transferred them to a bowl on the Lazy Susan Jane was preparing. "Are you sure we should do this here and not at the church? Seems like it would be less mess."

"It'll be finished in a moment. Then all we have to do is set it on the table when we get there."

93

I followed the sweet midgets with dill pickles and olives, then scooped out the dip Jane made and put it in the center bowl of the Susan. When she finished cutting the celery into sticks, she rearranged the dishes until she was satisfied with their placement. It might have been her artistic flare, or maybe it was her nerves.

"Will Steven be there this evening?"

Jane blushed. "He's going to try." She stood back and gave the veggie tray a nod. "Perfect. Now I'm going to get a quick shower. Do you need any help?"

I shook my head. "Go, enjoy. I have showering down to a science. Wish we would've thought of using the stall sooner."

As for clothes, that was another story. I'd been wearing either jeans or sweatpants I'd cut up to accommodate the cast. Though I'd worn an occasional skirt or dress, with my leg raised on the platform, they made me uncomfortable. That limited my choices.

"Just a few more days," I told myself, pulling out a pair of modified jeans. At least I could look nice from the waist up.

I picked out a soft pink shell with a matching sweater and then went off to shower.

* * * * * *

The church was already bustling, though it was almost an hour and a half before the dinner was to begin. I tried helping prepare the tables, but after running over a few toes, it was decided they'd be better off without me.

"Glory, dear, how's about we put you someplace safe." Gracie Naner, my former fifth-grade teacher, patted my shoulder as she pushed me down the large room away from the kitchen and serving areas. She was at least seventy-five, but her sweet voice was still strong and showed no sign of aging. In fact, her thin arms, cloud of white hair, and frail appearance belied Miss Gracie's fortitude altogether.

She handled the wheelchair as if the combined weight of it and me were insignificant. A remarkable feat considering the woman couldn't weigh a hundred pounds soaking wet. Made me wonder if she was secretly lifting weights, or at the very least, lying about her age.

She deposited me at the far end of the fellowship hall, patted my shoulder again, then hustled back to where they were preparing the serving tables. I hadn't moved like that since I was a kid. Even

Marla Hobbs and Jane would take a backseat to Gracie Kay Naner in more tables serviced, and they were twenty years younger!

I latched onto the bulletin for the night's praise session and was pleased to see the songs chosen. It was a good mix of traditional and contemporary, as usual, maybe even better.

Since a group of churches in the community coordinated their efforts in the Potluck 'n Praise program, you could attend one of these worship services at a different church each week. People from all over the community joined together, putting denomination behind and placing

Jesus at the forefront, as He should be. It was just one of the perks to living in a small town—and maybe the reason our little college was so popular. There was a sense of community, the joy of God, and the heart and soul of true Americana embodied in this combined effort.

People drifted in and out of the kitchen and fellowship hall, bringing in their dishes for the servers to later place on the tables. Marla Hobbs was in the thick of things, vying with my sister for the Betty Crocker Award for best hostess. Personally, I preferred Jane's eye for detail and artistry when it came to the food. It was more appealing than Marla's lean toward *Stepford Wives* perfection.

I was thrilled when Andi arrived with Seth and Chelsea in tow. They all had a fresh-scrubbed look to them, and their smiles were good for the heart.

Seth ran over and gave me a hug before joining a group of his pals in a section of the room designated for play. Plenty of trusted adults were around to make sure the kids were safe and stayed where they were supposed to. There were organized games, donated toys of all kinds and for all age groups, and even craft projects available for anyone so inclined.

I watched as Andi took Chelsea around and introduced her. Both girls were radiant, a sure sign Andi had recovered from her tree-climbing adventure and that Chelsea hadn't allowed what transpired between her father and me to upset her.

"Well, I'll be, Glory Harper. Are you ever gettin' outa that blasted chair?"

I grinned up into the weathered face of Olav Cawley. At eighty-two, he still farmed a small acreage on the outskirts of town. About a year ago, he finally brought in his youngest son to help him. Though Gavin Cawley was only sixty-four, he'd never been as spry as his dad and often seemed the older of the two. Still, they were a remarkable pair.

"Hi, Ollie, how are you tonight?"

"Great as always, little lady. As always." Pulling on his suspenders, he gazed out at the gathering crowd. "Looks like we're gonna bring down the rafters, maybe even convince a few angels to join in." He laughed. "You been takin' care of yourself, girl?"

"The best I can."

He laughed again. "Betcha Jane is keepin' you in line, if I know her. I was surprised she didn't call in the cavalry when you busted your leg. Haven't seen them around. Are they still off someplace?"

Our parents were somewhere in Yellowstone with a group of seniors sightseeing across the US. They called in once a week to let us know where they were and what they'd seen. Since both were in their mid-seventies, and this was the first time they'd done any real traveling, we didn't think it was necessary for them to know anything about their accident-prone daughter.

"Last we heard they were in Wyoming waiting for Old Faithful to do its stuff."

"Yep, yep. Saw that with the missus back in the fifties, I think it was. Mighty powerful experience. Hey, Glory-girl, who's that little gal over there with Andi?" Olav leaned down and pointed to where Andi and Chelsea were talking to our pastor, Connor Grant, and his wife, Madison.

"That's Chelsea Midas. She and her family just moved into the Stout place."

"Aha, that explains it." Olav rubbed a grizzled hand across his face. "She sure has a look of Henrietta when she was a girl. T'weren't anyone sweeter nor prettier, let me tell you. That one's a chip off the old block."

"Huh?" I stared at Chelsea.

That was it, why I had that strange sense of *déjà vu*!

"Looks like they're linin' up. I think I'll go grab me a space. Want me to bring you back anything?"

"That's okay, Ollie, I've got it covered," I said, unable to take my eyes off Chelsea Midas.

"All righty then. If'n you're doin' okay, I think I'll mosey on over to Miss Gracie Kay and see if I can't coax the little lady to have supper with me."

"Why, Olav Cawley, do I detect a hint of romance here?"

"Heh heh, might be. Might be." He grinned down at me. "Enjoy the angels, Glory-girl."

I chuckled, then found my attention drawn back to Chelsea. As Olav passed her, he stopped to briefly speak to the girl before bee-lining it straight to where Miss Naner stood behind the serving tables. I watched them for a moment, then searched for Chelsea in the crowd.

She wasn't difficult to spot. It seemed every available man in the place had found his way to her side.

I closed my eyes and concentrated on the Stout house, how it looked as you entered the front door, the old refectory table along the side of the wall just opposite the entrance to the living room. The Midases had the furniture, though it wasn't placed quite the same way. The large empty space above the fireplace was the biggest change of all.

The painting that hung above the fireplace had depicted Henrietta at nineteen with her newborn son. Though I hadn't seen the painting in years, my memories were sharp and clear; from the soft folds in the baby blue blanket wrapped around Rex, to his tiny fingers reaching toward Henrietta's face—a glowing face surrounded by a fall of brunette curls.

Could Olav be right? Could the twins belong to Rex? That would explain a lot. I mean, it was common knowledge that Henrietta's will stipulated the property was to remain within the family. We'd all wondered what Rex did to get around the constraint, how he'd been able to sell the estate. I figured it was the result of all the money he owed. This put a different spin on things.

If the twins were his daughters... It would also explain why he'd been bugging them.

"Hey, sorry. Excuse me."

Brought out of my reverie, I stared into the face of Nick Pearson. This was the first time I'd seen the kid in church in over a year. It'd been even longer since you could actually see his face. It was devoid of the usual white makeup and black lipstick he'd been wearing. He still had rings in each eyebrow, in his nose, and at the corner of his mouth, but at least he didn't look like he was dressed for a Halloween party.

"Hey, Mrs. Harper. You saved my butt."

"Excuse me?"

"The cops were looking at me for some robbery and junk at your neighbor's. Not cleared, you know, but they took what you said seriously. Got busted by the 'rents, but hey, when my payback is a free meal and staring at some legs..."

Rents? Ahh... parents!

"That's good." Why would Spencer tell him about me?

"Yeah. When they said someone up there heard my 'Stang, I knew it was you." He flashed me the peace sign—at least, it's what I thought of as the peace sign. "Later."

I didn't like the inference here. First, Darrell Midas calls me a gawking looky-loo, and now this kid was positive I was the one who told the police about his nightly runs. This wasn't how I wanted people to think of me.

"Are you going to sit here all alone or would you like some company?"

Speaking of Blue Eyes, there he was in the flesh, grinning down at me. I felt my stomach do a couple somersaults, and my mouth went dry.

"I didn't expect to see you," I told him, trying to remain nonchalant despite the growing swarm of butterflies in my chest.

"I don't often get the opportunity to join in on one of these meetings. There's a good turnout."

Detective Spencer was wearing street clothes, jeans and a shirt that looked new. His dark hair was a little damp, and he smelled of soap with a slight hint of a spicy aftershave.

"It's always like this. Busier when the college is in full session."

"It's a great tradition." He pulled up a chair and sat next to me. "You look a little shell-shocked. Are you okay?"

Shell-shocked. That was an apt term for it. Should I tell him my latest theory, or would it be better to keep it to myself?

"I'm fine. It's just a little noisy."

Which it was. I may not have been ready to spring the revelation on him regarding the twins, but I did have something he might be interested in hearing. I was about to speak when Pastor

Connor called for silence.

It took a few moments for everyone to settle down, and once they did, Connor blessed the meal and prayed for our service to uplift the hearts of all. *Amen* resounded throughout the hall and the feeding frenzy began.

Seth ran over, grabbed the arm of my chair, and jumped up and down. He had a sweet, silly grin that spoke of both joy and mischief.

"Hi Bouncy, Bouncy. Mommy says to ask if you've got a wet wipe, and if you don't, would you make sure my hands are clean." Seth was nothing if not literal.

"I think it would be easier for you to go wash them, kiddo." It would also keep me out of the path to the chow line.

Seth nodded his agreement and then glanced at Blue Eyes. "Hi, Mr. Spencer. You gonna eat with us too?"

Okay, what was this? First, I hear Andi state she has the detective's number on speed dial, and now my grandson acts like he knows the guy.

"I'd like to, if it's okay with you and your grandmother."

I don't know what it is, but whenever someone refers to me as a grandmother, Seth busts out laughing. I've always taken it as a weird kind of compliment, but that's just me.

Andi came up beside us and ran her hand across her son's head. "Hey, slugger, have you gotten those hands washed yet?"

Next to her, Chelsea Midas looked like the poster girl for the Joker's product, Smilex, from the first *Batman* movie.

"I don't think I've smiled and laughed so much in my life." the girl said, confirming her delight. "Everyone's so nice. They all act like they've known me forever. Even that sweet old guy over there."

She pointed to where Olav Cawley stood with his arm draped possessively around Gracie Naner's shoulders. "He told me I'm the spitting image of my grandmother. Isn't that a hoot!" She giggled. "I'm so glad you asked me to come."

Nobody else seemed to understand the importance of her statement—except me. I nearly choked.

No one noticed that either.

"I'm happy you're enjoying yourself." I patted her arm.

"Come on, bud." I took hold of Seth's hand to capture his

attention—the moment Chelsea arrived, all focus went to her.

As we meandered our way through the hall toward the bathrooms, I realized we weren't alone; Detective Spencer accompanied us.

"I'm big enough to do this myself, Gramma." Which he was, even though I hated to admit it.

"I understand, but you know how moms can be. Scoot," I told him. "You don't want to miss out on all that food."

"He's a kick," Spencer said, watching Seth shuffle into the men's bathroom.

"He is." I looked up at the detective, realizing for the first time how tall he was—six two at the very least. Even when I'm on my feet, I barely reach five two, a full foot shorter. Not that it made any difference.

"You know Andi and Seth." It wasn't a question. I'd seen the way he handled those, answering one question with one of his own.

"Jared too. We've fought a few fires together."

Tarryton wasn't large enough to support a full-time fire department. Instead, members of the police department, and all the volunteers they could get, comprised our firefighting force. Jared had been a member of the volunteers for several years now.

I recalled Andi's odd comment the other day when I'd asked if she knew Spencer. Come to think of it, her attitude and avoidance to give me a straight answer explained a lot.

Seth emerged from the bathroom, wiping his hands on his shorts.

"No paper towels?"

He shrugged. "Easier this way." He skipped off ahead of us.

"It was you, wasn't it?" I didn't look at Blue Eyes; I didn't think I could at the moment.

"Excuse me? Ahh..." He cleared his throat. "You've got me; I was your blind date the night of the, er..."

I raised my hand to stop him and turned, hoping my face wasn't as red as it felt. "Okay. Now we've got that settled, you don't have to feel obligated to go through with the date next Saturday."

"Obligated?" Spencer shook his head. "Glory, I didn't ask you on a date out of an obligation. I did it because I'd like to get to

THE CASE OF THE BOUNCING GRANDMA

know you."

"Because I struck you as being so sensible and down-to-earth when I reported a murder the other day?" Now I *was* being facetious. "The only time we've met, and—"

"That's not exactly true," he interrupted. "We've kind of run into one another off and on, though I don't expect you to remember."

How could that be possible? I mean, this was one guy you definitely didn't forget.

"The second time was about a year ago at a barbeque Jared and Andi had," he was saying. "I wasn't there long, got called away on department business. And we didn't actually meet, but I knew who you were."

A year ago? I vaguely remembered the barbeque but didn't recall him being there. If that was the second time...

"And the first?"

"When you, Jane, and Andi sang 'I Hope You Dance' here at the church. You had tears in your eyes—and everyone else's."

I know he heard my attempt to swallow, the huge intake of air, and the gulp. Right now I didn't care.

What am I saying? I could barely breathe.

We had performed that song as a tribute to Ike's life—on the first anniversary of his death.

Chapter 12

There have been few occasions in my life when I have been totally speechless. This was the second time in the last three days.

I didn't have a comeback for Detective Rick Spencer; I didn't have a voice to make one. I imagine the expression on my face and my gasping for breath showed my surprise. Blue Eyes, for his part, took it all in stride. He flashed me one of his dazzling smiles that made those cute crinkles around his incredible eyes. He gave my shoulder a gentle squeeze and then urged us forward to find a place at the tables.

Seth was already holding spots for us, and after the detective—Rick—was sure I was settled, he got into the chow line.

"Gramma's got a boyfriend!" The silly little song startled me back to reality.

"You think so, huh?" I tickled Seth in the ribs. His giggles restarted my brain activity and helped me focus. "What about you, kiddo? Where's Chloe tonight?"

Chloe Henderson had been Seth's girlfriend since preschool. She was a soft blonde, angelic confection of a thing, with a tiny voice and a smile that brought sunshine to the cloudiest day. Every church event found the two of them sitting together and planning for the next time they'd see one another.

"Ah, Chloe's just a kid, Gramma." Spoken like a young man smitten with his first big crush. I felt a little sorry for Chloe but figured Seth's infatuation for an older woman was bound to be short lived.

I wondered what he would do when he got the opportunity to meet Chandra. That might be enough to return his attention to someone his own age. Then again...

The dinner went well with plenty of jokes, laughter, and conversation. Chelsea was a hit, not only with Seth, but also with the slightly older males.

My poor little grandson held his own, sidling up to Chelsea whenever a potential suitor came by. I even saw him reach for her hand a couple of times. Chelsea would grin down at him and tell him a knock-knock joke, which reassured him of his place in her heart.

Watching them, I understood why she wanted the career she was anxious to train for. Andi said Chelsea had the heart and soul needed for a good day-care provider, and from what I'd seen, I had to agree.

Jane and Dr. Steven were more subdued than they'd been in his office the day before. He still made my sister blush every time he smiled at her, and when he winked, I thought she might faint. There was a little more hand holding than usual. I had a feeling that bling I'd joked about wasn't too far in the future. Good thing I'd soon be back on my feet.

I didn't talk a lot during dinner. It felt odd to have a man at my elbow, to have him lean close to talk with me or the others in our group. None of them appeared fazed that the cat was out of the bag, so to speak. To the contrary, they seemed relieved. Bottom line, someone should've said something about Detective—er—Rick long before. Or, at the very least, when he'd shown up at my door three days ago.

I'd have to talk to Jane about that.

I think Olav was right about the angels joining our praise worship. It was as though an entire choir of voices were singing off in the distance, yet there in the sanctuary with the rest of us. There was a whisper of sound—could it be wings?—and a sweet, nostalgic smell that had nothing to do with the leftover desserts in the fellowship hall downstairs.

Perhaps the most remarkable experience of all, though, was what happened during the closing prayer. The congregation stood and everyone held hands, stretching across aisles, pews, chairs, and benches, to form one gigantic circle. As Pastor Connor thanked our Lord for our time together and said a blessing over us, I felt a feather-light touch, a kiss, on my forehead. I opened my eyes to see who may have done it, but no one had moved. Heads remained

THE CASE OF THE BOUNCING GRANDMA

bowed, eyes closed, and hands tightly clasped throughout the church. Nevertheless, it hadn't been my imagination.

In the bustle of activity following the doxology, I kissed Andi and Seth good-bye, waved at friends and acquaintances, and noticed that Elsie Wilkes had been crying. I knew I couldn't fight the crowd with the wheelchair, and with Andi already gone, didn't have anyone to check on Elsie. I couldn't ask Jane even if I'd wanted to; she was back in the kitchen finishing with the cleanup.

"Anything wrong?"

Believe it or not, I'd almost forgotten about him. I gazed up at Rick—it was all right to call him that—and made my decision.

"There's a friend over there, center pews, midway to the aisle, turquoise blouse, red hair." I pointed at Elsie and hoped that between my description and my aim he would know who I meant.

"Got her. Looks like she's been crying."

Good observation. Of course, would you expect anything less from a cop?

"I'd like to know if there's anything I can do for her, but there's no way I can reach her."

Rick nodded. "Leave it to me. Will you be okay here?"

"Perfect." I backed away from the aisle so my chair wouldn't pose a problem for anyone trying to get by.

Even though Rick went against the flow of people, by the time I resituated, he'd already reached Elsie. I could tell she was surprised when he began speaking. She waved to me, tucked her hand into the crook of Rick's elbow, and allowed him to lead her through the crowd.

"Are you all right?" I asked when they were close enough I didn't have to raise my voice.

Elsie nodded as she pulled a tissue from her shoulder bag. "I—I almost didn't make the service." She wiped her eyes. "You know I was going to show Rex one of the new townhomes over on Baker? Well, I waited and waited, and he never showed up. I called both of his numbers and left messages, but..."

"He didn't answer." Detective Spencer was talking now.

Elsie agreed. "I know people are saying how unreliable and irresponsible Rex has become, but we've always been special friends."

That's because they'd been engaged three times since high

school. Every time the big day was in sight, Rex skipped town and came back married to someone else. Elsie would pick herself up, dust herself off, and wait for the latest Mrs. Stout to get bored. When it happened, she was waiting in the wings, ready to forgive, and back to grooming Rex to be the perfect husband. Even Henrietta's warnings hadn't changed Elsie's mind. Still, you'd think she would have learned by now.

"So this is out of the ordinary for him?"

I knew Detective Spencer studied Elsie, watched her eyes, the way she wrung her hands, and any other body language that might give him an indication to what may be happening.

"Well," Elsie sniffled, "Yes and no. I mean, he was adamant about the townhome. He despises that little apartment he was forced to rent. He wanted a nice home, and he'd been to see a client—ex-client there. He liked what he saw."

When had Elsie begun to look so old? Before tonight, I hadn't noticed the lines in her face or the slight sag to the skin on her neck. I mean, they'd all graduated together; Rex, Elsie, Jane, and Steven. The two couples most likely to be together in holy wedlock—at least, that's what their senior yearbook stated.

Jane and Dr. Steven would probably turn that prediction into a reality. I was afraid Elsie didn't have a prayer.

"When's the last you saw him?"

"Las-last night. We had dinner and talked about the townhome. I called him before noon with our appointment time. He was thrilled I managed to get it so quickly." Tears were forming in the corners of her eyes, and I couldn't help feeling sorry for her. I reached out and tucked one of her hands in mine.

"I'm sure everything's fine, Elsie. He probably remembered this was Potluck 'n Praise night and didn't want to be talked into coming."

Rex had never been a fan of church. I remembered when we were kids and how he'd shoot spitballs throughout morning services. No matter how many times Henrietta grabbed his ear to get his attention, it didn't stop him. I'd bet he spent most of his adolescence down on his knees in this sanctuary picking up each and every disgusting spitball he'd let fly.

"Perhaps you're right." She gave us a weak smile. "I'm sure there'll be a callback when I get home." Elsie pulled her hand from my grasp and rubbed the area. Had I held it too tightly?

"If you don't hear from him tomorrow, give us a call at the station, and we can check into it. Okay?"

Elsie nodded. "I appreciate your concern." She gazed up at Blue Eyes then, and it was as though she was only just now seeing him.

"Why, I know you." She gave him one of her best smiles, all sugar and syrup. A big change from the tears and distress of a moment before. "You're George and Mary Todd's grandson. You remember them, Glory," she said, turning to me. "Your folks lived next to them while you were growing up."

Rick Spencer's awesome blue eyes latched onto mine and held me as Elsie continued to talk.

"I think everyone in town loved George and Mary. You couldn't find two more friendly and charitable people anywhere. Pillars of the community. And your mother, Connie, isn't it? She used to baby-sit me when I was small."

I think Rick answered her. But other than knowing I was no longer held by his intent gaze, awareness of what was going on around me fled. Instead, thoughts of my childhood flickered through my brain like an old-fashioned home movie.

Yes, I remembered the Todds, the smell of out-door barbeques our family shared with them, the delectable popcorn balls Mary made every Halloween, and the tears in her and George's eyes when they joined us Christmas morning. I'd always been under the impression they didn't have any family—at least none nearby.

There was something more, just at the edge of my mind, but I couldn't grasp it right now.

"Well, I really must be going."

That's right, Elsie, old girl, drop your bombshell and then leave it for others to sort out.

She said her good-byes and rushed off to join the Hobbses, who were on their way out of the sanctuary.

We watched the trio until they were no longer in sight, then regarded one another with curiosity. At least, I was curious.

"Small world." It was inadequate, true, but what else was there to say?

Blue Eyes nodded. "Six degrees. That's what some people estimate separates one person from another."

"Ah." Wasn't that a movie, *Six Degrees of Separation*?

"So, what's your take on Stout?"

Was this the detective or the guy? Did they go hand in hand?

Why was I trying to separate him into categories, make him into some sort of multi-personality head case?

Why was I always asking why? After all, this seemed a far safer subject than trying to figure out some past connection—something I was certain was virtually impossible.

"Rex Stout is the most arrogant, egotistical, self-delusional megalomaniac that's ever lived—outside most politicians and lawyers."

Rick's hearty laughter rang through the nearly empty building. "Don't hold back, Glory. Tell me how you really feel."

Rolling my eyes, I continued my onslaught. "Did you know that Elsie and Rex were engaged three times? Henrietta was fond of her, tried to warn her about Rex, but it didn't work. Every time one of his marriages failed, he was back on Elsie's doorstep. Believe me, it's not something I understand."

"Well, he's still on probation, so he'll show up." Rick stretched, his eyes sweeping the sanctuary. "Terrific service. Very uplifting."

"Very." I listened for a moment for that whisper, for the flutter I'd heard earlier, but it was no longer there. "Do you have a few moments before you go?"

"For you, anytime." He leaned against one of the balcony columns, crossing his legs at the ankles. "Shoot."

"Um, bad pun coming from a cop," I grinned. "It does, however, have to do with your profession." I told him about Helen Midas's cool welcome and obvious anxiety over Jane's and my visit with the twins.

"I'm sure she's just trying to protect them, Glory. After all, their story was in the paper the night before."

"Okay, I can accept that. But there's more." I drew in a deep breath, looked toward the basement stairs, hoping I wouldn't see Jane, and then went on. "Chelsea went with us to Kelly's for flowers. We found one of her flats at our place, so I took it over." *Don't lose him now, Glory,* I thought. "They had an old, beat-up chest freezer outside with an extension cord leading into the garage."

"And?"

"They're multimillionaires. They brought home this—this reject from the dump yesterday, set it up outside, and plugged it in."

"Maybe they fish and didn't want the smell in the house."

"Then why not put it *inside* the garage? And why were they digging in their yard at three a.m.? And why was a cell phone ringing from inside that freezer?"

That last bit got him, as it should. He looked down at his hands, uncrossed his feet, then stuffed his hands in the pockets of his jeans.

"There's something more you haven't told me."

Ah. He was even more perceptive than I'd thought.

"Do you know Olav Cawley?" When he nodded, I went on. "Olav and his wife were lifelong friends of Henrietta's, grew up together. When he spotted Chelsea Midas, he couldn't keep his eyes off her."

"There was a lot of that going around. She's a beautiful young woman."

"True, but that wasn't the reason."

I stretched my back and tried to get more comfortable. It had been a long day.

"From the first time I laid eyes on the twins I've had this strange sense of *déjà vu* that I haven't been able to shake. Ollie put it into words tonight."

"Which are?"

"He said that Chelsea has a look of Henrietta, that she's a chip off the old block." I shook my head. "When he said that, I had a sudden flash to the painting that used to hang over the fireplace in the Stouts' living room. It's been a while since I've seen it, but I'm telling you, that girl definitely resembles Henrietta Stout."

"O—kay. That explains the comment he made to Chelsea."

So, someone other than me had heard it.

"The girls could be her grandchildren," he continued. "Rex's kids."

He wasn't getting it. Had I explained everything correctly? Had I filled in all the gaps?

There still *were* gaps, of course, but it tied together somehow. I knew it did. The foot, the freezer, the digging, Rex hanging around—it was all part of the same package. It had to be.

Rick was pulling his cell phone from his pocket. I could hear it vibrate in his hand as he flipped it open to answer the call. He held up a finger, and turning around, spoke softly into the phone.

"There you are!"

Jane and Dr. Steven were holding hands as they came toward me. They were both flushed, making me wonder if it had been hot in the kitchen or if they'd managed to make it that way.

"Ready to go?" I asked.

Jane nodded. "I'm exhausted. I want to go home, watch the late news, clean up, and crawl into bed for the next ten hours."

That was a laugh. Jane has always been an early riser, and no matter what time she got to bed, she would be up and ready to go by five-thirty without fail.

"Hey, Steve, ladies. It was a great night. I can't wait to do it again." Rick stared at me for a moment, advanced a step or two, began to lean down, then held his hand out to me. "Glory, I look forward to our date. In the meantime, feel free to call me anytime."

I took his hand in a brief shake. It was enough to bring on another swarm of butterflies.

When we got home, Jane was true to her word. She turned on the TV, found the news program she wanted, and curled up on the couch.

"I think I'll sleep in tomorrow. I'm not even going to set the alarm."

"It's a good idea, but your internal clock will get you up."

"Not this time," she said. The dreamy look on her face changed suddenly. "Hey, look, that's the woman I told you about. Angelina Verona. I wonder if they found her." Jane turned up the volume as the anchor stated this was their top news story of the day.

"Luisa Verona, mother of Angelina Verona, held a press conference earlier this evening with an appeal for assistance in finding her daughter. If you have any information regarding Angelina, who has been missing for almost a week, please contact the police hotline. This is doubly hard on Mrs. Verona as this marks the eighteenth anniversary of the disappearance of her twin granddaughters."

"That's right, Ed." The second reporter took over. "As you

THE CASE OF THE BOUNCING GRANDMA

know, Angelina Verona will long be remembered from the Parker surrogate scandal of nineteen years ago. At the time, Miss Verona was a maid for Kansas City real estate mogul Adam Parker and his wife Jeanette, an up-and-comer in haute couture."

Old photos flashed onto the screen behind the reporter.

I was tired and barely listening, but there was something that drew my eyes to the screen as still pictures and newsreels flew across it. The Parkers looked familiar somehow, the turn of the woman's head—did the man have a limp?

This was silly. As Jane pointed out, the story had been in the news a lot, and Adam Parker seemed to live in the limelight. Still...

"Health issues prevented the use of Mrs. Parker's egg, so special arrangements were made to artificially inseminate Verona with Parker's sperm. By the time the twins were born, the Parkers were in the midst of a divorce. When Verona pressed the issue of the surrogate contract, Adam Parker ordered a paternity test that proved he was not the babies' father."

Photos of two infants between their mother and grandmother took the screen.

"Babies Monique and Giselle were kidnapped shortly before their first birthday, eighteen years ago. Mrs. Verona says Angelina never gave up hope in finding her daughters and was in pursuit of a lead at the time of her disappearance."

"That poor woman!" Jane shut the TV off, and standing, stretched.

"Did you see that? Did you see it?" I thrust out my hand for the remote, but by the time I'd turned the set back on, the story was over. Frustrated, I shut the TV off and tossed the remote onto the coffee table.

"What's eating you?" Jane's former look of serenity appeared to hover on the oh-no-what-now-Glory expression she frequently got when dealing with me.

"Ollie said Chelsea looked like Henrietta when she was young."

"Cawley? He said that?"

I nodded. "He even told Chelsea she looked like her grandmother."

Jane sighed and shook her head. "Ollie's confused, Glory. It happens when a person hangs around you."

111

I let the comment slide, anxious to get back on track.

"Think back, Janie. Remember the painting of Henrietta and Rex that used to—"

"Hang above the fireplace. So?"

"He's right. There's a definite resemblance."

"Ah, Glory, not another mystery." She turned off the table lamp near her.

"Not another one, the same one." I blocked her path into the hallway. "Janie, you know this story, the one about the babies. Last night you were all over it."

"Your point?"

"When you think of Angelina Verona, of the photos you've seen of her, what do you see?"

"I'm tired, Glory. Beat with a capital B. I don't want to play your games tonight."

I moved out of her way and let her pass.

"Think about it, Janie. Think about Henrietta, the Verona woman, and think about those twins. And think about Rex suddenly being able to sell that property."

She didn't turn around. "I'm going to bed, Glory, to dream about the beautiful night I had. Take a hint and follow my lead."

I knew I was onto something big now. Gigantic. Where it all fit, how it all fit, I'd figure it out. But Jane was right; now it was time to settle down and get some rest. I drew in a deep breath, then closed my eyes and concentrated on slowly releasing it.

By the time I'd switched off the remaining lights and rechecked the front door locks, the agitation had lessened. In my room, I pushed the door shut, then sat in the dark and listened to the myriad of sounds coming from both inside and outside the house.

It was peaceful tonight, quiet. The ambient light filtering through the curtains was more than enough to see by. Yet even without it, I could easily find what I was looking for.

In the bottom drawer of the bureau that once belonged to Ike was a two-gallon freezer bag with a zipper lock. Inside was the last shirt Ike had worn before his death. I drew the bag onto my lap and slowly unzipped it.

When was the last time I'd held that brushed cotton against my cheek or sunk my nose into its soft folds? Six months? A year?

I'd had other pieces in the beginning—his robe, his pj's, and his pillow. Each of those had been a source of comfort, lying next to me night after night as I tried to get used to the loss of my one true love. One by one, however, they lost the smell, the essence that spoke of Ike. One by one, I had discarded them, telling myself I no longer needed a security blanket... and begging God to tell me why He'd taken Ike from me.

Tonight I held the last item. I closed my eyes, remembered that feather-light kiss on my forehead from earlier, then lifted the shirt to my nose.

All I smelled was plastic.

Chapter 13

When the phone rang a little after six the next morning, I shot up from the bed, my broken leg temporarily forgotten—but only for a moment. I grabbed the receiver as I wrestled the sheet from my cast.

"Mama?" Andi's voice was small and quiet on the other end of the phone.

"What is it, honey?" *Please, God, please have Jared be all right.*

"W-we got a c-call. They're w-wanting the families of Jared's unit to meet at the armory at eight this m-morning."

"I'll be ready—"

"N-no, Mama. Just me. Wives, you know. Of course, there's Jim Ingles because Sandi's in the unit." She cleared her throat. "Spouses, then. Anyway, there was no explanation. I—I don't know—"

"Baby—"

"I—I don't even know if Jared's okay," she said in a single breath, gulping afterward as though starved for air.

"He's fine, Andi. He's—"

"Mama, please, no platitudes, no words of comfort. Just pray, okay? And... and don't tell Seth when I bring him over. You and Aunt Jane have to act normal. That's important. I don't want Seth to be afraid for his daddy."

I wished I could be there with her, to hold her and give her the comfort she claimed she didn't want but really needed. Despite the hesitation, the fear reflected in her voice, there was also a sense of resolve and determination.

"We'll be here," I assured her.

Andi signed off with a simple good-bye that spoke volumes to anyone who knew her. She would prepare herself for the worst while praying for the best, turning it over to God to see her through. A faith that could move mountains.

I dragged myself out of bed and plopped into the wheelchair. Five more days and this thing would be history. Five more days and I would be able to bend my leg, wear regular clothing, and return to normal.

Well, as close to normal as I could be.

Jane was already in the kitchen, bustling around and putting away dishes that had been in the dishwasher. She had something cooking on the stove, probably one of the western omelets that she liked so much.

"Morning," she said as I wheeled to the refrigerator. "Who was on the phone?"

"Andi." I told her about the meeting. "She'll be bringing Seth over soon."

"Not a problem. I'm sure everything's fine, just some sort of update. After all, Jared told her their mission was hush-hush."

True, that's what he'd said. Still...

"What's that you're wearing?" I looked down and fingered the brushed cotton. "Just an old shirt." I grabbed orange juice from the fridge and rolled over to the sink for a glass.

"Not just any old shirt," Jane persisted. "That's one of Ike's, isn't it?"

I poured half a glass of juice and topped it off with water—loved the orange juice but between the calories and the acid, diluting it worked best for me.

"I've thought about going to Linda's for a cut and style. You think she might be able to work me in today?"

Jane blocked my path to the table. "You haven't been to a stylist since Ike died."

"I'm getting pretty ragged looking after three years of trying to cut my own hair, don't you think?"

My sister remained where she was, standing before me as though she were a sentry blocking entrance to a world-class exhibit.

"Want to tell me what's going on?"

"You want to tell me about Detective Rick Spencer?" I challenged.

That got her; she moved out of my way. Setting my glass on the table, I stared up at her.

"Why don't you check your omelet and then come over to talk."

"There's a good explanation, Glory." Jane slid the omelet from the pan onto a plate and brought it and her coffee to the table. She sat opposite me, staring me straight in the eye.

"What do you want to know?"

"Everything."

She twisted a bit under my gaze, but her eyes never left my face. "He heard us sing at church a couple years ago and asked Jared about you."

"So he said."

"Look, Glory, what do you want me to say? Do you want us to apologize for not telling you that this gorgeous man has been waiting the last two years to ask you out? Do you want to know that he's kind and considerate and didn't want to rush into anything because he knew you were still working through your husband's death?"

Okay, this was way more information than I'd expected.

"Slow down a sec," I told her. "You're telling me that—that this guy has been waiting to meet me, to date me?"

"I've already said too much." Jane shook her head. The sudden light in her eyes told me she'd come to some kind of a decision.

She pushed back from the table, drew in a deep breath, and let me have it. "From the moment he saw you singing that day, he's been asking Jared and Andi about you. I didn't know anything about it before they arranged for the dinner date six weeks ago. I didn't even meet him until he showed up here on Monday because of your foot-in-the-rug mystery."

"That's why you acted so weird." It was all coming together now.

"I didn't act weird," she protested. "I was in shock, but I wasn't weird."

"I still don't get it. Why would he wait around for *me*? I mean, look at me!"

Jane shoved her plate away, leaned forward, and grabbed my hands.

"I *have* looked at you, sweetie. Thing is, I don't think you've looked at yourself."

It was too early in the morning to deal with this. Besides, there were other things to think about right now—discussing my... um, attributes wasn't one of them. I attempted to remove my hands from my sister's grasp, but she held on even tighter.

"You are bright, funny, loving—"

"Not to mention, exasperating, nosy, and—"

"I'm being serious here, Glory." Jane's stern, no-nonsense voice got my attention. So did the tears at the corners of her eyes.

"You know, we have Andi and Seth to consider right now."

Jane released my hands and stood. She picked up the plate with her untouched omelet, went to the sink, and scraped the food into the garbage disposal.

"You know how I felt when Steven told me he'd been waiting his whole life to love me?" she said, her back to me. "I realized God had given me a special gift, a renewed chance for love in my life. There was no need to feel guilty about how I felt for Steven; I knew Don would want me to be happy. And if that meant having a man in my life—"

"I'm not arguing the fact, Janie. I wholeheartedly agree." I took a swallow of my juice, hoping it would give me strength. "I— this shirt was the last of my comfort blankets. I'd put it in a plastic bag to seal in Ike's smell. Last night I pulled it out, and—"

I swallowed the tears that threatened to fall. "I felt this touch at church, when we were all holding hands and praying. It was like a feather on my forehead, but I imagined it was a kiss."

I rolled away from the table and put my hands into my lap, my fingers rubbing the smooth cotton shirttails. "I hadn't needed the added touch of comfort, the smell for a long time.

But last night... I don't know."

How could I explain this when I didn't understand it myself?

"When I realized Rick *wanted* to know me, to *go out* with me, I was—thrilled." I met my sister's eyes. "Janie, I didn't think about Ike, I thought only about me, about the—wow, this guy wants to be with me! But later... later, I had to know, had to see if it was all right. Do you understand?"

She nodded slowly. "And?"

"I took the shirt from the bag and put it against my nose."

I felt the threat of tears abating. As strange as that seemed, it was stranger to realize I neither wanted nor needed the tears.

"It smelled like the plastic bag. Still does." I laughed a little. "I put it on, thinking that if I slept with it... I don't know what I thought."

"Are you okay, Glory?"

I smiled. "Better than I've been in the last three years. I don't know if I'm up to this dating thing, but it's flattering to know someone's interested. But this," I lifted the tail of the shirt. "This doesn't hold Ike here. He's in our hearts and always will be. Last night, well, I think God was telling me it was time to let go, time for us to get back on the same page."

Andi and Seth arrived, keeping me from having to face further introspection. I'd never been good at self-analysis on any level. I preferred things light, happy, fun. Too bad life couldn't always be that way.

"When he found out we were coming over early, he decided he wanted to have one of Aunt Jane's special omelets. Isn't that right, buddy?" Andi removed Seth's Chiefs cap and set it on the counter.

"With the little bits of bacon!" Seth chimed in, licking his lips. "But not those pepper things. Okay, Aunt Jane?"

"Sounds like a plan. How about you get the eggs and bacon from the fridge and we'll get it started."

Seth gave me a quick hug, then did as Jane suggested.

While he was busy gathering ingredients, Andi nodded toward the dining room. After a glance at Jane, I followed my daughter.

"Don't tell Seth where I've gone, okay?"

"Not a word." I promised.

"I'm going to pick up Mindy. She's so worried about Greg that I, well, you know. Besides, there's no reason for both of us to drive."

Andi drifted to the china hutch where her wedding photos were displayed. She picked up one of them, rubbed her fingertips over the glass, then returned it to the hutch.

"He's all right, you know," she said, turning to me. "I'd feel it if he wasn't."

"Of course he is."

She came into my arms, and we held each other. Prayers for

Jared and his unit filled my heart and mind. And as my daughter pulled from my embrace, I added a prayer that Andi would be given the strength to see things through no matter what transpired.

By the time Andi left, Seth was digging into his special omelet, and Jane was working on another one for herself.

With her encouragement, I put in a call to Linda's Styling Salon and left a message requesting an appointment. I think we both figured I'd better do it before I had a chance to change my mind.

After I'd showered and dressed, Seth and I went to the backyard to enjoy the sunshine. We tossed around a small plastic ball until Jane joined us. At her suggestion, he got his T-ball set from the garage. With my pitching and Jane's fielding, we were all laughing in no time.

"You're getting good at this," I told my grandson after he shot the ball past Jane to the back of our lot near the alley.

"It's 'cause I'm practicing for Little League. They say I'm not big enough, but I'm really strong."

I glanced at my sister, whose face was red from all the running.

"Maybe you should rein in a little of that strength, kiddo, so Aunt Jane doesn't pass out."

Seth giggled as he positioned himself once more into batting stance.

Jane tapped me on the back and handed me the ball.

"Hey, slugger, what do you say that after this one, we figure out something else to do?"

Seth nodded then donned a fierce expression as he prepared to take a final swing at the ball.

Maybe it was the way I threw it, the sudden breeze, or simply the way Seth stepped into the swing. Whatever it was, the ball popped up and over the privet hedge and into the Midases' yard. I heard it smack something in its descent—either the garage or the freezer—then there was nothing but silence.

"Oh, man! I'm sorry, Gramma."

"Don't worry about it, honey. I'm sure it didn't break anything."

"I'll go get it."

He dropped the bat and took off across the yard. There was no

THE CASE OF THE BOUNCING GRANDMA

way I could catch up to him.

And I definitely didn't want him going over there alone.

I needn't have worried; Jane was next to him by the time I managed to wheel myself a couple of feet. I continued to roll the chair into the front yard and onto the driveway. From there, I heard a deep, guttural voice, which sounded more like a growl than words—Darrell Midas, I was sure.

A few seconds later, Seth came bounding around the giant spirea bush and sprinted up to me. Jane followed closely behind, and from the rigid set of her shoulders, I could tell she was angry.

"Of all the unmitigated gall—"

"He wouldn't give the ball back, Gramma, even though I told him it was the last present my Pa-Pa ever gave me."

There were tears in my grandson's eyes, and that didn't sit well with me.

"He threw us off the property," Jane added. "Said he was tired of our interference. How rude—"

Okay, this was war!

After a reassuring hug, I set Seth away from me. As I started down the driveway, I noticed one of the twins and Mrs. Midas coming toward us. Seth's ball was in the older woman's hand.

"We came to apologize." Helen Midas still had that air of superiority about her, but her expression was less hostile than it had been the other day. "We—my husband and I—have been under considerable strain since the girls won the lottery. We've always been private people, and well—"

She held the ball out for Seth. He was about to reach for it when the other twin appeared. The child did a double-take, glanced at me, then practically dove for his ball. Once he had it, he backed up until he was standing between Jane and me.

"Thank you, ma'am," Seth said as he grabbed onto the arm of my chair.

There was a genuine smile on the other woman's face as she regarded my grandson. "You're welcome. And I apologize if my husband frightened you."

She turned to me, the smile now less evident. "I want to thank all of you for your kindness. Chelsea gave us glowing reports on last night's service. Chandra and I are sorry to have missed it."

"Next Wednesday it will be out at Valley View," Jane offered.

She was still tense, but her tone said the fury had abated. "Same kind of service, different location."

"Well, it sounds delightful."

The words were right, but the overall attitude didn't match. Helen Midas may have been trying to smooth things over, but she didn't intend to get too close, too friendly.

As for the twins, flanking their mother with their eyes lowered and cheeks flushed, I wondered why they were here. Had they come to make sure she was civil, to keep her in line? No, that couldn't be it; the body language was wrong, more submissive than assertive.

There was something off here, something... They looked more like a couple of teenagers who'd been punished for their misdeeds than the twenty-year-old women they were.

"We've had so much to clean up because of the vandalism," Helen Midas was saying. "So many things have been ruined and will have to be thrown out. It's been very difficult."

"I understand. I can't imagine going through that on top of your move. I hope they find who did this to you folks." Jane moved forward, her hand outstretched. I could tell Helen was uneasy with the gesture, but it didn't stop my sister from trying. In the end, they shook hands— after a fashion.

"Well, we should be going, girls. We need to leave for your campus tour."

Something about the way Helen Midas turned on her heel and strode off reminded me of a fashion model on a runway. It was a crazy notion that came out of nowhere and was gone just as fast.

The phone rang, and Jane left to answer it. I remained where I was, facing one of the twins.

"I wanted to personally thank you for everything," she said, finally raising her eyes to meet mine. "Chelsea had so much fun with y'all yesterday, she was bursting at the seams."

"They're twins," Seth whispered at my side.

I patted his hand, which was still on the arm of my chair. "We enjoyed her company. How were your campus visits?"

Chandra shrugged. "They were nice. I especially liked Northwest since it's in a smaller community."

"Channy?" Chelsea came around the giant spirea and stopped short of my property. "We need to go now."

Chandra waved at her sister, then turned back to me. "Daddy and Frank want to get the stuff that was ruined to the landfill or dump. Whichever it is."

"Channy."

Even from here, I could see the flush on Chelsea's cheeks. By now I knew her well enough to recognize the hint of desperation in her voice.

"We thought that winning the lottery would change things for the better, you know? Maybe cut the apron strings." The helplessness of Chandra's words tugged at my heart.

"Don't ever let anyone tell you that having money is the solution to problems," the girl said, tears filling her rich, brown eyes. "It only creates more."

Chandra ran to where her sister waited. Chelsea put an arm around her shoulders, gave Seth and me a quick wave, then disappeared behind the spirea.

124

ALICE K. ARENZ

Chapter 14

"Those people are beyond strange." Jane peered into the den, where Seth was preoccupied with a computer game.

"That's what I've been trying to tell you." I wheeled the rest of the way into the living room.

"You've been telling me they're murderers," Jane said, joining me. "That's a far cry from just being odd."

"I don't know; it seems to correlate with everything we've seen and with what I've found." I patted the folder in my lap that contained the information I'd gathered from the Internet. "One of the reporters who tried to do a story on them was literally thrown off their property in South Carolina. He even went to the cops to file charges."

"And?" Jane sank into one of the overstuffed chairs, turned sideways, propped her feet on the arm, and leaned back into its cushiony depths. I hadn't seen her do that since we were kids and she was settling in for a night of studying.

"He wasn't taken seriously. From the tone of the article, I figure he's a bit like Will Garrett."

"Ahh. What else have you got there?" Jane held out her hand, then withdrew it. "Before I forget, the call was from Linda. You've an eleven o'clock appointment."

"So soon?" Guess that meant I would have to follow through with the idea. Not that my hair couldn't use a proper cut and style.

"What else?"

"Huh? Oh."

I searched through the articles until I found my crime diagram. I had several lines that led nowhere, each with a name, but nothing definite to connect them to the body.

"Glory? I thought you wanted me to know what you've been

up to."

I bristled at the exasperation in Jane's voice. I *did* want her to know. I needed her input, but...

"Look, I promise not to make fun of it, okay?" She seemed sincere, so I handed her the file with the schematic on top. Jane studied everything for some time before she spoke.

"The diagram is interesting. Where'd you get the idea?"

"They use something like it on that TV program *Without a Trace*—sort of. I thought it would help map things out." I shook my head. "There are so many people involved, I really need a poster board."

"Okay." As she studied the diagram, her face went through a series of contortions. "The Midas family members make sense. I think I understand your listing Nick Pearson, but Elsie?"

"She sold the house. But mostly because of her connection to Rex."

She raised her eyebrows in a quizzical manner. "And Rex is here because..."

"I think he's the twins' father."

"You came to that conclusion as a result of Olav Cawley's remark?"

"Partly. He put into words what I've been trying to figure out from the moment I saw a picture of the girls. They definitely resemble Henrietta. Now, you combine that with what Chelsea said about Rex always hanging around—"

"And you come up with the reason he was able to unload the property." Jane nodded. "The will wasn't broken since he sold the estate to his daughters."

"Exactly." I grinned. Her tone and expression were thoughtful and sincere, which surely meant she was coming around.

"While that's a nice thought and would fulfill Henrietta's wish for grandchildren and keeping the house in Stout hands, it doesn't prove there's been a murder, or that the foot you saw was human."

Okay, I still had some convincing to do. I rolled over to where yesterday's paper still lay on the coffee table. Most of the front page was devoted to the missing Angelina Verona and contained some recent photos of the woman. After seeing the news last night, I knew I was onto something. The newspaper photos convinced me I was right.

THE CASE OF THE BOUNCING GRANDMA

"I know what you're about to say, and you're wrong, Glory. Angelina's daughters would be about to celebrate their nineteenth birthday. Nineteenth, not twentieth."

I held the paper out to Jane. "Have you taken a good look at this woman?"

"I don't need to. I remember the story, how she looked back then—"

"Janie, think about this. Those kids don't resemble Helen or Darrell Midas in appearance or personality. If the twins belong to them, if they are the parents, there should at least be a resemblance."

Jane swung around in the chair and sat upright. She took the newspaper from my hand and set it in her lap.

"It's possible they adopted the twins."

"If we were talking about other kids, maybe I'd see that as a possibility, but we're not. We're talking about *this* set of twins and Helen and Darrell Midas. From what I've gathered, they've always been dirt poor. How would they have gotten the money together to adopt? That's saying they could have gotten past inquiries into their background and met all the state requirements."

"There are other ways."

If anyone would know this, it was Jane. She and Don had checked into adopting. They'd even been part of a program that helped unwed mothers choose parents for their children. Jane and Don passed and exceeded every requirement, yet nothing had come of it.

"I'm sure you're right, but that's not the point." I needed to keep her on track, to help her see the obvious. "I only know one way for those girls to resemble Henrietta Stout *and* Angelina Verona."

"Where is everyone?" Andi called.

By the time she entered the living room, Seth had discarded his game in favor of his mom. He immediately hit her with his ball story.

"And they're twins, Mommy. Chelsea has a sister who looks exactly like her. Identical."

"That's right. Pretty neat, huh?"

I studied my daughter, watching for signs of distress. She was a little pale and a bit keyed up, but that was to be expected after the

127

morning she'd had. There was no indication she'd received bad news, for which I thanked God. Hopefully she'd feel better once we had the opportunity to talk about the meeting.

"Yeah, neat. And they made their dad give me back Pa-Pa's ball. Their mom brought it over, but I know it's 'cause Chelsea made her."

"At least you have it. I hope you thanked them."

While they went through the events, I could see Andi trying to hide her trembling hands. I knew she wouldn't want to discuss what she'd learned in front of Seth, so we'd need to convince him to return to his computer games or to go out in the backyard to play.

Andi was way ahead of me—she was already following him into the den.

"We'll discuss your theories later," Jane told me. "If you can convince me you've got something, I might be able to help."

I raised my eyebrows in question. What could she do to help prove or disprove my theories?

Jane's grin was on the sly side. "Just remember what I've always told you, little sister—never underestimate me."

Her wink said she had something up her sleeve. Knowing my sister, whatever it was could knock my socks off.

This subject might be closed, but there was another I was dying to discuss: Elsie's revelation about Blue Eyes. But right now, my daughter needed our attention.

Andi returned to the living room and sank onto the sofa. She raised her arms high above her head in a slow stretch, then rubbed her eyes on the downward motion.

"How about a Big Mac for lunch," she said. "My treat."

Whenever we took Seth to Micky D's, Andi opted for salads over the rest of the menu. Like Jane, she constantly checked labels for trans fats, partially hydrogenated oils, high fructose corn syrup, and all the other things we probably shouldn't eat. Between the two of them, they'd made getting a meal more of a chore than a joy.

"Ready to tell us what's going on?" I eased the wheelchair as close to her as I could get, which wasn't close enough for me—the coffee table prevented me from reaching her.

"Colonel Hammond was there. I thought he'd gone with

THE CASE OF THE BOUNCING GRANDMA

them." Andi rubbed at her eyes again. "There isn't much to tell, Mama. The Colonel said they got to their assignment, everyone was fine, and he was sure we'd hear more in a week or two. You know the colonel. He's an old softy as a civilian, otherwise it's 'Tough as Nails' Hammond."

"No mention of where they are?" Jane asked.

"The Middle East. No definites, no real explanations. The only reason they called us in was to tell us what they couldn't tell us."

"You know, it's probably for the best. I've often thought the media releases far more information than necessary when it comes to our military deployments. Playing it close to the vest better protects our servicemen and women. Especially since telling the public also means informing the terrorists we're after." Jane moved next to Andi and patted her knee. "We know he's okay, and that God has Jared in the palm of His hand. Right?"

"Right." There were no tears, no hesitation in her voice. Even the trembling subsided.

Andi smiled at us with a look of determination on her face. "I've added a request to the prayer chain, and Mindy's doing the same for Greg and the rest of the unit through her church. Now," she said, giving us one of her no-nonsense looks. "What about lunch?"

Jane looked at her watch. "It's only a little after ten, kiddo, and we've got to get your mom to the salon by eleven."

"You're going to—"

"Don't rub it in." I was already regretting my decision; I didn't need Andi's astonishment to press the issue.

"No rubbing." She held up her hands. "I think it's a terrific idea."

"Thanks, honey. Um, before we go, I'd like to talk a bit about Rick Spencer."

"We've already been through this, Glory." Jane frowned.

"Oh, Mama, I'm sorry. I should have said something the day he showed up here. It's just—"

"Relax, guys. I'm not out to accuse or attack anyone, so chill." I quickly related Elsie's story about his grandparents.

"I remember the Todds." Jane said. "We basically adopted them because they didn't have family nearby. They were a sweet couple."

"That's what I remember too."

"Rick mentioned visiting the area as a kid, but that's it. He's super honest, Mama, so if he'd ever met you, he'd have said something."

Blue Eyes's rating just went up a notch.

Jane leaned forward in her chair. "What was his reaction to the news?"

"Same as mine, I think. Surprise."

Jane nodded. "So what's bothering you?"

"I don't know. It's like there's a piece missing, but it's just beyond my reach."

"That's from spending too much time on your foot-in-the-rug mystery and all your other conspiracy theories."

I made a face at my sister and Andi laughed.

"You just need to relax, Glory. Not everything involves a secret or has a mystery behind it."

I chose to ignore her remark—something I was good at.

"You know, I remember Mrs. Todd's awesome popcorn balls and how Mr. Todd would help Dad with the barbeque, but beyond that..."

"It's not surprising. They moved away the summer you were nine." Spoken like a true big sister. "I don't recall seeing much of them that last summer, but I do recall the evening you got stuck in a tree—"

"I never!"

"You did too, Glory. I think it was the cottonwood."

Andi watched me expectantly, her eyes wide with amusement. I wanted to deny the accusation, but the memory emerged with a jolt.

"I'd taken the ladder and propped it against the tree." I felt a sudden rush of heat burn my cheeks.

"And the ladder fell, trapping you up the tree." Jane finished.

"I was stuck up there forever."

"Maybe an hour."

"You were in the house and Mom and Dad were gone—"

"And you were screaming your head off."

By now, Andi was laughing so hard I thought she'd fall off the sofa. "So that's were Seth gets it!" she cried.

"Had you any doubt?"

I refrained from sticking my tongue out at my sister—but just barely.

"In my defense, it was the only tree in the neighborhood I hadn't climbed."

They were both rolling with laughter, so I doubted they even heard me.

"I always thought you left me up there on purpose."

Jane wiped tears from her eyes and shook her head. "Not true. If it hadn't been for the boy who came by the house, I wouldn't have known what was going on."

"What boy?" Andi and I asked in unison.

"I don't know. He said he'd heard you..." Jane stopped and stared from me to Andi. "He said he was from next door."

"Rick!" Andi clapped her hands together and grinned from ear to ear. The implication sent a flush of heat throughout my body.

"On that exciting note, we'd better get a move on so you're not late for your appointment." Andi rose from the couch, came over, and gave me a quick hug. "Don't fret, Mama." She kissed my forehead. "I'm going to grab Seth."

Looking a little stunned, Jane got up from the chair, her eyes never leaving my face. "You think it was him?"

"You're the one who saw him."

Of course, that was more than forty years ago...

"All I can tell you is I didn't recognize the boy—or the man." Jane took hold of the wheelchair and pointed it toward the kitchen. "The only way you're going to know for sure is by asking him."

Which would mean telling the whole embarrassing story.

Not on your life.

Twenty minutes later Andi accompanied me into Linda's. While Seth and Jane went to Centerview Park so he could play, Andi agreed to wait until it was my turn in the chair.

"I'm so proud of you, Mama," she told me with a grin.

"Thanks, honey, but it's just a haircut."

I didn't want her to read any more into this appointment than the simple need to fix my botched attempt—attempts—at cutting my hair. I couldn't explain what brought me to this moment—I was having enough trouble assimilating that myself.

"I noticed how uneven I cut it last week and figured it was

time to give the professionals a crack at it."

"Right." She didn't sound like she believed a word.

"Glory, I'll be right with you." Linda Williams waved at us as she led a customer to the cash register.

"Guess that's my sign." Andi rose. "You have your cell phone?"

I nodded. "Sweetie, would you do me a favor?"

"As long as it doesn't entail my getting into trouble—"

"You're as bad as Jane! I just want you to look up some stuff at the library." I gave her the list I'd made out earlier.

"The Parker-Verona scandal?"

"Yeah. I've looked on the Web and haven't been able to find anything on the original case, just the bits and pieces they're rehashing because of Angelina's disappearance or in

association with Parker's shady real estate deals. Anyway, it happened about eighteen or nineteen years ago."

"I know. It's been all over the news since the Verona woman went missing. Mind if I ask why you're so interested?"

"Hi, Andi, Glory. Long time no see." Linda Williams joined us. She ran a hand through my bangs and lifted my ponytail. "I was going to ask if you'd been seeing another stylist, but—"

"Don't ask," I told her, grimacing.

"You definitely want it cut. How about a perm or color?"

"No perm, but maybe we could try the color. It's been a while, so we might have better luck this time." I turned back to my daughter. "Will you do it?"

"No problem."

Linda told Andi to return in about an hour, then started wheeling me to her work station. I stopped her and caught Andi just as she was heading out the door.

"And sweetie, let's keep it between you and me for now. Okay?"

Andi nodded, her perplexed expression telling me I'd have some explaining to do later.

But if she found what I was hoping for, no explanation would be necessary. In this case, a picture was worth far more than any amount of words.

Chapter 15

Why is it when you are least able to carry on a conversation, someone wants to talk to you? From the dentist who's numbed your mouth and filled it with cotton, to wait staff who appear to have an almost innate sense of timing, these people seem to know the exact moment to ask a question and try to engage you in discussion when there's no way you can answer them. Since it's too perfect to be accidental, it has to be planned—a kind of comic relief for their mundane world.

As I sat beneath the dryer, waiting for the color to take, activity in the salon not only increased, but also seemed to consist of dozens of people who wanted to speak to me. With the noise of the dryer, the drone of piped-in music, and my hands attempting to protect the tips of my ears from being fried, I was reduced to reading lips—something I wasn't very accomplished in doing at all.

I did a lot of smiling, nodding, and waving in answer to someone pointing at my cast or the wheelchair that was parked nearby. I checked my watch, wishing I'd forgone the color and stuck with a cut and style. I'd no reason to believe Linda's concoction would work any better this time than it had in the past. After three years of allowing the gray hairs to intermix with the blonde, it wasn't difficult to guess which would win.

When the tips of my fingers began to burn, I took my hands off my ears and scrunched further down in the seat. The last time I did this, Linda came over and readjusted the bonnet, lowering it to cover my head. Since she was busy at the cash register, I should have a few minutes' reprieve.

I watched the manicurist finish another client and briefly considered asking her to squeeze me in. I wasn't all that crazy about cuticle cutting, but the hand massage sounded good. A glance at my hands had me ready to signal for the girl's attention, but someone stumbling over my cast changed my mind.

A sensation of discomfort jolted through me, bringing me upright and slamming my head into the hair dryer. I shoved the thing off me and raised my eyes to the one person in town more accident-prone than I am.

"I am *so* sorry, Mrs. Harper. Are you okay? You're okay, right?" Ashley Tanner, a former classmate of Andi's, patted the air in front of my cast. Her fingers were spread wide and angled back, a sure sign she'd just had her nails done.

"I'm really, really sorry," she went on, not giving me a chance to reply. "I know I should have been more careful and watching and all. It's just that I was admiring my nails. Aren't they gorgeous? I think they're rad or bad or whatever." She giggled but still didn't stop for a breath as she wiggled her fingers in front of my face. "Whaddya think? I'm not really a waitress."

This was news to me; the girl had been working at her parents' truck stop just outside of town since she could walk—or stumble. The sudden cessation of her non-stop repertoire had my head spinning. Was I supposed to respond to her getting a new job or to the color of her nails?

"Then where are you working now, Ashley?"

She gave me one of her signature "duh" expressions then let out a high-pitched giggle accompanied by unladylike snorts.

"No, silly. The polish." Once again the fingers danced before my eyes. "That's the name of the polish: *I'm Not Really A Waitress*. It's by OPI. How cool is that!" With another hoot of laughter and a wave, the girl continued across the room to a waiting stylist.

I returned Ashley's wave, pulled my legs back as much as I could, and tugged the dryer down into place. I'd nearly dozed off when I sensed a change in the lighting. Linda and a woman I didn't recognize passed by on their way to the register.

The little wind chimes on the front door caught my attention, and I turned to see Rex Stout enter the salon. Though I knew several men used Linda's stylists, it surprised me to see Rex here. I figured him for something a bit more upscale than this little place.

As always, Rex was impeccably dressed with his comb over

THE CASE OF THE BOUNCING GRANDMA

cemented in place. He greeted Linda and her customer with one of his slimy smiles, and while this expression was

normal for Rex, I sensed something off in his demeanor. That was made even more apparent by his effort to appear patient while Linda and the woman visited. But the signs were there for anyone who knew Rex—the tightened smile, the hand that couldn't make up its mind to be in or out of a pocket, and most telling of all, the constant nod of his head.

Yes, something was definitely up with Mr. Stout, and I'd wager this wasn't a pleasure call.

When the customer's transaction was finally completed, Rex held the door open for the woman, then returned to the counter. They exchanged words when he tried to hand a wad of cash to Linda, and she refused to take it. She turned her back on him and began adjusting a display of shampoos. Rex, true to form, refused to be ignored.

He came around the counter, put a hand on her shoulder, and turned her toward him.

It was obvious they were arguing and just as obvious Linda didn't want him there. She kept pointing to the door, even pushed him toward it a few times, but Rex wouldn't budge.

Throwing her hands in the air, Linda returned to the counter and picked up the phone. Rex followed her, threw the money on the counter, then glanced back into the shop. When he spotted me, the heightened color in his face darkened.

He came at me like a bull chasing a red tablecloth. I just wasn't in a position to move out of his way.

"You haven't learned your lesson, have you, Glory Harper?" he said, bending down to my level and ensuring he spoke loud enough for me to hear. His breath stank of stale alcohol, and not the medicinal kind.

Since I wasn't sure what he was talking about, I had no idea how to answer him. I took note of the wild look in his muddy brown eyes, the way his mouth formed a particularly hateful sneer, and wondered what Elsie had seen in him all these years.

"Elsie was worried about you last evening."

"And you had her sic the cops on me."

Ah, so that was it. But I hadn't been responsible for...

"They rousted me out of the tavern on Willow because you

couldn't keep your nose out of my business. It wasn't enough that you caused me to lose the agency—"

"I didn't tell you to steal your clients' money."

"Why you—"

Linda came up behind him. "I've called the police, Rex."

She shoved him away from me, then went to work on the dryer. "They should be here in about five minutes," she said, switching off the unit, raising the bonnet, and checking my hair. "If you're still here, I'll file a complaint. If not, I'll say it was a misunderstanding. Your choice."

Rex Stout, the son of one of the nicest Christian women I'd ever known, swore like a sailor on leave. As he turned, he spotted my wheelchair, grabbed it, and sent it careening through the center of the shop, barely missing Ashley Tanner and her stylist. It struck the back wall with such force that it toppled over onto its side.

"That's you if you don't keep your nose out of my life, Glory Harper."

He ripped open the door and tore down the wind chimes that hung over it. He flashed a glare in my direction just before flinging the chimes into the waiting area. Apparently satisfied with the alarm this caused the shop's patrons, he turned and stalked out of sight.

Looking up at Linda, I saw she was crying. Though I knew I hadn't caused the scene, at least not directly, I still felt guilty.

"Sorry about that," I said, as she and another employee helped me to the rinse sink.

"Don't be silly, Glory. His attacking you was an afterthought, I'm sure."

They eased me down onto the chair, and after asking her assistant to right my wheelchair, Linda waved the other woman away.

"That man thinks he can make everything he's done disappear by shoving money at people," she said once we were alone. "He's been going around town and paying everyone

double what he stole from them. Of course, it doesn't come with an apology."

That sounded like Rex—the no-apology part. I doubt the words 'I'm sorry' are even in his vocabulary.

"Is it part of the court conditions?"

THE CASE OF THE BOUNCING GRANDMA

Linda positioned me in the sink, turned on the water, and sprinkled a little on my head. "He had to make restitution," she said, working the color into a lather. "As far as I know, he paid the court, then they paid us. We got a check a few weeks ago. As for this other stuff, it's my personal opinion that he's trying to buy his way back into the community. As far as I'm concerned he can take his money and—"

While I didn't hear the rest of what she said over the sound of the water pelting my head, it wasn't difficult to fill in the blanks.

"What I'd like to know," Linda said as she shut off the water and lifted me from the sink, "is where he came up with all this money he's throwing around. He didn't have it when they indicted him. Everything was tied up in his mother's estate. I know he sold the place, but it still doesn't make sense. I mean, he's rolling in dough."

I was interested in finding out the answer to that as well. Though I had my suspicions.

Thirty minutes later, I was staring at myself in a mirror.

"I guess the texture of your hair changed enough for the highlighting to work this time." Linda ran her fingers through the hair at my crown. "Looks natural, don't you think?"

I nodded, dumbfounded at the transformation. Natural waves and soft curls that fell to the top of my shoulders replaced the scraggly locks I'd come in with.

"Mama, you look terrific!"

"Hey, Bouncy, Bouncy, they cut off your ponytail."

I tore my eyes from the mirror, thankful they'd saved me from making more of a fool of myself.

"I know you don't like spending a lot of time on your hair, Glory, so this cut should suit you. It's pretty much wash and go."

Exactly my kind of do! I handed Linda a check, and she gave me my scrunchie.

"You won't need that for a while," she said with a grin.

Andi helped me into the car, and while she put the wheelchair in the trunk, Jane sat staring at me.

"You look a good ten years younger," she told me, making me blush. "Once you get out of that cast, you'll have to beat the guys off with a stick."

"Then thank goodness I'll have a pair of crutches for a while."

Jane and Andi laughed at my retort, but it seemed to confuse Seth. "Why are you going to hit people with your crutches, Gramma?"

As Andi explained my sarcastic remark, I stared out the window to avoid my sister's sidelong glances. While all this attention was flattering, it was also embarrassing. I wished I hadn't followed through with the idea of going to the salon—until I spotted a Crown Vic from Tarryton's police department. Then I couldn't help but wonder what Detective Blue Eyes would think when he saw me.

"Chelsea and Chandra came through the park right before we left," Jane said as she turned into the McDonald's parking lot.

"Walking?"

Jane nodded. "All that money and they still don't have their own cars. It's a little strange."

More than a little, I thought. But then, what about that family wasn't?

"That was a fast campus tour." I knew our school. They went all out for prospective students and their families.

"They had to cut it short. Some family thing," Andi said.

"I asked them to come to lunch with us." Seth beamed. "They're going to meet us there."

Seven years old and he was already asking girls out! He was growing up way too fast.

True to his word, the twins were waiting for us inside. They no longer appeared the submissive children they'd seemed when accompanying their mother in the delivery of Seth's ball a few hours earlier.

Chandra and Chelsea mimicked the others' comments regarding my hair but unlike my sister, knew when to change the subject.

"Lunch is our treat," Chelsea announced with a wink. "I think we can afford it."

Chandra agreed with her sister, glanced at her watch, and then went to the entrance of the restaurant to gaze out the windows. Though her show of friendship was genuine enough, she appeared restless and anxious.

"We've got about forty-five minutes before Frank gets here," she said when she returned.

THE CASE OF THE BOUNCING GRANDMA

"If this isn't a good time—" I started.

"That's not what I meant." Chandra stood back to let me pass. "I just don't want y'all to think we're rude if we have to leave before everyone's finished."

"Oh, Channy, chill." Chelsea pulled a cell phone from her purse and started punching in numbers.

"No, don't use the phone!" Chandra grabbed it and flipped it shut. Seeming to realize her behavior was a bit extreme, she blushed and let go of the phone. "I mean, there's no reason to bother him. You know how he can be when he gets calls on his cell from numbers he doesn't recognize."

It seemed a weak excuse to me, but I wasn't about to interfere. Once again it was obvious there was far more going on here than met the eye.

"Whatever." Chelsea replaced the phone in her purse, then grinned at me. "Our first cell phone. It is so cool. It can download videos, send text messages, access the Internet, and take pictures too."

"Is it a phone or a computer?" I asked, trying to put a little levity into the conversation.

"Oh, Gramma, you know it's both." Now it was Seth's turn to act embarrassed. His exasperation was so obvious, I was surprised he didn't reprimand me for playing dumb.

At the counter, Andi actually ordered a Big Mac. Though that was unusual, the bigger surprise was her choice of water to drink over her favored Dr. Pepper. As she stood aside so Jane could order, I took a good long look at my daughter. Andi caught me staring, blushed, and tugged Seth to stand in front of her.

I got this fluttery feeling deep in my belly that told me to sit up and take notice. Call it a mother's intuition, but the more I looked at her, the more I sensed an underlying excitement. And I knew it wasn't just Jared's absence.

An idea sent a sudden thrill through me. Was it possible? Could Andi be pregnant? It was all I could do to contain my own excitement, but I resolved to behave and not press the issue.

We found a section of the restaurant where we could sit together. Seth, like the man he would be one day, finagled a seat between the twins. When I rolled up opposite them, he glanced up and gave me one of his lop-sided winks that contorted the side of his face.

"I thought you girls had a campus tour today." Jane picked through her salad, checking out the ingredients, as she always did, before taking a bite.

"It was at nine. More of a formality, you know. Channy and I had gone out there before. This was so Mama could see the place and talk to people. As it turned out, she had to cut out early." Chelsea shrugged. "No biggie, though. We'll be back."

"I think she wishes we were still in Brees Run," Chandra rolled her eyes. "Heaven only knows why."

The answer to that was simple enough; Helen Midas wasn't ready to let her daughters go. I couldn't believe she'd managed to hold onto them this long.

"Well, I'm thrilled to death to be away from there. Did you know we were working two jobs before we won the lottery?"

Chelsea nibbled at her Quarter Pounder. "My day started at the Gas 'N Go at five-thirty in the morning. Channy came in at one, and then I was on to job number two—McDonald's. It was the only restaurant in town."

"There wasn't much else there, other than a grain store that doubled as a grocer." Chandra laughed. "We only had McDonald's 'cause we were close to the highway. Anyway, my schedule was just the opposite. We'd been doing that for what?" She looked at her sister. "Two years, right?"

Chelsea nodded. "After the factory closed where Daddy and Frank had been working, they had trouble finding jobs. Mama tried to pick up a few more houses to clean, but it wasn't enough to make ends meet. That's why we stuck around rather than going off to college. It's also why we took the chance and bought the lottery tickets."

"God was smiling down on us that day, that's for sure."

While I was trying to imagine Helen Midas cleaning houses for a living, Seth continued watching his beautiful companions, barely touching his Happy Meal. Usually ravenous, he toyed with his chicken nuggets and fries as he gazed in undisguised rapture from one twin to the other.

"Are you going to eat while it still has some semblance of warmth or are you going to wait for the grease to congeal it into a solid mass?"

THE CASE OF THE BOUNCING GRANDMA

Jane always had such a wonderful way with words. The picture she painted had me looking at my plain hamburger and fries with a lot less enthusiasm.

"Mind if I ask where you girls were born?" It was the first thing Andi had said since placing her order. She glanced over at me, flashing me an odd little smile.

"Braydon, Mississippi. We don't remember it, though." Chandra smiled. "They decided to move inland after a hurricane nearly wiped the place off the map."

"Oh my!" It was a lame response, and I knew it. I just wanted to keep them talking.

"The wind was so bad the day we were born, they couldn't get to the hospital," Chelsea volunteered. "They hadn't been living there very long and were staying with Aunt Kimmie, Daddy's sister. She was a nurse at the local hospital—before that hurricane destroyed the place. She delivered us right there in her home."

"That's quite a story," Jane joined in. "It's a good thing your aunt was around."

Both girls nodded.

"We loved hearing about it when we were little. It made us feel special, being born in the middle of a hurricane and all. It was hard on Mama and Daddy, though. The records were so messed up, it took them years to get our birth certificates and social security numbers. Weird, huh?"

"Hey, Channy," Chelsea pointed to the television mounted on the wall adjacent to us. "Doesn't that look like the woman who was asking us all those questions before we left South Carolina?"

My eyes flew to the screen along with everyone else's. You didn't need the sound to know what the program was discussing: Angelina Verona's photo with a running footer said it all.

"Hmm, I think you're right." Chandra squinted. "I can't quite make that out."

"She's missing," Jane told her. "The last her mother heard from her was sometime last week."

"Oh... well, then it's probably not the same person at all." Chelsea studied the TV a moment longer, then turned to her sister. "We left Brees Run almost two weeks ago. Well, ten days, anyway."

"Is that all it's been?" Chandra shook her head. "So much has happened since then. We're just a little over a thousand miles from Brees Run, yet it seems a lifetime ago." She took a swallow of her Coke. "The trip itself wouldn't have been so bad if the moving van hadn't broken down in Kansas City."

"That doesn't sound fun to me," I said, still chewing over the information regarding Angelina Verona. "Having to unload your things from one van to another."

"We didn't have much, and what we didn't absolutely need, we put into storage. Once we got a van to pick up the things we bought from the former owner of the house, Frank trotted it right down to the city to get our stuff. It's kind of silly, the roundabout way we did it, but it worked."

I wouldn't call it silly. Bizarre, maybe, but not silly.

"I didn't recognize the van's logo. Was it from here in Tarryton?"

Jane's question surprised me. I would have given her a high five if it could have been done on the sly.

"That's where the silly part comes in." Chandra giggled. "Daddy was so frustrated about not finding a van to rent immediately, that he decided to buy one. Isn't that just the funniest thing you ever heard? I mean, he drove an empty van all the way from Kansas City to Tarryton just so Frank could turn around and go back a day later to get the rest of our stuff!"

I didn't think it was funny, nor did I believe in coincidence. Frank Midas hadn't returned to the city *just* to pick up items they'd left in storage. It was my guess he was after one thing in particular... a body.

Chapter 16

"What are you doin' in here?" Frank Midas stood over our table, his hooded blue eyes hard and cold, his face red with fury as he glared at his sisters. "I've been waitin' out front for fifteen minutes."

The overpowering odor of sweat, mixed with strong cologne, wafted from his body with every movement. It didn't go well with the smell of burgers and fries.

"We decided to have lunch with friends," Chelsea told him evenly. "If you think you can act a little less like a caveman, you could join us."

Chandra blanched. I hoped Andi and Jane were up to CPR; the poor kid looked like she might pass out any second.

Frank fingered his soul patch as he stared across the tables. He flexed his biceps, which bulged out of his dirty muscle shirt. There were tattoos on both shoulders; one was the silhouette of a very shapely, very naked woman, the other an indistinguishable design that made my flesh crawl. He sneered at Jane and me, but his attitude changed when he spotted Andi.

"Hey," he said, raising his ragged eyebrows and grinning at her in a way that raised my hackles. His salacious expression made me wish I had one of the crutches I'd spoken of earlier.

"You girls goin' ta introduce me to these... ladies?"

"This is Frank," Chelsea said. Her posture stiffened as she watched her brother. "He's always this rude."

"Why you little—" Frank loomed over Chelsea, his hands clenched in fists.

Jane stood suddenly and circled around the man to stand protectively behind Chelsea. As she settled into place, Seth jumped out of his seat, scooted down the other end of the tables, and flew over to me. His eyes remained on Frank Midas the entire time. I pulled my grandson close and patted his back to reassure him.

Chandra leaned into Andi, the last of the color draining from her face. Andi propped the poor girl up, then turned her icy gaze on Frank.

"Unless you want the management to call the police, I suggest you take it easy, Mr. Midas." My daughter's eyes bored into him.

His insolent expression didn't alter when he turned his attention from his sister to Andi. "Well now, pretty lady, all I wanted was an introduction. I didn't expect my sister to be so bad-mannered." His attempt at Southern charm was poor at best. And keeping his hands fisted and inches from his sister didn't help endear him to any of us.

"I'm Mrs. Wheeler, and I don't appreciate your attitude." Andi continued holding onto Chandra. Though the girl was no longer as pale as she'd been a moment before, she still didn't look well.

Jane placed a hand on Chelsea's shoulder, narrowed her eyes, and cleared her throat. "We were in the middle of our lunch, Mr. Midas. We were talking and time got away from the twins. I'm sure they meant no disrespect in failing to meet you at the appointed time."

"You're some kinda schoolteacher, huh?"

The smart-aleck remark only made Jane bristle. Frank Midas may be tough, but I'd lay odds that Jane was tougher. After teaching for thirty years, Jane could go head-to-head with the best of them—as long as it was a war of looks and words, anyway.

"We... we really should go." Chandra sat up, gave Andi a weak smile, and began placing the remains of her meal on a tray. Chelsea followed suit, but not with the same meek expression her sister had.

Seeing he'd cowed his sisters, Frank Midas pushed out his chest, folded his arms across it, and backed away from the tables. He glared at the girls as they walked past him to the trash bins, then turned his impudent gaze on us.

There was a hint of triumph to his smirk as he stared at Jane and me. But what really bothered me was how he ogled Andi. If I had one of those crutches now, I'd bean this idiot.

"Thanks for lunch, girls," I said, meeting Frank glare for

THE CASE OF THE BOUNCING GRANDMA

glare. "It was fun."

Frank Midas laughed, turned on his heel, and walked away. Chandra, still looking like she might cry, gave us a weak little wave, then followed her departing brother. Chelsea, however, hung back.

"I hope y'all still want to be friends. I know my family hasn't treated you very well, and I apologize for that. We—" she hesitated as if she was searching for the right words. "We've always kept pretty much to ourselves, with the exception of going to church. Even then, we didn't join in on the activities or anything. That's why I loved attending the Potluck 'n Praise. It was like nothing I've ever been to before. Why, if Daddy and Frank hadn't lost their jobs and all,

Channy and I wouldn't have been working outside the home. I mean—" She shook her head. "I know it's gotta sound strange to y'all, but you're the first real friends we've had."

"You're not going to lose us," Andi assured her.

Chelsea nodded, then looked in the direction her sister and brother had gone. "I'd better go before he gets into another rage. Thanks for everything."

"Why do they have to go home with him?" Seth snuggled a bit closer to me. "He's meaner than their dad."

"It's okay, honey." I hugged my grandson as I too wondered why the twins put up with such abuse. "I'm sure the girls will be fine."

I hoped I was right. But with someone as volatile as Frank Midas, anything was possible.

"Did you see the way Chandra reacted?" Andi's hands shook as she gathered up the remnants of our lunch. "We should call later to make sure they're all right."

"Unless you've some way to get her cell number, that won't be possible." Jane stuffed Seth's uneaten lunch into the box it came in. "When we were at the park they mentioned not having the phone or cable connected."

"After this long? That's not right." Andi picked up Seth's Chiefs cap and set it on her son's head.

"I doubt it has anything to do with the utility companies." I maneuvered the narrow aisle and joined the others near the trash bins. "I think they want the girls to have as little outside access as

145

possible. That's a problem now they have the lottery money."

"But to still be so isolated at their age... it's hard to believe they'd allow it. Especially after they'd gotten a taste of being out in the world." Andi pulled Seth in front of her and pointed him toward the doors.

"I don't know if Brees Run would be considered out in the world, sweetie. Whether they were working two jobs or not."

Andi glanced back at me, shook her head, then followed her son.

"I think we need to discuss your theories, Glory," Jane said as we headed toward the car. "It's time we took a closer look at what you've got."

The drive home was far quieter than any time we'd spent together. The underlying excitement I'd sensed in Andi had been subdued by the encounter with Frank Midas. Even my stalwart sister was affected by the brute's behavior. Our concern mirrored Seth's, even if we didn't put it into words.

"You going to come in for a while?" Jane pulled around Andi's car and into the garage.

"Please, Mommy? I was in the middle of a game when we left."

"Just a little while, slugger. We're going over to Mindy and Nathan's for supper."

"Cool!" Seth hopped out of the car. " 'S okay if I go finish my game?"

Andi agreed, and he dashed into the house while she and Jane got my chair and helped me out of the front seat.

"What's he playing that has him so anxious to get back to it?"

Jane wasn't a big fan of computer games, unless they were educational in nature. Though I agreed with her for the most part, I've been known to waste more than a few hours playing Spider Solitaire.

"It's one of those games you got him last Christmas," Andi told her. "Maybe it'll take his mind off what just happened in McDonald's."

"I'm still trying to figure that out." I rolled in through the kitchen door and grabbed a bottle of water before heading to the living room.

"What's there to figure out? The man's a bully and a letch,"

146

THE CASE OF THE BOUNCING GRANDMA

Jane said. "He likes to watch people squirm."

"Well, I dare him to try anything with me. I'll cut him down with a roundhouse before he knows what's hit him."

"I'd as soon you stay as far away from him as possible, Andi. The man's been in prison for assault with a deadly weapon."

Jane picked up my file from the coffee table where she'd set it earlier. "I think that family uses intimidation the way most of us use love and decency." Tapping the folder against her leg, she moved to the overstuffed chair and sat down. "It's a wonder those girls are as nice as they are."

"Which brings us back to what I said before."

My sister cocked an eyebrow in my direction. I had to find a way to convince her.

"The twins don't resemble the Midases in looks or personality."

"That's because they actually *have* personalities." Andi smirked.

"Oh, sweetie, you don't know the half of it. Until you've met the father—" Jane shook her head. "I'll give you that much, Glory. But just because the girls aren't surly and obnoxious doesn't mean Helen and Darrell Midas aren't their parents."

"There's the resemblance to Henrietta."

I watched as Jane flipped through the articles I'd printed off the Web. Her concentration on the documents in front of her gave Andi the opportunity to slip me a wad of papers. I mouthed a thank you and received a wink in response.

"What's this about Henrietta?" Andi took a seat on the couch and gazed from Jane to me.

"Your mother took a remark from Olav Cawley and turned it into one of her mysteries."

That hurt. Here I'd thought Jane was coming over to my side.

"When Ollie saw Chelsea last night, he said she looked like Henrietta. That got me thinking—"

"The portrait!" Andi's face lit up. "That's it—what's been bothering me." She nodded and smiled. "I *knew* there was something familiar about those girls, just couldn't put my finger on it. And after Chelsea said someone at the church told her she looked just like her grandmother—"

"Not you too." Jane sighed. "While I have no doubt Rex has

offspring running around that no one knows about, I find it difficult to believe..."

I couldn't see which of the articles had gotten her attention, but I could tell from her face that the information bothered her in some way.

"It sheds a new light on how Rex was able to sell the house, doesn't it?" I directed my comment to Andi, who had moved closer to her aunt in an obvious attempt to see what captivated her.

I took the opportunity to glance through the papers Andi had given me. The photos that accompanied most of the articles on the Parker-Verona scandal were smudged and grainy. Still, I easily recognized Angelina Verona and Adam Parker, even though I'd only seen the latter in recent news reports. Shifting to the best of the photos, I tried to make out Jeanette Parker's features but found myself drawn to another individual hovering in the background. Closer inspection had me sputtering for attention.

"What's up, Mama?"

"You guys might want to take a look at this." I wheeled over to Jane and held out the page.

"Where'd you—" Jane took the paper. "This was taken outside the courthouse when Parker proved the Verona babies weren't his."

Andi scooted to the edge of the couch and peered at the paper in her aunt's hand. "Sorry it isn't very clear. They had the newspapers on microfiche, and the printer connected to the machine was horrible."

"It's okay," I assured her. "I just want you both to take a good look at the people in this photo."

As my daughter and sister concentrated on the grainy photograph, I closed my eyes and pictured it in my mind: Angelina Verona crumpled in the arms of a man I assumed was her lawyer; a triumphant Parker glaring at the cameraman; the expressionless Jeanette Parker, and the man, barely visible behind her, whose hand was on her shoulder.

Opening my eyes, I stared at Jane and Andi, watching for the moment of recognition to come.

"Could it be? I mean, I don't see how, but..."

"What? Who?"

That's right, how could Andi identify someone she hadn't

met?

I didn't want to say it aloud, didn't want Jane to think I was trying to influence her or create yet another mystery.

"I might be mistaken," Jane said, raising her eyes to meet mine. "But I think that's Darrell Midas."

Chapter 17

While I was rejoicing in the moment, Jane was busy trying to minimize its importance.

"*Might be,* and I stress those two words."

"You saw the resemblance. That's good enough for me."

"It doesn't prove a thing."

"It does beg the question of why he was there and in what capacity." Andi took the page from her aunt and studied it. "I haven't had the honor of running into Mr. Midas, but after the up close and personal with his son, I'd have to say this guy bears a slight resemblance to Frank. Though I have to admit, the quality of the copy's so poor there's no way to say anything for sure. And there's nothing here to identify him."

"Which is why there's no reason to get excited," Jane said in her best matter-of-fact voice.

"I'm just thrilled to know you saw the same thing I did—without my putting the idea in your head."

"True," Jane admitted. "You didn't say anything. I have to wonder, though, if this morning's run-in with Midas, followed by our wonderful experience with the son, might have influenced me."

"So you're both saying all thugs look alike?" Andi's question stopped us cold. I guess our looks of surprise amused her because she stuck out her tongue and giggled.

"Well, neither of them looks like Rex Stout, so that's not quite true."

"Ah, but Rex isn't a thug," I told her. "More of a bully and a slimy Lothario wannabe." I gave them a quick rundown of what had transpired in the salon.

"We all agree he's not a nice guy. And age hasn't improved his disposition." Jane shook her head. "He's always been a piece of work. Rex has been using the misunderstood, angst-filled, bad-boy routine since high school."

"Sounds like an attempt to imitate James Dean," I said dryly. "A poor imitation, anyway."

Jane shrugged. "Most likely. It didn't impress anyone—other than Elsie, of course."

"Of course."

"Yes, well, trying to live up to a movie legend didn't work when the real tough guys kept beating him up."

"The bully being bullied," Andi said. "Sounds like a life changing ordeal."

"For most people, yes. For Rex," Jane shook her head. "I'm not sure. A part of me always wanted to feel sorry for him, but he never made it easy to like him. He wore his bruises with pride, like they gave him the right to be nasty and cruel to others."

Though gaining more insight into our resident bad guy was interesting, I really wanted to get back on track.

"It's hard to believe his insurance agency did so well."

"That was Henrietta's influence in the community," Andi interjected. "Very few people in Tarryton really like Rex."

"You're probably right," Jane agreed. "Bottom line is it's difficult to find a single redeeming quality in Rex. Well, that's not altogether true; he really did love his mother, so he can't be all bad."

"A redeeming characteristic, Janie, but it doesn't mean he's innocent."

"Maybe not, but there's no reason to go off half-cocked." Jane tapped the file in her lap. "You've collected some interesting things in here, Glory, but I don't see anything to support your allegations about the twins' parentage—or your determination to prove someone's been murdered."

How could she say that after everything I'd shared with her?

"What about our observations? Andi sees the resemblance to Henrietta too."

Jane drew in a deep breath before responding. "I don't remember the painting well enough to argue one way or the other. But there are major things wrong with your theory regarding the

THE CASE OF THE BOUNCING GRANDMA

twins. First, their age. As I said before, the Verona twins would be turning nineteen—"

"So they futzed around with the birth date. You heard that story about being born in the middle of a hurricane—"

"Second," Jane continued. "Angelina agreed to the surrogacy because her mother was ill, and they didn't have money for her care."

"What has that to do with anything?"

"Third, and this is a biggie, despite the fact Parker got the courts convinced he wasn't the father—"

"Of course he wasn't; they're Rex Stout's."

"Angelina claimed she was a virgin at the time of the insemination. Your theory would have her already pregnant, which even the doctor finally admitted wasn't a possibility."

That took the wind out of my sails. I looked down at my hands, trying to come up with an explanation, knowing there was a logical rebuttal but unable to put my finger on it at the moment.

"As interesting as this is, Seth and I have to get going." Andi came over and kissed my forehead. "Keep working on it, Mama, you'll figure it out. And you know what? You look terrific."

Seth appeared at my side. The way he snuggled into me said he hadn't gotten over the restaurant encounter. I put my arm around his shoulders, reached down, and tickled his ribs. He squirmed and giggled, then came after me with what he called his spider fingers. He tickled my neck and the tops of my shoulders until we were both laughing so hard we cried.

"Can I have an apple, Gramma?" he said through a fit of giggles.

"I'll bet you're hungry. You were so busy watching Chandra and Chelsea you didn't eat a thing." Jane's observation mirrored my unspoken one.

Seth blushed. "I've never known twins before."

"What do you think, Mom, is it all right for him to have an apple?" I asked, giving him another squeeze.

"You can grab it on our way out, kiddo. We need to run home before our dinner date."

Although Seth didn't look happy about leaving, he didn't argue. He gave Jane and me a quick hug then ran to the kitchen to get his apple.

153

"You two need to put your heads together on this Midas thing," Andi told us. "Mama's right about the girls resembling Henrietta, Aunt Jane. And there's a definite resemblance to the Verona woman too. Between that and the fact they've ended up next door, it's just too weird to be a coincidence."

"You've got that right." I glanced over at my sister and found her once again engrossed in one of the articles from my file.

"Let me know what you come up with. And Mama, try to check on the twins later, okay?"

I told her I would, and with a wave, Andi left. I listened as the garage door opened and closed. A moment later, I heard Andi's car start, followed by the sound of it backing out of the driveway. When I could no longer hear the car, I turned to Jane.

Her head was still bent over the file. She reached up to tuck a strand of her dark hair behind her ear. When she began tapping the nail of her index finger against her teeth, I decided it was time for her to share what she found so fascinating.

"So?"

"I'm sorry; did you say something?"

"You've been studying that article for some time now. I just wondered what was so interesting."

I could see her hesitation and was a little perturbed by it. After all, they were my articles, and if she'd found something important in there...

Okay, Glory, stop, breathe. It had been a long day, and it was only a little past three. There was no reason to jump down Jane's throat just because I was tired and a bit overstressed.

"It's the story about the twins' birth. It sounds—contrived. Of course, when you take everything into consideration..."

"It all sounds odd," I finished for her. "I know. When this whole thing started, I was looking for a murderer, and what I've discovered is a convoluted story no one wants to believe."

"That's because you have a bunch of theories with no real answers." Jane raised a hand to keep me from interrupting. "You have no way to prove the parentage of those girls, Glory. You and Olav Cawley can state they look like Henrietta until the cows come home, but that isn't proof."

She stood and brought me the file. "You can tell everyone in town you saw a foot in that carpet, but you haven't got the proof

THE CASE OF THE BOUNCING GRANDMA

you need to convince the police or anyone else to take you seriously."

"What about the cell phone in their freezer?"

"Did anyone else—outside the Midases—hear it? And who's to say Frank or Darrell hadn't accidentally dropped his phone when they were putting food inside?"

I wasn't enjoying her portrayal of the devil's advocate.

"What about the girls' comments about Angelina Verona? I mean, the news reports stated Angelina was following a lead."

"And you think it led her to Chelsea and Chandra?" Jane's expression remained doubtful. "Remember, the girls weren't even sure if she was the same person they'd spoken with back in South Carolina."

"Yeah, it's another of those weird resemblance things you don't believe in."

Jane patted me on the back. "It's not that I don't believe in it, Glory. All you have are coincidences and theories with no supporting evidence to substantiate your claims." She grabbed up her purse. "I'm going over to my place to water plants and check on things. You want to come?"

I shook my head. I needed some alone time. "Go ahead, and take your time, Janie."

"You want me to help you to the patio or anything?"

I could tell from her tone that she regretted the role she'd played in shooting down my theories. While I might be down, I wasn't out of the game.

"I'm fine," I told her. "I'll put in the roast while you're gone. I saw it in the fridge this morning."

I followed her into the kitchen, rolled over to the refrigerator, and opened the door.

"Not too much seasoning, okay?"

I waved her on and pulled out the rump roast she'd already put into a ceramic dish. I wheeled away from the fridge and over to the stove as Jane went out the kitchen door into the garage.

"You really do look terrific," she said, peeking around the door.

"Get out of here before I have to hurt you." I blushed and made a show of concentrating on what I was doing.

By the time she started her car, I had the oven on. Without

waiting for it to preheat, I stuck the roast inside.

I wheeled through the living room to the den with my file in hand, determined to get the information I needed to support my theories. If Jane wanted proof, then that's what I'd get her. Though how I could accomplish that, I didn't know.

Once in the den, I spread the different articles across my computer desk. I held onto the pages Andi had copied for me on the Parker-Verona scandal, deciding to concentrate instead on what I'd gotten from the Web. Spotting the article Jane had been so fascinated with, I grabbed it to take a closer look.

Accompanying the article was an exceptionally good color photo of the Midas family. I scanned the picture, then settled in to read the article. As Jane said, it mentioned the story the girls told us about their birth in the midst of a hurricane. Though the author quoted the twins, he posed several questions of his own that had remained unanswered. Among them, the fact that Kimberly Midas had died at the community hospital when the hurricane destroyed it—the day following the miraculous delivery of her brother's babies. When the girls related their story to us, they hadn't mentioned this last bit either.

No wonder Jane had found the story so interesting! The only person who could substantiate the Midases' story of the twins' birth was dead. If that wasn't a glaring red flag, I didn't know what was.

I gazed down at the photo, into the warm faces of Chelsea and Chandra. Their rich dark eyes were in sharp contrast to the icy blue of their mother's.

Eyes. Something about the...

"Blue!" Helen Midas had blue eyes, and I was positive her husband's were the same milky blue as Frank's.

It had been a long time since I'd had a genetics course, but I was almost positive that two blue-eyed parents could not have brown-eyed children—or at least it would be a very rare occurrence.

A quick Google search left my head spinning—genetics was definitely not my thing. But even after all I read about changing genes, unreadable genes, and a multitude of other things, belief in my original conclusion remained firm. I may not be able to prove that the twins were the missing Verona children or that Rex Stout was their father, but I was sure of one thing: Helen and Darrell Midas weren't their biological parents.

Chapter 18

An epiphany, that's what it was, a sudden and unexpected insight that couldn't have been more welcome.

I hugged the article and would have danced a jig if I'd been able to. I didn't think it'd be wise to attempt it in my current condition. Still, there was no reason not to celebrate.

Beating a tattoo on my desktop, I wished Jane or Andi were around so I could share my discovery. Eye color wasn't the only thing to consider here either. I had to side with that reporter. The story of their aunt delivering the twins the day before her death seemed a little too coincidental. Of course, I wasn't big on coincidences, anyway.

The doorbell rang, forcing me out of contemplation and into action. Anywhere else in the house, the time it took to reach the front door was more than most people were willing to wait—I'd lost visitors because of taking so long to wheel myself over the carpets. The den was just off the entryway—carpet to floor in thirty seconds flat. Almost.

I opened the door to find Blue Eyes on the porch with his back to me. He was in uniform again today, and even from behind, he looked good.

"Hello?"

"Oh, sorry."

He turned to me with one of his engaging smiles. Within a fraction of a second, his expression changed to one of startled appreciation—at least, that's how I read it.

"You... your hair... wow."

"I'll take that as a compliment." I grinned, moving aside to allow him to enter.

"You look... great."

He appeared at a loss for words, which made me feel a bit giddy inside.

"Thanks. You too."

"Huh? Oh," he laughed. "Sorry if I'm being rude, Glory. I didn't mean—"

"To stare?"

"Yeah. I mean—"

"Yes?" Oh, this *was* fun.

Was there a little hint of red in his cheeks? And while I was on the subject, did he have to shave a couple times a day to keep his face so smooth? Those high, rugged cheekbones, firm chin, and those awesome eyes...

Snap out of it, Glory! He was supposed to be going all dreamy, not me.

"You wanna sit?" I led him into the living room, wondering why he'd come over and absurdly happy he had.

"I can only stay for a moment. I understand you had some trouble with Rex Stout earlier today."

Ah, so that's it. Linda must have told the police what happened at the salon.

"He was just being the Rex we all know and tolerate."

"Linda Williams said he threatened you."

"He threatened my wheelchair. And beat it up too." I laughed. "I appreciate your concern... Rick," *Okay, now breathe.* "I've known the guy all my life and have never taken

him half as seriously as he takes himself."

"That may be, but I don't think you should underestimate the man. After all, there are a lot of people who thought they knew Stout and could trust him. Myself included. None of us expected to get burned by our insurance agent."

His serious tone told me I'd better shape up.

"When you put it like that—Okay, yes, I guess he threatened me. But then, so have Darrell and Frank Midas. They all want me to mind my own business. Which is what I thought I was doing at the salon..."

"Excuse me? Did something else happen?"

Concern was etched across his face and in the way he held himself. While it was nice to see, I had to remind myself it was also a part of his job. Besides, did I really want to get into this?

"It's nothing," I said, shrugging and hoping he wouldn't pursue the bone I'd thrown. "Just more of the same."

"So you haven't given up trying to prove they've hidden a body on their property?"

I wasn't sure how to interpret the gleam in his eyes. But his doubt hadn't deterred me before, and it wasn't about to now.

"Of course I haven't. I know what I saw, Detective." I grinned up at him. "Now, may I ask you a few questions?"

He sat on the corner of the overstuffed chair and nodded.

"Do you know anything about the Angelina Verona case?"

"Some," he said, drawing out the word like he was hesitant to answer.

"I'm not going to ask you to reveal anything that would compromise your position, okay? I just wondered if you knew she'd been to South Carolina, that she'd spoken to the Midas twins."

His back, always straight, appeared to stiffen, and there was a sudden twitch at the corner of his mouth.

"I believe the information about South Carolina has been in the news."

"Oh, I hadn't realized." I blushed. Maybe I should have paid more attention to the news. "Was that where she disappeared?"

Blue Eyes pushed up his sleeve to check his watch, then returned his attention to me. "Have you any idea what the conversation with the twins was about?"

"No. Do you always have to answer a question with another one?"

He gave me a sheepish grin. "It comes with the job. Look," he said, standing. "I have to be going. I just wanted to make sure you were all right."

"I appreciate that and would appreciate it even more if you answered my question." I followed him to the door, careful to stay back so he could open it without my being in the way.

"Authorities tracked her back to Kansas City."

"Back? You mean she disappeared after she got home?"

He shook his head. "She never made it home. She was near the Independence Mall on I-70 the last anyone heard from her. That's all the information I can give you."

"Thanks." He may not realize it, but this little tidbit fit very nicely with the scenario forming in my brain.

"Remember what I said about exercising a little caution, okay?" His tone was filled with far more concern than his job required. Once again, I felt a little thrill of excitement chase along my spine.

I smiled up at him, put two fingers together in what I hoped was the Boy Scouts' promise, and nodded.

Blue Eyes grinned at me, crossed the threshold to the outside, then turned back. He squinted as he scanned my face.

"You were the girl in the tree!" He studied me so closely I was certain he could see right into my head. I wondered if he realized just how mortified I was.

"Which would make you the boy who alerted my sister to my predicament. It's a little late, but thanks."

"Wow." He had a nice, easy laugh that helped put me at ease. "And you're welcome. Anytime."

I was relieved he didn't stick around to discuss the incident. It was like he knew the little confirmation was all that was necessary. That put another plus mark in the detective's column.

As Rick pulled the patrol car out of my driveway, I spotted Darrell Midas peering around the giant spirea. When he realized I'd seen him, he slunk out of sight.

Icy fingers scraped their way down my back and across my shoulders. I shut the door and made certain the locks were engaged before I returned to the den.

A gentle breeze set the curtains dancing, and it occurred to me that the open windows made the house accessible to intruders. It wasn't something I'd considered before now, but I found myself wondering if it might be wiser to forego the fresh air for safety's sake.

Wait a moment. This was my home and had been for the last twenty years. I wasn't going to lock myself behind closed doors and windows and cower inside for anyone. Especially for a couple of bullies like Darrell and Frank Midas.

I was brave, but I wasn't stupid.

Making my way back into the living room, I hunted for Jane's knitting basket. When I finally found it tucked between the sofa and the overstuffed chair, I searched until I found the fourteen-inch plastic needles. They weren't as deadly as the smaller metal ones

THE CASE OF THE BOUNCING GRANDMA

but were still capable of doing a little damage if yielded as a weapon.

I couldn't very well carry the thing in my hand all the time, but I did have a perfect hiding place.

With considerable care, I worked the needle beneath the cast until just the head was showing. Wheeling back to the den, I pulled out the packing tape I always kept on hand. No, there was a better solution. One that would even keep Jane from becoming suspicious.

I rolled down the hall, through my room, and into the bathroom. Many of the items usually kept in the medicine chest were now within easy access on the counter next to the sink— including a large box of water-resistant Band-Aids. I soon had the head of the knitting needle taped against my leg with a couple of Band-Aids. It would be simple to retrieve in an emergency—day or night. If anyone asked about the bandages, I'd say it was a scratch from the roses out back.

Satisfied with my inventive means of protection, I went to the living room, snagged up yesterday's paper, and returned to the den.

Just as Rick had stated, Luisa Verona last heard from Angelina a week ago today. She'd called from her cell phone at a gas station near Independence Center—less than thirty miles from home.

"It was late in the afternoon," Mrs. Verona was quoted as saying. "And she said she'd be home for dinner. When she didn't arrive, I called her, but it went right to voice mail. She never turns the phone off, so I knew right away something was wrong."

Did that work? Did turning off your cell send a call directly to voice mail?

My landline rang, and I grabbed it up.

"Hi, Mama." I heard Seth holler out a "hey, Gramma" in the background. "I wanted to let you know that Chelsea just called."

"Are they okay?"

"She was quiet, but I don't know if that's because she was upset or trying to keep the call from being overheard. Anyway, Chandra was sick after they got home, and they were both worried about how Seth was doing. Isn't that sweet?"

"Very considerate. Makes you wonder how they learned to be so nice living around people like that."

ALICE K. ARENZ

"Yeah, well, I wanted to give you her number. You have a pen?" She read it off, then continued, "Thing is, Chelsea doesn't want us to call unless it's an emergency. She hasn't told anyone she has the phone and doesn't want them to know. Does that sound logical? I mean, I just don't get it."

Neither did I. But after what I'd seen of the family so far, I could understand Chelsea's concern.

"I'm sure she knows the best way to handle her family, kiddo. It's weird to us, but we aren't in their shoes."

"Thank the Lord for that! I managed to give her both of your numbers—cell and home—as well as Aunt Jane's cell number. She and Chandra want to go to church Sunday. I assured her that you and Aunt Jane would love to take them. I hope that's okay."

"Of course, it is. So will they come here or what?"

I hoped we wouldn't have to go over to their house. I wasn't certain about Helen but was pretty sure neither of the men would welcome us.

"I told her what a stickler for punctuality Aunt Jane is, and she said they'd be at your place by eight-thirty. Chelsea said they wanted to get into a Sunday school class and involved in all the activities. I really hope we can help them, Mama. They need to get a life of their own."

"We'll do what we can, honey, and leave the rest to the Lord. Now, I've a question for you. If your cell phone is off, is the call transferred directly to voice mail?"

"Mine is," she said. "I don't know about all the plans, of course, but it makes sense. Why?"

"Just wondered. What about the battery; how long would it last if you left the phone on?"

"Maybe two days with a lot of use. I leave my phone on all the time, you know, just in case. But I don't use it all that much."

"Would it last a week without recharging—if you weren't using it?"

"I don't know. What's this all about?"

"Oh, uh, nothing, really," I hedged. I heard my grandson in the background, asking about what he could and couldn't take to his friend's house. "Sounds like Seth is ready to leave for Nathan's."

I could tell Andi wasn't satisfied with my answer, but I wasn't

164

THE CASE OF THE BOUNCING GRANDMA

ready to divulge what I was thinking. After telling me that she and Mindy would be taking the boys to Worlds of Fun in Kansas City tomorrow, Andi signed off. They thought the theme park would be a perfect place for all of them to get their minds off Jared and Greg—if only for a few hours.

I resumed the study of my supporting evidence—at least, that's how I liked to think of it. Snoop, busybody, looky-loo, or buttinsky were not titles I associated with myself—they were more Elsie's style. However, in this particular case, I didn't much care what anyone labeled me—I was a sleuth out to solve a case.

Um, I liked that. Sleuth.

Don't let it go to your head, Glory. It was time to find some of those answers.

I reread my original articles, studied the photos accompanying them, read the remainder of the story on Angelina from yesterday's paper, and skimmed what Andi had gotten me from the library. When I was finished, I studied my crime diagram and came to a startling conclusion.

It was all wrong.

Pulling down some printer paper, I taped together four pages, stowed my files out of the way, and set to work. This time, I'd use solid lines for things I was sure of, dotted ones for questionable items. Since one person seemed to connect all the others, her name went across the top of the diagram: Angelina Verona.

I drew a solid line to the right and wrote, "Luisa Verona," with a notation of the date and time she'd last spoken to her daughter. Moving to the left of Angelina's name, I drew two solid, diagonal lines and labeled one Adam Parker and the other Jeanette Parker.

Okay, it was looking pretty good. Who next?

Of course!

Beneath Angelina's name on the right side, I placed another solid diagonal line, labeling it Darrell Midas. Though I didn't have proof that it was Darrell lurking in the photo from eighteen years ago, if I was a betting person, I'd have laid odds on its being him.

From that point, it got easier to fill in the schematic. A dotted line connected Helen Midas to Darrell; another one ran from Darrell to Frank, then from Frank to Helen. Straight down from the center of Angelina's name, I drew a dotted line and wrote,

"Chelsea and Chandra," with 'Giselle and Monique Verona' in parentheses with a question mark.

Rex Stout received a solid line to the twins and a dotted one joining his name to Angelina's. Elsie Wilkes was also given a place in the diagram—a questionable dotted line with

the notation of "sold house" next to her name.

Beneath it all, I wrote, "Foot In The Rug/Body," and proceeded to draw dotted lines to Frank, Helen, and Darrell. As an afterthought, I plugged in another over to Rex.

I picked up the drawing and pinned it to a nearby corkboard, then sat back to examine my handiwork.

"Very impressive."

I jumped at the sound of my sister's voice.

"Sorry, didn't mean to startle you." She placed a hand on my shoulder. "You've been working hard."

"Do you see what I see, Janie? Do you see how it all connects?"

"It appears to, yes. But there are still a lot of holes and even more supposition."

I continued to study my schematic. "Maybe there are, but I know I'm onto something. And it's a lot bigger than I originally thought."

Jane patted my shoulder then perched on the corner of my desk. "Well, if you're up to it, you may have a chance to get some of those answers."

I peered over at my sister, more than a little curious.

"What are you up to, Jane Marie Calvin? You have a sneaky expression on your face."

"I resemble that remark!" She gave me one of her stern teacher looks before she broke into a smile. "Remember when I told you not to underestimate me?"

"I've heard that recently from a couple of people. So?"

"So, Glory-girl, this is your lucky day." She leaned forward slightly, grinning like the Cheshire cat. "We're heading to Kansas City first thing in the morning, so you'd better organize your thoughts and questions. We've got an appointment with Luisa Verona tomorrow at ten."

Luisa Verona—Angelina's mother and the woman who might be Chandra and Chelsea's grandmother.

"That's... great, but how?"

"Remember that group Don and I were involved with, Mother and Child Reunion?"

"The one that helps women find homes for their babies rather than simply placing them up for an anonymous adoption?"

Jane nodded. "I've remained in touch with the director, Emily Garry. She counseled Angelina after the Parkers refused to take the twins. Anyway, to make a long story short, I asked for a favor, and now you've got the opportunity to speak with Luisa."

"Th-thanks. Wow." I swallowed the sudden surge of emotion. "Does this mean you believe me about the girls?"

Jane stood and walked to the corkboard. She traced the myriad of lines, said an occasional "hmm," then turned back to me.

"Frankly, I don't know what to believe. But I'll tell you what I hope." A single tear rolled down my sister's cheek. "I hope those girls really are the Verona twins."

Snuffing, Jane left the den. I listened as she shuffled down the hallway to her room, wondering what she would think of my most recent theory.

Grabbing the pen from the desk, I moved to the corkboard to draw another dotted line. This one went up from 'Foot In The Rug/Body' and stopped on the one name that seemed the most logical conclusion.

Angelina Verona.

168

ALICE K. ARENZ

Chapter 19

"I imagine it's already occurred to her, Glory, but let's keep your theory to ourselves. All right?"

Jane's death grip on the steering wheel turned her knuckles white. She was upset, but I wasn't sorry I'd told her.

"I wanted to say something last night, Janie, but didn't want to risk your canceling this appointment."

She gave me a sidelong glance, then returned her gaze to the road. "I'm sure you don't need to be reminded of how it felt when Elsie told everyone Ike had died. I know he got a kick out of it, but you were furious."

She wasn't kidding. I'd been livid over Elsie's outrageous mistake while my husband, weak from his latest round of chemo, had laughed until he cried. Seeing Ike walk into church the following Wednesday night nearly gave Elsie a heart attack. She hadn't spoken to the family after that—until Ike's funeral a month later.

"What was it Mark Twain said? 'Reports of my death have been greatly exaggerated,' isn't that it?"

Jane nodded.

"Ike was tickled to be in Twain's league. But you're right; I was angry and hurt. It was as though we'd been betrayed." The memory was not one I was fond of. "We'd been holding on, praying, and hoping for healing for so long, then..."

"I know, sweetie. At least Ike enjoyed it." Jane patted my shoulder. "While it's not the same thing, Glory, there's the same element here. Luisa Verona knows her daughter is missing, knows that with each passing day the chance she's still alive lessens. She's been here before, remember, when her grandchildren were kidnapped."

ALICE K. ARENZ

I couldn't even imagine the heartache Mrs. Verona had been through. First those darling babies, now her only child. It had to be devastating.

"You don't have to worry, Janie. I didn't intend to tell her that I think my neighbors have Angelina's body in a freezer in their backyard."

We rode for a while in silence, allowing the rhythmic sound of the highway to lull us. When we passed the exit for KCI Airport, Jane asked me to read the directions to Luisa's home in Gladstone.

"She's not too far from Midwest Seminary," Jane said. "We'll take the 152 east exit, over to 169 sou—"

"That's okay, I trust you to get us there."

I didn't come to Kansas City enough to know street names or the location of specific neighborhoods. I knew how to get to the airport and to several of the malls, and I believed I could find where Jane and Don used to live if I had to. Beyond that, it was just confusing.

I was happiest in a small town with a close-knit community— and the ability to get across the entire town in a matter of minutes was a plus. Not that I didn't enjoy going to the city once in a while—I loved the shopping and excitement of KC; I just didn't want to live there.

In no time, we pulled into an older neighborhood with well-kept yards and beautiful trees lining both sides of the street. If I hadn't known better, I'd have thought we were back in Tarryton or any other small town across the Midwest rather than in the midst of a large metropolitan area.

We stopped before a smaller ranch, which had dozens of rose bushes lining the front of the house. The deep reddish brown of the bricks skirting the lower half of the home were the perfect backdrop for the vibrant colors of the roses, giving it a welcoming, homey feel.

"Smells like heaven," I said as we made our way up the sidewalk.

"It's beautiful. Even better is the no-step porch."

Since the porch was small, Jane left me on the sidewalk while she rang the bell. Within seconds, a tiny woman opened the door. She had just a hint of an olive complexion, abundant snowy white hair, and deep chocolate eyes.

THE CASE OF THE BOUNCING GRANDMA

"Yes?" She may have been little and gave the impression of advanced age, but, like Gracie Naner, the voice belied the impression; it was strong and firm.

"I'm Jane Calvin and this is my sister, Glory Harper."

"Oh, yes, the people Emily Garry sent. Please, come on in." Luisa Verona pushed the inner door wide open then came onto the porch to hold the screen.

Once we settled in her spacious living room, Mrs. Verona offered us iced tea she'd had waiting for our arrival.

"When Emily called yesterday, I didn't quite catch all she was saying. I'm sure you understand how distracted I've been."

She held out a glass for me, and I noticed how lovely her hands were. She had to be in her late seventies, but only a few age spots marred their beauty.

"Thank you." I smiled. "We've been following your ordeal and have been praying for your daughter."

"That's very nice of you, dear."

While she served Jane, I gazed about the room, which was warm and cozy with its soft earth tones and touch of old-world Italian charm. But what really fascinated me were the unusual photos that looked like a composite of drawings and something computer generated. Each photo progressed in a natural flow, aging the subjects slightly from one to the next. It wasn't difficult to recognize who they portrayed—from toddler through childhood, these were someone's renditions of Monique and Giselle Verona.

"I don't know if you remember me, Mrs. Verona," Jane was saying. "But my husband and I spoke with you and Angelina about the babies."

That got my attention. I stared over at my sister, trying to understand what I was hearing.

"When she was considering adoption?" Mrs. Verona nodded. "So I have you to thank for that year with my grandbabies. Don't look so surprised, dear. She only spoke to the one couple. Whatever you said made her determined to raise those girls. You restored her faith in herself and God. And after all these years, through the kidnapping and everything else, she never lost it."

"I—I don't know what to say," Jane sputtered. I'd never seen my sister at a loss for words and found it rewarding in a strange kind of way.

171

Mrs. Verona's face seemed to glow from within, and I wondered if she might be remembering the time she'd spent with her grandchildren. I imagined that's how I looked every time I thought about Seth.

"I noticed you were admiring our display of photographs," Mrs. Verona said, turning to me. "They truly are something, aren't they?"

I nodded. "I'm sorry, it's—they're fascinating."

I noticed Jane was taking in the collection lining the walls. She suddenly paled when she spotted whatever was behind me. I twisted around and found myself staring into faces that mirrored a slightly younger version of the Midas twins.

"The moment Angie heard of the computer programs that could do age progression, she was on it," Mrs. Verona told us. "We have the twins listed in every national database, with Missing and Exploited Children, you name it. As the programs advanced in capability, she had someone progressing the girls every year. Of course, they were so little when they were taken that it's unlikely they look much like these, but it's been nice to have the pictures around. It's almost like they're home."

"Mrs. Verona—"

"Luisa, please, dear."

"Right, thank you."

Even though I'd been certain of Chelsea's and Chandra's true identities, faced with the sudden revelation, I was finding it difficult to breathe. I was faring better than Jane, however; I could tell she was struggling to hold back tears.

"I don't want to pry, but... I understand that Angelina was following a lead when she disappeared."

"That's right. She'd received an e-mail from one of the BTH people."

"BTH?" I was proud of Jane. She was not only keeping it together, but she'd also managed to don a formidable expression of determination.

"Yes. It stands for Bring Them Home." Luisa sipped her tea. After setting the glass on the coffee table and making sure it was securely on a coaster, she continued. "It's a volunteer network of everyday people who try to match photos and computer renderings to missing persons reports. If that sounds like I've memorized the information, I have." She gave a little laugh. "From what I understand, it's just one of such organizations that help police departments across the country."

I'd seen something about one of these groups on a TV news program. The idea had fascinated me. They could take a forensic reconstruction of a skull, photograph it, and put it into a database to search against actual photos. During the hour-long telecast, they'd shown how a John Doe was matched to the photograph of a man who'd been missing for several years.

"Had she gotten a recent update on the progression photos?" Jane asked.

"About two or three weeks before she received the email. I haven't had the opportunity to put them in frames. Would you like to see the pictures?" She was out of her chair and off to get them before either of us said a thing.

"You know they'll match," I whispered. "You can't have any more doubts."

Jane sent me a stern look. "Not a word, Glory. Promise me."

I knew she was right. It wasn't my place to tell her about her granddaughters. But I knew someone who could.

"I couldn't find the originals, but I've some copies Angie left behind." Luisa handed one of the age-progression photos to me and another to Jane. "You may keep these if you like. The original is in color, you know, much more lifelike."

"Did you give the police a copy?"

I was surprised to find my voice so normal. By this point, it was amazing I hadn't swallowed my tongue. Especially after I'd had the chance to look over the latest progression—

even without color enhancement, Chandra and Chelsea were dead ringers for the photo in front of me.

"I did. But they don't believe Angie's disappearance has anything to do with her lead on the twins." She sat back down in a nearby chair. "I know they checked out the person who sent the e-mail and found nothing that could help them. The woman was very cooperative, I was told, and hadn't understood why Angie wanted to see her in person." Luisa sighed deeply. "But that's my girl. There have been so few leads the last couple of years that when anyone contacts her she's off and running. You know, she's worked at least two jobs since the babies were kidnapped just to have funds available to continue the search effort."

"She's a remarkable woman, Luisa. I could tell that when I met her."

Luisa Verona nodded and gave my sister a wan smile.

"My husband had recently passed away when I got sick, and Angie was about to graduate from high school. I didn't want her to quit school, but she was bound and determined to take care of me. She'd done some part-time work for Jeanette Parker, running errands and such for her boutique, and had grown fond of the woman. Jeanette knew we couldn't afford the medical bills and offered Angie a job in their home." She leaned back in her chair and stared out into the room. "I think Jeanette already had her pegged for the surrogacy, though Angie's never agreed with me."

When she shook her head, her tiny frame shook as well. "I am sorry to be going on like this. When you reminded me of working with Mother and Child Reunion, everything came back so clearly. Please accept my apology and tell me what I can do to help you."

Jane and I exchanged a glance. I had no idea how to proceed from here. I wasn't entitled to ask her a lot of probing questions, though I would have liked to. To be honest, I was surprised she'd volunteered as much as she had.

"We're not working with a group or anything right now, Luisa, but we—I've been following the case from the beginning. I hated the way the Parkers used and discarded your daughter and the babies, and it broke my heart to see her so despondent when she came into Mother and Child." Jane gave the older woman a tremulous smile. "When I heard Angelina

was missing, memories of what you went through flooded back. And I... I just wanted you to know we care."

"That's very sweet of you, dear. Few people remember Angie's ordeal, and if they do, they point fingers and repeat Adam Parker's nasty accusations. My daughter is, and always has been, a good Christian girl, willing to give of herself to help others. She would never have slept with a man out of wedlock, and for that man to accuse her of doing so after she'd signed the surrogacy contract is a slap in the face.

"Angie's lawyer had Mr. Fancy Pants on the run, though. We'd gotten proof Parker had duped the doctor and used a donor for the insemination. We would have gotten the name too, if the

THE CASE OF THE BOUNCING GRANDMA

babies hadn't been kidnapped."

I'd read this in the articles Andi copied for me. Angelina had wanted to pursue Parker and get the name of the donor, but Parker's lawyers had succeeded in getting the case thrown out of court. No babies, no reason to release confidential information—especially when it might get Parker in trouble.

Jane had been doing a great job obtaining information, but it was obvious Luisa was getting tired. I didn't want to wear her out or cause her any further distress, yet I felt a need to understand what had happened before Angelina's disappearance.

"Mrs.—Luisa, I don't mean to be forward or nosy, but I wonder if I could ask you a couple of questions about the lead your daughter received."

"If you think it can help, I don't mind."

"You said the police checked on the individual who sent the e-mail."

"Yes, a woman from Athens, Georgia, I believe it was. Her message stated she might be able to help Angie and listed her telephone number."

"In Georgia? Not South Carolina?" From Jane's expression I could see she was just as confused as I was.

"That's right. Angie called while I was at mass, and by the time I got home, she was already packed and ready to leave. And no, she didn't tell me what the woman said."

"But this woman talked to the police?"

She nodded. "It appeared to be a misunderstanding. She'd contacted Angie to see if she'd be interested in hiring her to help with the search. She didn't have any actual information about the twins."

"Did Angelina call you after she'd spoken with the woman?" Jane was getting into it now. I could see the wheels spinning and knew we were finally on the same track.

"Almost every day. There were a couple of calls from Georgia and one—no, two—from South Carolina. She was very up, very hopeful. She wouldn't give me any specifics, but I had the feeling she'd stumbled onto something. As a matter of fact," Luisa Verona leaned forward and stared thoughtfully from Jane to me, "when she called from Independence, she was so happy it made my heart sing. That's why her disappearance has been so difficult, you see. I know she found something. I just wish she'd told me what it was."

If she had, perhaps Angelina and her daughters would be celebrating with Luisa right now.

"Have you any idea how she ended up in South Carolina?" I asked.

Luisa smiled. "Whenever Angie travels she tries to make connections with other parents of missing children. If she can offer comfort and support to someone else, or point them toward our Savior, then she feels her trip hasn't been in vain. Angie's met a lot of people over the years."

"We can't make you any promises, Luisa." Jane reached out to the older woman and took her hand. "But we want to help."

Tears filled Luisa Verona's dark chocolate eyes as she turned to my sister. "You helped once before when my daughter was lost and despondent. You reminded her that God was bigger than any problem and that through the love of our Lord Jesus even a mountain could be moved."

Tears slid down her cheeks. "I'm eighty years old, and my wish before the Father calls me home is to see my precious grandbabies with their mother so we can be a family once again."

We had no promises or platitudes, no words of comfort that could help alleviate her pain. But what we could do was to pray— which is exactly what we did.

Chapter 20

"Thank you." Jane's voice was so soft I barely heard it over the sound of the traffic.

I had so many questions, so much I wanted to know. But her tears stopped me. We sat in silence as she made her way out of the neighborhood, onto North Oak Trafficway, and finally onto I-29. She headed south on the interstate instead of going north toward home and still I said nothing. Something told me that Jane needed the chance to think, to assimilate the information we'd gotten from Luisa—and come to terms with the twins' true identity.

Jane swiped at the latest round of tears and pulled a tissue from her purse, all the while keeping her eyes on the traffic. When she took the exit for I-35 South, I decided it was time to speak.

"Where are we going, Janie?"

"To try our hand at exposing a weasel," she snuffed. "I don't have the restraints of the law holding me back."

Since Rex Stout wasn't in the vicinity, I figured she must be referring to Adam Parker, the man behind the surrogacy scheme.

"I take it you know where to find Parker?"

"His office used to be near the Plaza, along J. C. Nichols Parkway. If I can't find it, we'll stop somewhere and look it up."

I was all for taking the bull by the horns, but the little I'd read about Parker told me he was the ultimate in slime. Allegations had raged for years, though nothing ever came of them. He'd been accused of everything from bribing city officials to obtain property rights to stealing homes out from under the owners—all in the name of progress. He was touted as a real estate developer, a man with vision, and an entrepreneur. If he was so terrific, why did he constantly face the possibility of indictment?

Jane took the Southwest Trafficway exit, keeping pace with

other cars that merged onto the road.

"You know, I'm all for the truth coming out. But what makes you think you can get this guy to own up now? He's gotten away with his lies for nineteen years. I don't see any incentive for him to change his tune. Besides, we already know Rex Stout is the twins' biological father."

"Maybe Parker hasn't been confronted with the right information."

Okay... I searched my memory for something that might give us ammunition. Granted, my mind wasn't as sharp as it should be. I'd been up most of the night thinking about the possibility of Angelina being inside that freezer in the Midases' backyard.

We wove in and out of traffic that often slowed to a crawl. Jane drove with the expertise of a city dweller—something I'd never accomplished.

"Before we get there, I've a question."

"Don and I thought about adopting the twins."

My sister's uncanny ability to read my mind never failed to surprise me. Her expression didn't alter, nor did her eyes stray from the road in front of us.

"Angelina came to Mother And Child right after Parker won the paternity case. She and her mother were broke. Between Luisa's medical bills and trying to fight Parker in court, they didn't have anything left—including faith."

"And?"

"We met with her... them. After we talked with Angelina alone, she introduced us to Luisa and the twins. The moment we saw them together, it was obvious Angelina loved those babies. And her mother—it was tearing her apart."

"So you convinced Angelina to keep her children."

Jane nodded. "Simply put, yes. It was a bit more involved, but the end result was the same." She turned into a parking lot near a massive office building. "We prayed with them, comforted them, and then arranged with Mother And Child so we could make anonymous donations to their family."

She pulled up before a covered parking garage, grabbed the ticket, then proceeded into the narrow, darkened recesses of the structure. As we wound our way from one level to the next, I studied her in the dim light, marveling that she'd never

178

THE CASE OF THE BOUNCING GRANDMA

told me about this time in her life.

She finally pulled into a parking space, and shutting off the car, turned to me. "I know you're wondering why I never said anything." She swallowed. "You know we were crushed when I miscarried. We had the nursery ready and no baby to use it. Then here were these beautiful little girls with all this controversy surrounding them. I thought maybe... But after

meeting Angelina and Luisa, all I wanted to do was make their lives easier, give them the chance to make a good life for the twins. We had all that money we'd put away for the baby we'd have one day—"

I wrapped her in my arms and let her cry. Had she met with anyone besides my sister, Angelina might have gone through with the adoption. Instead, Jane and Don gave up their own dream and desire to be parents in favor of helping the girl and her mother. Was it any wonder Jane was my hero?

"It's getting stuffy in here." Jane pulled away with a wan smile. By the time she got the wheelchair from the trunk and came to help me into it, she was composed and ready to go.

The building directory listed Parker Enterprises on the tenth floor. Going up in an elevator wasn't my idea of fun, but under the circumstances, we didn't have a choice. Confined in the small space with several other people, I felt like a sardine. Jane understood my claustrophobia and recognized my anxiety as more people got on the car. She took my hand and gave it a reassuring squeeze.

We arrived on the tenth floor to find the area nearly deserted. Arrows pointed us toward Parker's suite of offices, where a reception desk and waiting area blocked entry to the great man's domain. Jane's step quickened, and she donned her no-nonsense expression as she approached the desk.

"Adam Parker, please."

The young woman behind the desk studied us before answering.

"Was Mr. Parker expecting you?" Her crisp tone said she already knew the answer.

"No, but I'm sure he'd want to speak with us. We're here about the Lantana project."

What's that? Lantana?

179

I glanced at my sister, hoping I didn't give away my confusion.

"Ah, yes, of course." The receptionist flashed Jane an apologetic smile. "You must not have gotten the message, Ms.—"

"Scott. We're last-minute replacements for the community representatives. We're a little late, I know, but the meeting was scheduled for eleven—"

"Yes, Ms. Scott, however, Mr. Parker was called out of town. I *did* leave a message with—"

"I'm sure you did. So..." Jane looked down at me as though she expected me to say something. I was still marveling at her nerve and couldn't have said anything to save my life. Well, maybe if it came to that...

"I *did* want the opportunity to speak with Mr. Parker myself," she continued. "You wouldn't happen to know if he has any free time later today."

The girl checked her appointment book, then picked up her phone to make a call.

Never again would I accuse my sister of not having guts or going out on a limb. This incident proved she was far more daring than she let on. She may not go for jumping on a trampoline or riding on a skateboard, but when it came to going head-to-head with someone, she was aces in the bravery department.

"I'm sorry, Ms. Scott, his assistant doesn't show anything available. However—"

"That's okay," Jane interrupted. "I'll call later for an appointment. Thank you for your assistance."

"What was that?" I asked, once we were out of earshot.

"Just trying to keep up with you, Glory." Jane grinned. "I read about the Lantana thing and figured it would be a way to get in to see him."

"And what would you have done if the meeting hadn't been cancelled?"

Jane punched the elevator button. "Faked it."

"Faked it?" She wheeled me into the back of the empty elevator. "Janie, what's gotten into you?"

"I don't know. Maybe you're rubbing off on me, or maybe I just want some answers."

"Though I'd like to take credit for this, you and I both know

I'm not that gutsy."

"To be honest," she said, leaning down so the people who'd just come onto the elevator couldn't hear her. "I feel like I could barf."

We both started to laugh and soon had our companions pulling away and giving us dirty looks. By the time we reached the first floor, we'd settled down.

"How about lunch? We can eat alfresco on the Plaza."

"Lead on, MacDuff. You're on a roll."

It was nearing one o'clock, and my stomach was growling when we finally found a parking space that wasn't blocks from the nearest restaurant. We decided on an Italian place that offered a food bar where you could sample various dishes or order from the menu.

It was disappointing to find their outside tables were filled, but that was to be expected at this time of day. I was thrilled they found a place for us inside.

While Jane went to the buffet to get our food, I looked out across the restaurant at the other patrons. When I spotted Adam Parker and another man in a nearby booth, I almost dropped my glass of water.

Jane was still occupied with filling our plates, and I was bursting with curiosity. Without realizing what I was doing, I found myself in front of Parker's booth.

"Adam Parker, I'm Glory Harper, and I was wondering if I could ask you a few questions." My mouth was dry and my hands shook so badly I was certain my entire body must be quaking.

"Excuse me?" The superior tone and condescending look he gave me didn't steady my resolve—but it did make me want to wipe that smirk off his face.

What had gotten into me lately? All this talk of fighting wasn't a good sign.

Of course, it might have something to do with the company I'd been keeping.

"I'd like to take just a moment of your time, Mr. Parker." I smiled, hoping he would consider how it might look being unkind to someone in a wheelchair.

"I'm not giving any interviews, Ms—"

"Harper. And I don't want to interview you. I just—"

"Have a few questions. So you stated. But as you can see, I'm having a meeting."

Mr. Prim and Proper's manner gave me the impression I was dealing with a mega-tycoon wannabe. His perfectly styled and obviously dyed hair, the suit that looked like it might be silk, and the haughty attitude spoke volumes.

Only I wasn't about to listen.

I drew out the progression photo Luisa had given me and held it up for Parker to see.

"Do you recognize these girls, Mr. Parker?"

The smirk on his face changed to a sneer as he reached toward the photo. I snatched it back and stuffed it into my fanny pack.

"I know where to find them, Mr. Parker, and so do the authorities." Well, they would, just as soon as I could get the information to Blue Eyes.

Adam Parker turned to his companion. "Would you excuse me?"

"Hey, I was about to go back to the buffet anyway."

The man slipped out of the booth. Once he was out of earshot, Parker's demeanor changed... and not for the better.

"What do you want, lady? Do you think you can blackmail me?" His eyes were cold, his expression filled with hate.

"No, sir. I don't believe in blackmail, tricking innocent young women, or any of the other things that appear to be second nature to you." *Dear God, help me now.*

"Why you—" Parker jumped up from the booth and loomed over me.

Though I cringed inside, I actually found myself straightening up and staring the man full in the face.

"Ah, Glory, there you are. And look who you've discovered." Jane took hold of my chair and moved me back a little.

"What kind of shakedown is this?" the man demanded.

He scanned the area nearby, nodded to someone behind us, then returned to his booth... limping.

"We're looking for your ex-wife, Jeanette. Would you happen to know where we could find her?" Jane asked. I wished I could see her expression but that would mean turning around and missing the series of contortions that Parker's face went through.

"In hell for all I know."

Rather than acknowledge his comment, Jane continued her own line of attack. "We already know you arranged for Rex Stout to father the Verona babies. Now we would like the opportunity to ask your ex-wife a few questions."

"We're done here... ladies." The caustic tone was like fingernails on a blackboard.

"That's where you're wrong, Mr. Parker. When you're punished for what you did to Angelina Verona, exposed for the despicable liar and fraud you are, *then* we'll be finished."

Jane pushed us past Parker's returning companion and up to the nearest waiter.

"I'm sorry; we seem to have lost our appetites. Could we just have the bill?"

We followed the young man, and while Jane paid for food we hadn't eaten, I kept my eyes on Parker. Despite the return of his dinner companion, Adam Parker continued to watch us.

And he kept on watching until we left the restaurant.

Chapter 21

It takes nearly two hours to go from Kansas City to Tarryton when the traffic is good. And though it had been hours since either of us had eaten, after the encounter with Adam Parker, food just didn't seem important.

"Did you see his face when I mentioned Rex?" Jane was so exhilarated I had to remind her to focus on the road. "I thought he was about to tackle us."

"He probably would have if there hadn't been so many people around as witnesses."

I was still trying to figure out what had gotten into both of us. We'd been so calm and collected during our visit with Luisa Verona. What happened?

"I owe you an apology, Glory. I don't know why I wanted to confront Parker." Once again, Jane read my mind. "Every time that man's in the news, it brings the whole sordid ordeal back to me. I've never understood why they followed through with the surrogacy when they were having so much trouble with their marriage."

"I know you're more familiar with the incident than I am, but it seems obvious to me. I mean, Parker knew his wife wanted a baby and maybe he thought it would help the marriage.

But like the slime ball he is, he also wanted an out. If the baby wasn't his—"

"He still would have been responsible for the child, so that doesn't make sense."

"Not to normal people like us," I told her. "But God only knows how people like Parker think. And speaking of the man, has he always had that limp?"

Jane pulled into the passing lane and sped by a semi

185

struggling up a hill. "I think he has. Why?"

I had no idea if she remembered my telling her about the mysterious man with a limp who'd been hanging around the moving van in the middle of a downpour, but I was determined to remind her.

"So you think Parker's the guy?" The doubt in Jane's voice was obvious. "Be honest now, Glory. Can you see that man standing around in the rain?"

As much as I didn't want to admit it, she was right. Adam Parker didn't seem the type to forego the comfort of a lush limo and opt for getting soaked. Still...

"He's roughly the same build." I wasn't going down without a fight. "From what I could tell, anyway."

"I don't want to burst your bubble, little sister, but I just don't see it." She reached over and patted my leg. "You can't be right about everything, Glory. But I thank God I finally listened to you about the twins."

When we finally entered Tarryton's city limits, it was like a breath of fresh air. Even though we had another confrontation ahead of us, this one was at least with a far more pleasant individual.

We pushed in through the main entrance of Tarryton's police department and became part of a madhouse. I saw officers Roberts and Bradley leading away a couple of angry teenagers, whose painted white faces and black lips reminded me of Nick Pearson. As two older couples followed the teens—probably their parents—I said a quick prayer on their behalf.

"Sit tight," Jane told me. "I'm going to see if we can talk to Rick."

"Hey, Mrs. Harper!"

Speaking of Nick, there he was across the room on a bench, his hands in cuffs behind his back. I rolled over to him and asked what was going on.

"Aah, a couple homies got busted for taggin' some places across town. Since I run with 'em, they busted me too."

"Tagging?"

"Yeah, no harm in it. Your generation did graffiti. We just step it up. Besides, no one cares about a junkyard."

"Unless, of course, you're the owner of the junkyard."

THE CASE OF THE BOUNCING GRANDMA

I'd recognize those silken tones anywhere. I gazed up into Detective Rick Spencer's gorgeous blue eyes.

"Hi!"

"What are you doing over—" Jane frowned at Nick, then turned back to me. "Well?"

"Look, girls, I'm swamped, so whatever you need to tell me—"

I handed him the progression photograph, a little worse for wear having been in and out of my fanny pack. I was sure it was still in good enough condition for him to understand why we were here.

"Where'd you get this?"

Blue Eyes indicated for us to follow him. He led us into a room just off the main entrance that contained a single table and a couple of chairs. I wondered if it was an interrogation room.

"We had a visit with Luisa Verona, Angelina's mother. That's the latest age progression of Angelina's missing twins."

"I've already told you what Olav Cawley had to say about Chelsea Midas," I added to Jane's explanation. "Now you've got supporting evidence."

"It's not that easy. We'll contact the right people, and it will be checked out. But right now this department's stretched. I was heading out the door when Jane stopped me. Your friend Elsie Wilkes has been shot, and Rex Stout is missing."

"Elsie's been what?" The news refused to sink in.

"Shot?" Jane steadied herself by grabbing the back of a nearby chair.

Rick nodded. "She's probably in surgery by now. Look, I'd like to help you solve this mystery, but it's not my jurisdiction. I'll see to it that the photo and story get into the right hands. I promise. And now I need to get back to the crime scene."

"Of course," Jane said, wheeling me back into the main room.

"I'll talk to you later." He patted my shoulder. "In the meantime, stay away from the Midas family."

We drove home in a mental fog. Once we got there, Jane called the hospital to check on Elsie. She was out of surgery but would remain in ICU—with limited visitors—until further notice.

I couldn't get my brain wrapped around what was going on. We listened to local news on the radio, but the reports of the

187

shooting were so vague they only added to our questions. The one thing that came across was that Elsie had been shot while she was showing Rex a condo. He'd called the police and made sure an ambulance was on its way, then mysteriously disappeared.

I was antsy the rest of the evening, unable to get comfortable in the chair or in my skin. Jane wasn't much better.

She'd sit in front of the TV for a while and then get up and pace about the house. By ten that evening, worrying and a lack of sleep had taken their toll on me. I was exhausted. As I tried to settle down in bed, my thoughts turned to how much my family meant to me. I wished it were possible for me to kneel but since it wasn't, I figured God would understand.

"Thank You, Father," I prayed aloud, tears streaming down my face. "Thank You for every minute You gave me with Ike. Thank You for his love, for Your love, for my wonderful daughter and grandson, and for Jane. Forgive me for doubting You, Father, for blaming You for Ike's illness and death. I come before You humbled, Lord, and ready to hear Your voice and obey—at least, I'll sincerely try to do so. Please be with Elsie and heal her wounds. And, Father, this is a biggie, but I know You can do it.

Please help us bring Luisa Verona's grandchildren back to her."

Chapter 22

Seth ran down the soccer field with the agility and grace of a practiced athlete. He set up for a pass, captured the ball, and kicked it past the goalie and into the net. The small crowd cheered, and my grandson shot us a grin and a thumbs-up.

"Attaboy boy, slugger!" Jane yelled before turning to Andi to exchange a high five.

I'd no idea where she got her energy; she hadn't slept any better than I had last night. Still, I was antsy. And the caffeine I'd downed since getting up this morning hadn't helped that feeling of wanting to jump out of my skin. Maybe that's what was driving Jane as well.

I waved at Seth and signed, "I love you," before he was back into the thick of the game.

"Wasn't that something, Mama?"

Behind the glow of pride on Andi's face was a pallor that concerned me. She managed to avoid my questions about her health with the pretense of assisting the soccer mom in charge of this week's drinks for the exhausted players.

As the teams of seven and eight-year-olds battled for the ball, I couldn't help but wish I had a way to expend my pent-up emotions and nervous energy. They ran the length of the field as fast as their little legs could carry them, slipping on the wet grass as it continued to drizzle, laughing with glee when someone splashed through a puddle, and just being kids. I was stuck in this blasted wheelchair with no way to work out my frustration and anxiety. And it wasn't going to get better any time soon.

I checked the time and wondered again what was going on in the investigation of Elsie's shooting. I'd been warned off the case. Actually, I'd been told to stay as far away from Elsie as possible.

"So she's doing all right?"

When I didn't say anything, Andi poked me.

"Mama? Is Elsie doing okay?"

"Yeah, I guess so. I thought you were talking to Jane."

Andi pointed to where my sister had gone to speak with Pastor Connor and his wife. Their daughter, Kelsey, was on the opposing team in today's game, but in a town this size, it didn't make much difference—we were all family.

"Did Elsie actually have Rick Spencer call you?"

I nodded. "We called the hospital to check on Elsie and a half hour later got an official request to leave her alone."

"What's up with that?"

A roar went up from the crowd as Kelsey Grant scored the winning point. The coaches ran out to the field, shook hands, then formed each team into a line. The kids raised their right hands and proceeded to walk past one another, giving each member a high five as they went by.

"I guess Elsie's blaming me for the shooting," I told Andi as she folded her lawn chair.

"How's that?"

"You've got me. With the enemies Rex has made in the last few months, she picks me. I don't even own a gun!"

Seth ambled across the field toward us. He was filthy from head to toe, but the smile on his face said it was all worth it.

"I wish it would just rain and get it over with." Jane rejoined us at the same time Seth arrived. "You look like a drowned rat, slugger, but you did an excellent job out there."

"We're supposed to go for ice cream, Mommy. Coach Noah's gonna pay."

Andi gave him a wan smile, her face taking on a hint of green.

"Hey, Gramma, did Mommy tell you she threw up this mornin'?"

Jane put her hand on Andi's forehead. "You're not warm, but you do look a little peaked."

"I'm fine. Really."

Andi frowned when I winked at her. She grabbed her tote off the ground, brushed at the dirt and grass, and held a hand out for Seth.

"We'd better get a move on if you want that ice cream. We're going over to the Wheelers' this afternoon," she said, turning to me. "I don't expect to be back until late."

"Yeah, Mad Gramma says we don't spend enough time with them."

"Seth David Wheeler, what have I told you?"

"Sorry, Mommy." Seth took his mother's hand and lowered his eyes. "She just looks like that," he said under his breath.

"Have a good day, guys. See you tomorrow at church."

I did my best to keep from laughing. Looking at my sister didn't help.

As they turned to go, Seth whirled around and hollered,

"Don't forget Chelsea and her sister!"

"That young man has a one-track mind," Jane commented, struggling to push the wheelchair through the wet grass.

"What do you expect? It comes with the territory."

Jane was in a hurry, so she didn't wait to visit like she did most Saturdays. It was fine with me; if I didn't talk to anyone, I was unlikely to spill what was happening with the twins.

We didn't talk on the way home, and the drive was so peaceful I started to doze off. I jumped at the sound of Jane's voice.

"Do you want to check with Andi about going with them? I'd invite you to come with Steven and me," she continued. "But..."

"Three's a crowd? I'll be fine by myself," I told her.

"So Rick gave the progression photo to the FBI?"

"He faxed it last night. He doesn't expect to hear anything for a while, though he did say an agent called asking about Rex. It was all pretty vague."

Jane pushed the button for the garage door. "You can't expect much more than that, Glory. The wheels of justice, yada yada yada."

The moment we got into the house, Jane went to get ready for her big date. She had a busy day ahead of her. Steven's parents had invited them over for the afternoon and an early dinner. If they managed to survive that, they had tickets for a play out at the college. With Andi and Seth at the Wheelers' and Jane occupied with Dr. Dreamboat, I'd be on my own.

I could take a nap, but being so antsy, that was pretty much out of the question. So I grabbed the latest Brandilyn Collins suspense novel, fixed a sandwich, and settled at the table with my book.

Later, when the doorbell rang, Jane called that she would get it. She made a detour into the kitchen, showing off her new sundress, a coral, cotton-polyester number that enhanced her tan and the rich brown of her hair.

"You look terrific, Janie, but don't you think you'd better let him in before he changes his mind?"

She swiped one of my chips and left the room with a swirl of her skirt. She returned a moment later with Steven, her cheeks already crimson.

"I know you can get in and out of the front door all right, so I've set a pitcher of lemonade and some glasses on the porch with a cooler of ice—just in case you want some air.

Also, I've written the Acklins' number on the bulletin board in the office as well as out here in the kitchen. If you—"

"Will you go, already?" I pushed back from the table and said hello to my doctor. "Get her out of here, will you?"

It was bad enough she treated me like a kid when we were alone; I didn't need her emphasizing the fact in front of her boyfriend.

"My pleasure." Dr. Dreamboat slipped an arm around Jane's waist. "What happened to you?" He pointed at the Band-Aids just above the cast.

I'd almost forgotten about the knitting needle. I touched the area just to make certain it was still in place, then looked up at my doctor.

"Just some scratches from a rose bush," I said. "I didn't want to risk an infection this close to getting the cast off."

"Perhaps I should take a look." Steven removed his arm from around Jane's waist and knelt in front of me.

"No! I mean, it's nothing, really." I put my hand over the bandages. If they discovered what the Band-Aids were hiding... well, that just didn't bear thinking about. "You're not my doctor until Monday," I told him. "Until then, you're my sister's boyfriend. And I'm not in the habit of allowing strange men to touch my leg."

Used to my quirkiness, he didn't argue. I'm sure he figured it wouldn't do him any good.

I followed them to the living room, then remained in the archway between it and the front door. "You kids have fun now."

I winked at my sister and received a scowl in return. As I watched them drive away, I wondered how I was going to amuse myself for the rest of the day.

194

ALICE K. ARENZ

Chapter 23

The Collins book was good, but reading about murder and mayhem when there may be a body in the freezer next door doesn't exactly set your mind at ease. I put the book down and searched my shelves for something a little less intense. When nothing captured my attention, I switched on the computer for a little more research.

I knew Jeanette Parker had owned a fashion boutique in Kansas City during the ten years she and Adam were married. Her designs had been in demand throughout the Midwest, and at the time of the divorce, some big-name designers were courting her. That was all the information I had in the articles Andi copied for me. Unfortunately, Jane had been unable to add anything.

I wondered about Jeanette Parker's past, where she was from and where she'd gone following the divorce. I figured if anyone else knew the true story behind the twins' conception, it had to be Parker's elusive ex.

I logged onto my account and pulled up Google. To narrow my search, I added the word *fashion* after Jeanette's name. Within seconds, I had over two hundred hits. I know of nothing more tedious than checking through a list of possible Web sites, hoping to find one or more with the information you need. Still, there was a long afternoon ahead and a lot of time to kill. Perhaps that wasn't the best terminology, especially under the circumstances...

I spent more than an hour reading about Jeanette's promise, how hot her old designs had become, and even found her stuff on eBay. There were monologues that mourned Jeanette's passage from haute couture and others stating she'd dropped out of sight to avoid being exposed as a fraud. I found photos of elaborate gowns she'd designed but none of the woman herself. It appeared that Jeanette Parker ceased to exist after her divorce. With all the rumors about her ex-husband's ruthlessness, it made me wonder if he'd done something to her.

By four o'clock the drizzle had stopped, and the sun broke through the clouds. The humidity was rising, and so was the temperature in the house. Rather than switch on the air, I decided to go onto the front porch. Armed with my crime files, extra paper, and pens, I stopped in the living room and retrieved the cordless phone before going outside.

Jane had moved a small wrought iron table close to the door, giving me just enough room to park the wheelchair next to it. The ice in the lemonade had long since melted, but Jane had thought of everything—including a sassy note on the Tupperware container reminding me of the small cooler of ice on the lower shelf.

Lifting the cooler, I noticed a box of crayons Seth left behind. To keep them from melting to mush in the heat, I tucked them inside the cooler.

It was abnormally quiet for a Saturday, especially at this time of the day. The Devlins, who lived across the circle drive, usually mowed around four every Saturday afternoon. While Ken fired up the grill in their backyard, Joyce would be on their riding mower. She'd once told me they had a standing bet on which of them could finish first. No matter what she did, Joyce always had more yard to mow after supper. Since they weren't in the yard, the rain must have been sufficient to change their schedule.

The lots were larger at the top of the cul-de-sac, making the rest of the neighbors almost half a block away. It made the area a little more private, and while I'd enjoyed that aspect in the past, since Ike's death it had become lonely—and until recently, too quiet.

The phone startled me, and I nearly dropped it.

"How're you doing?"

My heart skipped a beat. Though this was the first time I'd heard Rick's voice on the phone, I recognized it immediately.

"I'm fine," I told him. "Let me guess. Jane asked you to check on me."

He laughed. "Is it a problem?"

"Not at all. I'm staying out of trouble and behaving myself."

"That's good to know." Blue Eyes drew in a deep breath.

"I've been to see Elsie, and she's refusing to talk. I think she knows where Rex is, though she insists otherwise."

"Is she still blaming me for what happened?" I couldn't understand this no matter how hard I tried.

"I'm afraid so. I think she's just repeating what Rex told her. At any rate, I wanted to remind you to be cautious. Make sure your doors and windows are locked, and don't let anyone in while you're there alone."

I didn't need a babysitter—especially the guy who wanted to date me.

"I really *can* take care of myself, Detective Spencer, but thanks for the warning." I tried to make the statement light, comical, but wasn't sure it came across that way.

"I know you can, Glory. But you've gotten some people riled up, and it might be best if you lay low for now. Understand?"

"I've already promised I wouldn't say anything to the twins. I'll wait for your investigation—"

"The FBI is looking into it. The agent I spoke with had a meeting with Mrs. Verona today. I was assured he'd keep me in the loop."

I heard some noise on his end, then the sound was muffled like he'd covered the mouthpiece. "I've got to run. I'll be out of the office the rest of the day, so let me give you my cell number." He rattled it off, but before I had a chance to read it back to him, he was gone.

After programming Blue Eyes's cell into my phone, I set it down and picked up my file. Flipping through the pages, I studied every photograph, searching for details I may have overlooked.

A car came up the street—a gold Continental of indeterminate age. I recognized it as the vehicle Helen and Darrell Midas often drove. Sure enough, it pulled into their driveway, disappearing behind the giant spirea. I idly wondered if they'd request the bush be trimmed, then laughed at myself. True, it had grown so large that the only part of the yard I could see from my place was a small patch next to the street. But with neighbors like Frank and Darrell, the monstrous bush was a blessing.

Getting back to my file, I lifted up the photograph of the Parkers and Angelina coming out of the courthouse. If I had a magnifying glass it would be easier to study the features of the man behind Jeanette, the one we thought was Darrell Midas.

I heard voices and looked up to find Helen and Darrell standing in front of their mailbox. I couldn't hear what was being said, but Darrell's stance and arm movements appeared threatening. Helen didn't seem afraid of her husband, but she didn't look happy either. At one point, she covered her face with her hands and leaned into him. Darrell didn't hug her. Instead he put a hand on her shoulder for a moment before he turned and walked away.

I glanced at the grainy photo I held and retrieved Seth's crayons. Selecting a reddish-brown, I colored in Jeanette Parker's hair, a growing excitement building inside me. Finished, I held up the photo and glanced from it to where Helen Midas stood by her mailbox.

It might be grainy, but it was enough that suddenly everything fell into place.

I used the one-button dial I'd assigned to Blue Eyes, tapping my good foot faster and faster as I was switched to voice mail. I could barely wait to leave my message.

"Rick, it's Glory. Helen Midas isn't who she says she is. Call me."

Helen had closed her box by the time I was off the phone. I knew it wasn't the wisest thing to do, but I couldn't help myself.

"Helen, Mrs. Midas," I called, rolling over to the railing so she'd be able to see me.

I was surprised when she waved.

"Would you like to come over for a glass of lemonade?"

I saw her hesitation, the quick glance toward her house. I didn't have anything to entice her—at least nothing I wanted to shout across the street. I smiled and waved, then motioned for her to join me.

When she finally headed in my direction, I was floored.

"How are you today?" she asked, coming up the stairs.

"Hot and tired." I invited her to pull up a chair, retrieved ice cubes from the cooler, and poured her a glass of lemonade.

"Will you be coming to church in the morning?" I asked, handing her the glass.

"I'm not sure. We've still so much to do." She took a sip and smiled. "Fresh squeezed. Very nice."

"I'll tell my sister you like it. She insists on making it as tart as possible."

"It does have a kick." Helen pulled her chair around to face me rather than the street. "I believe you're good friends with our realtor, Elsie Wilkes."

Um, good friends? I wasn't sure Elsie would classify me as such right now.

"I've known her most of my life." That worked, and it wasn't a lie.

Helen dipped her head in what I assumed was her version of a nod. "We heard she was shot yesterday. Have you any idea how she's doing?"

"The last I heard she's in ICU." I answered quickly, trying not to show my surprise at the casual way she'd related the incident. "We may be a small community, but we've got an excellent hospital and doctors."

"That's good to know. Well, I suppose I should be going," She stood and handed me her glass.

"Do you have to? I was hoping we'd have the opportunity to get to know one another."

Her tight smile told me she'd already gotten the information she'd wanted. She brushed off her khaki-colored capris. "Perhaps another time."

She turned to leave and was at the top of the stairs when I couldn't hold it in any longer. I knew it might be a mistake, but...

"I just wanted to ask why you took the babies when you could have gotten them legally."

She stopped but didn't turn around. Her hand sought the banister as she stood stock-still.

"I've tried to understand what happened, Jeanette, why you left your career and disappeared. The divorce was horrible, I'm sure, but you had your talent and people who wanted to see you succeed. But you gave it all up."

She still hadn't moved. I wondered if she'd even drawn a breath in the last few minutes.

"That's when it hit me. You did it for the babies." I didn't know if this was going anywhere but knew I couldn't stop now. "Help me to understand why you took the twins, Jeanette."

She sank onto the top step, her back to me. "You've no idea what I went through," she said evenly. "The humiliation at the hands of that monster."

Helen/Jeanette rose from the step and returned to where she'd sat a moment before. "He used my desire to have a baby to rip out my heart—and I had no idea he was doing it, that he planned to divorce me. The surrogacy contract he'd drawn up was filled with loopholes." Tears coursed down her cheeks. "If even the smallest thing wasn't followed, the arrangement was void. That's why he arranged for a donor."

"Rex Stout."

She met my eyes with an appraising glance. "I knew you'd figure it out. The house, the furniture... when I saw the portrait of Stout and his mother in the storage rooms, I knew it was only a matter of time until someone guessed. I'd hoped people would just think I was guilty of a little indiscretion and let it pass."

"But then Angelina found the girls." I thought she'd be surprised, but nothing seemed to faze her.

"That's right. They'd gone to pick up their last paychecks." She laughed. "Here we were with all that money, and they wanted those blasted checks. I couldn't believe it when they brought her back to the house."

Where was Blue Eyes? Here this woman was confessing, and no one was around to hear it but me.

This was *not* something she needed to know, that I was alone. I reached down to the Band-Aids, prepared to draw my weapon if necessary.

"I'm assuming you know Angelina's missing."

"Yes. But I swear she was fine the last time I saw her. We made plans to meet once we were settled here. She realized Adam had played both of us, used us in one of his twisted schemes for the sheer pleasure of watching our pain. She was determined to confront him despite my warning to leave it alone."

She shook her head then raised her eyes to mine. "Yes, taking the girls was wrong, *but they were supposed to be mine.* I had the contract. That agreement was legal as far as I was concerned—as far as Angelina was concerned as well. I'd held up my end of the bargain, paid her a retainer, helped with her mother, and supplied her with the best ob-gyn money could buy."

I pulled a wad of tissues from my pocket and assured her they were clean. She didn't seem to hear me, just grabbed at them and

THE CASE OF THE BOUNCING GRANDMA

mopped her face.

"So Darrell helped you kidnap them."

She was taken aback, but only for a moment. She didn't ask how I knew, didn't ask a thing.

"I object to the use of that word," she said tightly. "We reclaimed what legally belonged to me."

She must have realized how hard she sounded, and once again, dissolved into tears. The sobs racked her body so hard all I wanted to do was comfort her.

"Have you... have you told anyone?"

"My sister and daughter." *God, forgive me for lying.*

Helen dabbed at her eyes, blew her nose, and made a brave attempt at regaining her composure. "I know you've friends in the police department. I, well, I'd appreciate if you wouldn't say anything until I can speak with the girls. It's... this will be hard on them. They deserve to hear it without a bunch of cops around."

Her tears, the story, sucked me in. Could I trust her? I'd tried to pierce her shell, but to no avail. The guttural sound of Frank's Dodge pickup caught our attention. Jeanette stood and hurried to the porch steps as the pickup sped up the street. She was halfway down when Frank brought the vehicle to a screeching halt in front of my place. He slammed out of the cab, stomped across the yard, and grabbed his stepmother by the arm.

"You ain't got no business with these looky-loos."

He threw me a hateful glare and pulled Helen out to his truck. After depositing her inside, he sneered up at me. "I'm sure y'all knows what happens to the curious." He snickered, slammed the truck's door, and sped the rest of the way up the street, disappearing behind the monstrous spirea.

I seized the phone off the table and backed my way to the screen. Reaching behind me, I twisted the knob, threw the door open, and pushed myself over the lip and into the house. I closed the inside door and locked it in record time.

As I rolled into the living room to shut and lock the windows, I punched the button for Rick Spencer's cell. Once again it went directly to voice mail.

"Rick, I've got a really big problem here. Helen Midas just admitted to being Jeanette Parker, and she confessed to kidnapping the twins. And I think Frank Midas threatened me."

201

I hung up and continued the task of closing all the windows in the house—making sure the doors were locked as well. I switched on the air-conditioner, then returned to the living room to close the blinds.

Elsie was shot yesterday while showing Rex a condo. She'd been inside the building when it happened.

Father God, help me. I've gone too far this time.

And yes, I knew what happened to curious people... probably the same thing that happened to curious cats.

They were killed.

Chapter 24

I closed every blind in the house—something I'd never done before. Afterward, I sat in the strange half-light, avoiding the windows. With no TV or radio for company, I felt cut off from the world. Sure, I could turn them on, but if I did, I might miss the warning sound of an intruder's approach.

Better to remain in silence.

I thought about calling Jane but didn't want to spoil her evening—nor did I relish the thought of her righteous indignation for my rash behavior. As for Andi, I didn't want to put her in harm's way. Besides, if her father-in-law so much as detected the scent of danger, he'd rise to the occasion like the ex-marine he was. Calling Matt Wheeler was tantamount to ordering up the cavalry with a take-no-prisoners decree.

As twilight fell, I went from room to room, turning on lights as I progressed through the house. I wasn't indiscriminate about the lights—I selected the ones least likely to cast shadows that could be seen from outside.

Back in the living room, I weighed the pros and cons of remaining in total silence. After hours of nothing but ambient house noises and the few sounds that drifted in from outside, I'd had enough. I switched on the TV, turned down the volume, and searched for something to watch. I settled on a rerun of *Monk*, the genius detective with the worst case of obsessive-compulsive disorder anyone could have.

However, after two nights of little to no rest, the soft lighting and drone of the television lulled me to sleep. Jane's arrival woke me a little after midnight.

"Hey, kiddo, what's going on at the Midases'? It looks like they're moving out."

It took a moment for the words to sink in. I whirled around—
if the term is applicable to turning a wheelchair on carpeting—and
moved toward the window, shutting off the lamp as I went.

Peering through the slats in the blind, I saw Frank and Darrell
loading the old freezer into the back of Frank's pickup.

"Quick, punch in speed-dial five," I told Jane, as I continued
to watch the men.

"You want to tell me what this is all about?"

"Call, Janie, it's Blue Eyes's cell number."

"Blue Eyes?"

"Yes! It's Rick's—Detective Spencer's cell."

I heard her move to the phone table followed by a sigh of
exasperation. "I'd be happy to call, Glory, but first I need the
phone."

Without taking my eyes from the men, I searched my lap for
the handset. I nearly panicked until I felt the odd lump against my
right thigh. I pulled out the phone and handed it to her.

"It's gone to voice mail. Quick, what do you want me to say?"

I thrust my hand behind me and rushed the phone to my ear.
"Rick, it's me again. The Midases are getting rid of evidence.
They've already loaded that old freezer in the truck, and I'm pretty
sure a roll of carpet is sticking out of the tailgate. Innocent people
don't wait until after midnight to move things. Call me!"

I hung up just as Frank's old Dodge rumbled to life. His father
hopped into the passenger seat, then they took off down the street.

"Glory, what's going on? Has something else happened?"

When I turned to face my sister, the light from the TV drew
my attention to an object on her left hand that glinted when she
moved. I switched on the lamp and stared at the engagement ring.

"When were you going to tell me?"

"I don't know. When are you going to tell me what's going
on?" As much as she tried not to blush, not to show how ecstatic
she was, it didn't work.

In the midst of the craziness around us, Jane had finally gotten
the bling she deserved.

* * * * * *

We took turns on sentry duty the remainder of the night. We
never heard Frank and Darrell return, and I began to wonder if
they'd taken off without Helen and the twins.

THE CASE OF THE BOUNCING GRANDMA

By six, with the sun rising and filtering in through the blinds, all thoughts of sleep fled. While Jane showered, I called the police department to check on Blue Eyes, only to find he was "unavailable."

After a lot of hemming and hawing, I convinced the operator to leave him a note. As further backup, I called his extension at the station and left yet another voice mail. It may have seemed excessive, but I figured the circumstances warranted it.

When Jane finished dressing, she came to the living room to relieve me. I immediately noticed she wasn't wearing her engagement ring.

"Where's the bling?"

She shrugged. "I'm not quite ready to share my news with the world."

I was concerned about the hesitation in her voice and hoped she wasn't having second thoughts. Ordinarily I'd have teased her about it, but this time I decided to refrain. This was an important step for my sister, and I didn't want to risk messing it up for her.

After telling her about the new messages I'd left for Blue Eyes, I went to get ready for church. I wondered if the twins would make it—if they were still around.

Though neither of us had detected any further activity in the neighborhood, there was no way to know what might have happened during the few hours I'd slept before Jane got home. For all we knew, the family could be anywhere—or at least as far as you could get in about eight hours.

Jane was nibbling on some toast when I rejoined her.

"Now aren't you glad you cut your hair? It looks terrific, and I'll bet you didn't do more than shampoo and blow it dry."

"Wash and wear hair; my style to a T."

The sight and aroma of her toast made my stomach churn. I hadn't eaten since lunch yesterday and was too queasy to even consider doing so now.

"Andi called. Seth wanted to remind us to pick up the twins." She shook her head. "I'm not sure this infatuation is good for him. He's so preoccupied—"

She was about to take a bite but stopped with the toast halfway to her mouth. "What am I talking about? The poor kid's your grandson. No wonder he's become so fixated."

I stuck my tongue out at her, then dug into a cabinet for the crackers. If they were recommended for the queasy stomachs of expectant mothers, they should do the trick on mine.

Time passed slowly as it is wont to do when you're waiting for something. Though we'd gone over everything repeatedly, it didn't stop me from thinking about it.

The facts were simple: Helen Midas was really Jeanette Parker. She'd kidnapped Monique and Giselle Verona with the assistance of Darrell Midas. They'd used his sister's death in the hurricane to fabricate an elaborate story about the girls' birth.

From there, things became more complicated.

Somehow Rex discovered the twins and used them to his advantage. He'd sold the house to "family" to pay off his debts, maybe even blackmailed Helen for extra cash.

Then there was Angelina. It was obvious one of the Midases had killed her—at least it was obvious to me.

"Glory, it's a quarter to nine. If we don't go, we'll be late for Sunday school."

Brought out of my musing, I shook myself to get my blood pumping. I rolled into the living room and over to the window. There was no activity on the street. Of course, the spirea blocked my view of the Midas house, so I couldn't tell if the girls were on their way. I hated the thought of missing them.

"Maybe we could wait a little longer. I mean, we could miss Sunday school."

Jane wrung her hands. "I'm as worried about them as you are, Glory, but I—we—need this time, the fellowship."

"And we'll get it. Just not in Sunday school. Okay? If they don't show up in half an hour, we'll leave. We can attend the Bible study they have in the sanctuary before the service. Yes, we'll miss our regular class, but Janie, this is really important. We're the only sanity those kids have right now."

Was my argument a little over the top? Maybe, but I believed every word.

"I thought you trusted that Helen—Jeanette... whatever... would protect the girls."

"I do. But considering her history, protecting them might involve taking off to parts unknown."

"She might convince Chandra to go with her, but I'm betting

Chelsea would refuse. That kid's tired of all the hassles. I don't think she looks at the lottery money as a way to happiness but as a means to be free."

While I agreed with her, I figured neither of us could put ourselves in the twins' shoes. They'd been living with lies and intimidation their entire lives, and it might not be so easy to break from the mold.

Time was wasting. We were down to fifteen minutes.

Chapter 25

I've always thought Paul was at his best when he wrote to the Corinthians. It was one of those times you *knew* God was the pilot, and Paul was just along for the ride.

I hadn't expected to have the patience to sit through the service, let alone the thirty minutes of Bible study beforehand.

Now, as Jane drove us home with Andi and Seth chattering in the backseat, I marveled at the messages we'd heard.

The Bible study concentrated on 1 Corinthians 13, one of my all-time favorites. This lesson in love continued through Pastor Connor's sermon, with an emphasis on verses eight and twelve.

"For now we see in a mirror, dimly" reverberated inside my brain. God's message that *love never fails* filled my soul to overflowing. No matter how many times we push Him away, no matter how many times we fail Him, His love will never cease. And through His grace, mercy, and love, we can move mountains.

Or, in our particular case, a bunch of shady characters.

"We need to check on the girls," Andi insisted. "We had a message from Chelsea on the machine last night. She said they'd definitely be at church."

"She was whispering, so it sounded funny," Seth added.

"What time was the call?"

"A little before three, Mama. You talked to the, er, mother at what time?"

"Four-ish."

"Now we've got the times established," Jane said, "what do you propose?"

As she turned onto our street, I had a sudden, overpowering urge. "Duck!"

"What?"

"Andi, Seth, duck down."

"Mama—"

"Do it, guys. Do what your mom said." Jane glanced at me. "You felt it, too?"

"What're we doin', Gramma? Is this a game?"

"Yep, it's a game, kiddo. Just stay down until we get into the garage."

"First you won't let me bring my car over, and now you're making us hide. What's going on, Mama?"

I reached behind me and caught one of my daughter's hands. "Trust me, okay?"

Once the garage door was down, Seth popped up like a jack-in-the-box.

"Are we still playing, Gramma?"

"We sure are. What do you think of the game so far?" I peeked back at Andi, whose face had paled. "You all right?"

"A little carsick. I'm not used to riding with my face against the floor."

Seth darted into the house the moment the engine shut off. While Jane got my chair, we filled Andi in on our adventures in Kansas City.

"So you confronted Parker on Friday, turned the progression photo over to the police, then after being told to stay out of it, you got a confession from Helen yesterday. You've been busy." Andi got out of the car and stretched. "Instead of waiting around for Rick to return your calls, why didn't you just call 911 and report her?"

"Your mother call 911? With her track record?"

"Hey, Gramma, these aren't workin'. Do we have any batteries?" Seth met us at the kitchen door, holding up an old set of walkie-talkies I'd given him.

"As a matter of fact we do." I rolled over to my junk drawer and pulled out a new package of double A's.

"I'm not sure I like the look on your face." Jane set her Bible on the table, took one of the units, and removed the old batteries. Seth handed her new ones, jumping up and down in anticipation.

"Are we gonna be spies?" he asked.

"That's what I'm afraid of," was Jane's droll answer.

"Look." I turned around and handed Andi the other unit. "We

all agree that we need to check on the girls. After everything that's happened, I simply think we should take precautions."

"Precautions?" Andi eyed me warily. "Why is it I get the feeling this is going to be more elaborate than simple?"

"Oh ye of little faith!"

I didn't know where the ideas were coming from or what was driving me, but I had a feeling of urgency I couldn't shake off.

"Seth, honey, run and get a pair of those shorts you keep here."

"Mama, maybe we should just leave—"

Seth bounded back into the kitchen and over to me. I took the shorts, grabbed a pair of scissors from the junk drawer, and started cutting off the belt loops.

"Oh, cool!" My grandson's face shone. "Are we gonna have an adventure?" Despite Jane's and Andi's misgivings, Seth was enjoying himself.

"Right again, kiddo."

I handed him the shorts and told him to go change.

When he was out of the room, I faced my disapproving audience.

"Okay, this is what we'll do. Jane, you'll go to the house to find out about the twins. I'll keep a lookout from behind the spirea—"

"Keep a—Glory, what are you talking about?"

"You'd better change first. Put on shorts or jeans and your sneakers." I turned to Andi. "You'll be posted on the porch with one of the walkie-talkies, and we'll have Seth in the oak with the other one." As an afterthought I added, "I'll give him my cell phone with 911 ready to dial with a single touch."

"Oh, boy!" Jane rolled her eyes. "I'm going to change—but not because it's part of your scenario."

When she'd left the room, Andi came over and felt my forehead.

"You're not warm, so we can rule out your being delirious."

I captured her hand and gave it a gentle squeeze. "I'm not doing this because I want attention or because I'm looking for a way to preoccupy myself so I don't have to think
    about your father."

Andi knelt in front of me, studying my face. I caressed her

ALICE K. ARENZ

cheek and tickled the spot beneath her ear as I'd done countless times when she was small. A hesitant smile touched her lips.

"You really think they're in trouble?"

I nodded. "I believe they need help. And right now, I think we're the ones to give it." I drew in a deep breath. "You remember the movies where people know there's danger, know a killer could be waiting to nab them, but they go off alone or out in the dark like they're invincible?"

"And wind up dead. So?"

"They're extras, expendable to the movie. This is real life, and none of us are expendable."

"So we prepare like we're going into battle?" Jane stood in the doorway. She'd changed into jeans and a T-shirt—and was wearing her sneakers.

"Better to be safe than sorry when dealing with people like Frank and Darrell Midas, don't you think?"

After we fine-tuned the plan, we called Seth in to brief him. He would be our captain, Andi told him, and as the commanding officer, he needed to pay close attention to his instructions.

"Like Daddy!" he said proudly.

"Right." Andi saluted him. "Can you repeat what we just said?"

He stood with his back straight and his chest pushed out. "I climb the oak tree and hide in the branches. I take my walkie-talkie and listen to you guys talkin', but I don't say anything. If you sound scared, or talk about the police, I use Gramma's cell phone and call them."

"That's perfect, slugger," Jane patted his shoulder. "Just one more thing. Don't come out of the tree unless one of us comes to get you. Got it?"

"Got it. Can I take a sandwich with me?"

While Jane made his lunch, I dumped the contents of my fanny pack and put a small bottle of water inside, followed by the freshly made peanut butter and jelly sandwich.

"If this gets caught on a branch," I said, cinching the bag around his waist. "All you have to do is press this little button and it'll unclip. Okay?"

"Got it, Gramma. I mean, General," Seth giggled.

"This sure is a lot of trouble to go to," Jane whispered.

212

THE CASE OF THE BOUNCING GRANDMA

"Pretty silly too."

"You thought they should hide as we drove up the street."

"Yeah, but I've been living with you for nearly seven weeks, and you're beginning to rub off on me."

"Hey, Gramma, I think this walkie-talkie is the one you use 'cause it's broken."

"Broken?" Jane asked, sounding a bit alarmed.

"It gets stuck on." I took Seth's unit and inspected it.

"You're right, honey. I'm glad you caught that." Andi passed the unit she held to her son, watching me closely as she did so.

"What are you up to, Glory Harper?" Jane gave me the evil eye.

Ignoring my sister, I grinned at my grandson. "You're all set, champ. You ready?"

"You bet, General!"

As he darted for the back door, Andi caught him in her arms. "When you get in the tree, call us on the walkie-talkie."

She gave him a quick hug.

"But you said—"

"That's the only time you're to use it. That's the game. Okay? Now scoot."

She stood at the back door, watching him run across the yard, her arms wrapped around her waist. "I hate tree climbing."

"He'll be fine, honey. Don't worry." I fiddled with the talk button on the unit I held.

"If that thing doesn't work—" Jane started.

"It sticks with the channel open, which will work perfectly for our purposes. Seth will be able to hear everything we say."

"So even if he forgets he's not to talk to us—" The light went on in Jane's eyes.

"No one will hear him or know he's listening," I nodded, keeping my thumbnail beneath the button to hold it in place.

A few minutes later, our walkie-talkie crackled to life.

"This is Captain Seth reporting. I'm in the tree, over and out!" Though the message was formal, the laughter was all Seth.

I lifted my thumb and handed the unit over to Andi. "It's all yours. Just talk."

"We read you loud and clear, Captain," Andi replied, flashing me a weak smile. "Remember you're just to listen, no talking.

We'll come get you in a little while. Mom signing out."

A few minutes later, Andi was on the porch, I was stationed behind the spirea, and Jane was on her way to the Midases' front door. I peeked through the thick branches and watched Jane push the doorbell. After a few minutes, she rapped on the door. When no one answered, she tried the side door.

I heard something behind me and swiveled around to take a look. I didn't see anyone down the street, and there was no activity at the Devlins'. By the time I'd turned back to the spirea, Jane was coming around it.

"It doesn't look like anyone's home. That old pickup's gone, and the car wasn't in the garage."

I wheeled the chair up the driveway, trying to keep pace with my sister. "Andi must have gone inside already."

"She probably saw me coming home and went to get Seth."

Once we were in the garage, Jane closed the door, then helped me maneuver around the cars and into the kitchen.

"There wasn't anyone home, An—"

I stopped in mid-sentence as my daughter came into view. Helen Midas's arm was clamped around Andi's neck, and she held a gun against her temple. Out of all of them, Helen was my least likely suspect.

"Ladies. It's nice of you to join our little party." Helen's tone matched the icy blue of her eyes. "We're going to take a little ride, so let's go." She used the gun to motion toward the back door.

"I'm afraid I can't—"

"You either figure it out or I'll push you down the steps. Your choice."

I got the feeling she wanted to do a lot more than push me. I started to say something, but Jane stopped me with a tug on my hair.

"Not a word," Jane whispered as she took charge of my chair. "When we get to the door, lean back. We'll try to work this thing like a stroller."

We were almost to the door when Adam Parker burst into the kitchen.

"Where's the kid?" Helen barked.

"There's no one else here." Parker wiped a hand across his forehead.

214

THE CASE OF THE BOUNCING GRANDMA

I couldn't believe the way he was dressed: designer jeans, a fancy polo shirt, and shoes that probably cost several hundred bucks. Nice outfit for a kidnapping.

When Helen tightened her hold on Andi's neck, Jane leapt forward only to be intercepted by Parker. He slapped her so hard she flew back, landing in my lap.

"I c-can't breathe—" Andi cried.

"Don't hurt her, she's pregnant!" I yelled, trying to help Jane and keep an eye on my daughter at the same time.

Andi's eyes went wide, whether from fear or because of my statement, I wasn't sure. As far as the crazed woman was concerned, nothing mattered.

"Once more." Helen shoved the gun in Andi's cheek. "Where's the bo—"

"He went home with a friend from church. We're to pick him up in a couple hours." I stared straight into the woman's eyes, determined to show no fear. "How about you let her go now, huh? We'll do whatever you want."

"Let's just get them out of here, Jeanette. She can help get her mother down the steps." Parker brushed his hands across his jeans. "It's getting late, and I'm running out of patience."

Helen/Jeanette laughed and pushed Andi toward Jane and me. "Like you have any say in what's going on," she sneered at her ex-husband. "I'm in charge this time, Adam, and don't you forget it."

Andi stumbled into my arms. I hugged her tight while I continued to watch our captors. The left side of Jane's face was swollen, her eye puffy. I took her hand and gave it a reassuring squeeze.

"Now you've had a family reunion, it's time to go." Helen waved the gun at us and motioned toward the door.

It took a while, but Jane and Andi managed to get the wheelchair down the steps and onto the patio. During the process, the Parker-Midas duo continued to argue about what they were going to do with us. I didn't care for any of their suggestions.

The back of my property borders on a small alley that provides access to the field beyond. With the privet hedge on one side and a six-foot privacy fence on the other, there was no one to witness what was happening—with the exception of my grandson. I prayed for God to keep him up that tree.

They herded us across the backyard, cursing every time the wheelchair hung up in the grass. Jane and Andi were on either side of me, sharing the chore of pushing the chair with one hand while I held their other one. We'd formed a tiny circle, and as we moved forward, Jane began reciting the Lord's Prayer.

I knew He was there, that He listened. I just hoped He was paying close attention to what was happening.

"So which of you killed Angelina?" My question caused Jane to falter in her prayer and succeeded in stopping our captors' argument. I received a smack across the back of my head from the woman.

Wincing from the pain, I turned slightly, still clasping my daughter's and sister's hands. We were almost beneath the oak, and I needed to keep our captors' attention on us and not our surroundings.

"And here I thought we were becoming friends!"

"Keep your mouth shut or I'll give you something to put in it."

Parker trudged ahead, limping badly across the uneven ground, and disappeared down the alley toward the Midas property.

"I'll take that as a confession." I turned back around. "So all that stuff about waiting to go to the police was just for show."

"I told you to *shut up!* You have yourself to thank for this mess, always gawking out your window, prying in other people's business. You'd no right to interfere with my daughters—"

"Angelina's daughters, if we're getting technical. You can't possibly believe I haven't said anything to the authorities. They already have the FBI on the case. Once they test Rex Stout's DNA—"

Helen shoved Andi out of the way, ripping her hand from mine, and tossed her aside. Jane released my other hand and ran to Andi as Helen flew at me. The chair toppled backward, and while I was attempting to pull myself out of it and free the knitting needle, Helen ground a knee into my chest, and shoved the gun in my mouth.

"You have a question now, lady?" she screamed. "You and Angelina destroyed my family with your interference. You want answers? How about this: That blackmailing piece of garbage

Stout has finally gotten what he deserves. And you and your little family will be joining him."

She pulled the weapon out of my mouth and stood. "Get her up," she ordered, turning to Andi and Jane.

They staggered over to me, tears coursing down their faces. As they struggled to help me back into the wheelchair, I could swear I heard a siren off in the distance. Their expressions told me they'd heard it too.

A nondescript utility van appeared in the alley. Parker climbed from the driver's seat and sauntered around the back to open the doors.

"Hurry up!" Helen prodded Jane in the back with the barrel of the gun.

As we stumbled forward, Jane and Andi resumed the Lord's Prayer. I could no longer hear the siren and knew if we got into the van, our chance of survival was unlikely. If Andi had managed to hold onto the walkie-talkie, Seth would know we were in trouble and would follow through in calling the police. I reached toward my daughter and tugged at her arm until she leaned forward.

"Is the message getting through?"

Andi met my eyes, straightened, and patted her stomach.

There was a small bulge in the waistband of her slacks that could only have come from the walkie-talkie. She rumpled her shirt to cover the evidence up again.

Stall, Glory, stall.

I picked at the bandages above my cast until I could feel the head of the knitting needle. We had a weapon; the problem would be using it without getting someone shot.

"So you were the one who shot Elsie Wilkes. Let me guess, you were aiming at Rex."

Neither of them commented; they were too busy shoving Jane and Andi into the van. While Parker made certain his captives remained where they were, his ex pushed my chair to the open doors.

"Either you two pull her up or I shoot her here. Your choice."

"So cold and heartless. No wonder the twins are trying to get away from you." I received another rap in the head for that.

Jane and Andi each grabbed one of my arms, then someone pushed me from behind so hard the three of us toppled over.

"Dear God, if You're listening, we could really use Detective Spencer *right now!*" I shouted as the doors slammed shut.

Lying on the floor of the van, we hugged one another and continued to pray aloud. We waited there for our captors to reappear, rocking back and forth, absorbed in the promises of Christ.

I worked at the knitting needle until it was free of the cast. Jane's mouth dropped open, and Andi's eyes widened as I wrapped my hand around the weapon in readiness.

Keep my hands steady, Lord.

The door finally opened...

The most beautiful dark blue eyes I'd ever seen lit with joy when he saw us. Detective Rick Spencer held out his hand and smiled.

"You girls need some help?"

Chapter 26

Seth was a hero, and he had the medal to prove it. The moment he saw Helen Midas and her ex go through the yard and into my house without knocking, he knew we were in danger. When they pulled his mother off the porch and threatened her, he called 911, told them what was happening, and asked for Detective Spencer.

Six days later, my grandson had a citation for bravery from the mayor, we were recovering from the scare of a lifetime… and I was preparing for my first date with Blue Eyes.

I hobbled into the living room with my new crutches and sighed when Jane started fussing over my choice of clothing.

"Stop!" I pushed her hands away and grimaced at her and Dr. Steven. "I've already changed five times. This will have to do." I was wearing a navy chiffon dress that made me uncomfortable enough without Jane's coddling.

Her face was still a little swollen, but it was hardly noticeable behind the smiles and laughter whenever Steven was near. Now officially engaged, she wore his ring with pride, showing if off every chance she got.

"I just want you to look your best, Glory." Jane touched my cheek, then returned to Steven's side.

"Are we too late?" Andi and Seth slipped in through the open front door, the screen banging shut behind them.

Seth flew at me, wrapping his arms around my waist.

"Hey, Bouncy, Bouncy. You sure look pretty. Smell good too."

"Thanks, honey. I see you're wearing your medal." I returned his hug while gazing at Andi.

"Careful, kiddo. You know Gramma's still unsteady on her

feet." Andi winked at me. "He's right, Mama; you're beautiful."

I hated blushing but seemed to do it a lot lately. The elaborate plan that kept Seth in a tree during our confrontation with felons had earned me a commendation as well.

But we hadn't been the only ones to show courage in the face of adversity. Rex Stout had surprised everyone.

After Helen/Jeanette failed to kill him, shooting Elsie instead, he'd realized time was running out on his blackmailing gravy train. Who would've guessed Rex possessed a conscience?

We knew that Rex had gone to Adam Parker for help and been shot for his efforts. It was a good thing Parker was a better swindler than he was a marksman, or Rex would be dead.

Afterward, Rex decided to do the right thing and save the twins. His participation in his old buddy's scheme had made him a father—biologically speaking—and he figured the girls should know the truth.

Somehow, Rex managed to get Chelsea and Chandra out of the house and to the police without anyone being the wiser. Since he thought he was dying, he gave a full confession of his complicity in the surrogacy scandal. He also admitted to blackmailing Darrell and Helen Midas after he'd recognized the twins from a news story.

I wondered how he felt when the doctor told him his wound wasn't life-threatening.

Helen/Jeanette wasn't talking, and Parker did what came naturally—he hid behind a slick, fast-talking attorney.

Frank Midas declared his ignorance, which didn't come as a surprise to anyone. He swore he was innocent of any wrongdoing; he'd only been following his father's and stepmother's orders.

Darrell was discovered at the local landfill where he and Frank dumped the carpet used to wrap Angelina's body. During the process of unloading the freezer, Darrell had suffered a massive heart attack and died. Authorities found him after Nick Pearson and his pals spotted Frank attempting to stuff his father into the empty freezer.

Though forensics proved Angelina had spent time in both the carpet and the freezer, it took excavating most of the two acres next door to find her.

"Glory? You're staring."

"Sorry. Got lost in thought."

"You're not brooding again, or having second thoughts, because—"

"Don't start, Janie." I grinned at my sister before turning to my daughter. "We've been waiting all day. Don't you have something you'd like to share?"

"We heard from Daddy," Seth volunteered. "He's being a spy, but he's just fine."

I raised my eyebrows. "A spy, huh? What makes you say that?"

"Mommy said it was secret."

"That's right, kiddo. Everything's still on the QT, but we know he's all right. Colonel Hammond said if things go the way they hope, we'll be getting mail soon."

"That's wonderful news."

Jane was as anxious as I was about Andi's doctor visit, but she was too preoccupied with Dr. Dreamboat to pry. I didn't have that problem.

"So," I prodded. "What else?"

Andi and Seth exchanged grins, and then she gave him a nod.

"We're gonna have a baby!" my grandson announced with glee.

There was a rap on the screen door, and since I was the only one standing, I went to answer it.

Rick's entire face lit up when he saw me. "You look incredible," he said, opening the door.

"Thank you." I raised my hand to stop him from coming inside. By the time I'd grabbed my purse from the hall table, everyone was in the entryway.

"Don't you want to ask him in?" Andi giggled.

"Not on your life!"

I didn't want to sit around with all of them staring at us. I was already nervous and didn't need additional incentive for the butterflies to churn up my stomach.

Rick held the door, and my family followed us outside. I could feel their eyes on me when he assisted me down the steps. It didn't boost my morale.

"Make sure you bring her home early!" Seth hollered as Rick helped me into his car.

"Have you heard from the twins?" he asked, pulling onto the street.

I knew he was trying to put me at ease, but I doubted it would work; the butterflies seemed to be multiplying.

"They've called both Andi and me," I told him after clearing my throat several times. "They're still pretty confused, but they already love their grandmother. Luisa has invited us down for a picnic next weekend."

Tarryton has several fast-food places, but aside from Tanner's truck stop on the edge of town, only one real restaurant.

It didn't take long to get there—another plus to living in a small community. Even though it was early in the evening, the place was busy. But Rick had left nothing to chance; they had a table waiting for us.

I was glad when the hostess led us toward the back and out of the way. I needed somewhere to prop the crutches, and the wall next to the table was perfect.

Pretending to study my menu, I asked, "So what sounds good?"

The old wood floor creaked when a server came by. I noticed the crutches sliding and reached out to keep them from falling.

I managed to catch one of them.

Everything happened in slow motion. The second crutch fell as another server was heading to a nearby table, his arms laden with plates of spaghetti. It smashed onto the dishes, sending broken china, sauce, and noodles everywhere. While the server tried to recover, he slipped in the mess on the floor and slid into a customer passing by, sending them both to their knees.

I covered my face, mortified. Peeking between my fingers, I saw Blue Eyes grab up the crutch and slide it under our table.

Prying my hands loose, he gave me a sheepish grin as he lifted a piece of spaghetti from my hair. "At least you're not the one going to the emergency room this time."

He punctuated the statement with a kiss.

Don't miss The Case of the Mystified M.D.

www.ingramcontent.com/pod-product-compliance
Lightning Source LLC
LaVergne TN
LVHW012015060526
838201LV00061B/4317